ABOUT THE AUTHOR

Maureen Gallagher was born in Monaghan. She spent much of her childhood in Donegal. Her stories, poetry and literary criticism have been published widely in magazines and journals, and she has won many awards for her work. Her debut collection of poetry, *Calling The Tune*, was published by Wordsonthestreet in 2008. Maureen Gallagher lives in Galway. Her website can be viewed at maureen-gallagher.com

LIMBO

MAUREEN GALLAGHER

POOLBEG
CRIMS●N

Published 2022 by Crimson
an imprint of Poolbeg Press Ltd.
123 Grange Hill, Baldoyle,
Dublin 13, Ireland
Email: poolbeg@poolbeg.com

ISBN 978-1-78199-701-7

Main front and back cover image by Peter Trant
Author back cover photo by Peter Trant

Printed and bound by CPI Group (UK) Ltd, Croydon CR0 4YY

www.poolbeg.com

ACKNOWLEDGEMENTS

First of all, I would like to thank Paula Campbell and Poolbeg Press for publishing my debut novel *Limbo*. Thanks also to Gaye Shortland for her warm support, her insightful feedback, and exceptional editing.

I am grateful to Averill Buchanan for her input at an early stage. A big thank-you to Ciarán Parkes for the wonderful conversations we had and for all his help. I would like to thank Margaret Faherty, Patrick McGinley and my Peer Group for feedback and encouragement on some of the chapters. I would especially like to thank Pete Morriss, whose inspired feedback was time and again enormously helpful, not least because of his remarkable ability to see a plot idea through many moves ahead, like a great chess player.

Above all, I want to thank my sister Ita Trant, who read draft after draft with the care and attention of a forensic scientist and whose imaginative and astute comments were invaluable.

I am grateful also to Peter Trant for his excellent photography.

For my family
with love

CHAPTER 1

Gweedore, Donegal, May 1989

Liam Patsy Joe Brannigan stumbles into the bar. He orders a pint and a chaser. The first of several. To obliterate the day.

"Terrible business that, out on the strand," the barman remarks, swiping the counter with a rag. Word has got around.

Brannigan's gut is on fire, inflammation on a villainous mission to do him down. To think, godammit, the reinforcements they're sending from the city includes a *woman*. A battle-axe, no doubt, built like a barn. He scowls into his beer as he reruns the events of the morning.

* * *

The phone rings. This border business is annoying the shit out of him. And those Biddies from Umfin – friggin' communists! He continues writing his report for the Super.

The phone rings again just as a pallid youth appears at the hatch. Brannigan looks up. Mike effin' MacAllister, IRA sprog.

"Yes?"

MacAllister shifts from foot to foot, runs his hand over his shaved head. "I want to report a case of domestic violence."

Brannigan sighs and opens the Incident ledger. The phone continues to ring.

"It's my father ..."

Brannigan gazes into MacAllister's watery eyes.

"He's threatening my mother," the sprog continues, worrying the zip of his fleece.

The phone stops ringing.

Brannigan starts to write. Stops. Holds the biro at arm's length and stares at it. He shakes it vigorously, flicks to the back page of a notebook and scribbles, then looks up and, as if seeing MacAllister for the first time, frowns.

"And what exactly is the nature of this threat?"

"He's painting graffiti on the gable end of my mother's house."

"Hold it, not so fast." Brannigan writes something in the ledger.

Suddenly, there is loud screeching outside the window. Brannigan and MacAllister turn to see two seagulls struggling over a fish. The attacking black-headed gull wins and soars off with the prize. When the hell will the department build a new barracks in a decent location?

Brannigan switches off the transistor – friggin' Madonna. He consults the ledger again, remembers what the question was, registers the juvenile before him. "Is she his wife or ex-wife?"

A bright red flush spreads up MacAllister's neck and along his face until it reaches the top of his bald punk head. He clenches and unclenches his fists. "*Wife. Wife. Fuck's sake!*"

Garda Brannigan peers over his glasses at the youth. A mean mood connects the two like hostile lovers.

Brannigan concludes the statement. He slaps the book closed and thumps it with his fist for effect.

"I've duly recorded the incident. We'll have an officer drive by." He picks up the biro, scribbles again on the back of his notepad, squints at the tip. "Friggin' biros – they never last." He throws it into the bin.

"Is that all?" demands MacAllister.

Brannigan glances up at the youth. Christ, if the Shinners are relying on the likes of this waste of space to free the North, how come the Brits haven't kicked the shite out of the whole shaggin' lot of them years ago?

"That's all we can do for the moment." Brannigan reaches to pull over the hatch door.

MacAllister sticks his hand in, blocking the door from closing fully.

Brannigan glares at him. Is this little frigger for real?

The phone starts up again.

"Kindly remove that hand, sir."

MacAllister glares back. "Something needs to be done," says the republican die-hard, eyeballing the Garda sergeant. "*Now!*"

"*Kindly remove that hand!*" Brannigan spits, his voice black with charge.

The phone rings off.

A mob of gulls has swooped to the harbour in the hope of pickings from the fishermen's haul. Neither garda nor youth pays any attention to the cacophony.

MacAllister glowers. "This isn't good enough. I'm going to report –"

"I'll ask you once more –"

"My bastard of a father is – is – and you don't give a flying fuck!"

Spittle lands on Brannigan's chin.

With a dexterity and lightness of foot that belies his enormous bulk, Brannigan quicksteps out the side door and grabs the young man by the arm.

"Listen, you little fucker," – the sergeant brings his face right up to the punk's, their foreheads almost touching – "I've just come back from Ballybofey. Full of shitheads conspiring to blow us all to kingdom come – so, as you can appreciate, I'm up to here with lowlifes, which means I'm not going to listen to a little runt like you blathering on about his mammy and daddy fighting over some friggin' writing on the wall."

The phone rings again. Brannigan scowls at it.

MacAllister tries to shake himself free of Brannigan's grip. "I'm going to report –"

Brannigan hauls the struggling teenager out of the room and into a corridor. He unlocks the door to one of the cells and flings MacAllister in. Breathing heavily, he backs out and straightens his uniform.

"You have attempted to obstruct the work of a Garda Síochána in a Garda station. You will wait here until the Superintendent gets back."

He slams the door, turns the key in the lock and goes back to answer the ringing phone.

"Bunbeg Barracks. Brannigan speaking." A searing pain emanates from his gut. "You *what*? Speak up!" A pause. "The line is very bad." Another pause. "*Jesus H. Christ!*"

It's the last thing he wants to hear.

CHAPTER 2

"So who found the body?" asks Frankie.

The police car pulls out of Dublin headquarters, Detective Anto Moran at the wheel.

"A tourist. Some geezer who visits Donegal every May." Moran puts the boot down. "Likes to mop up bargain breaks at the seaside village." He lights a cigarette and inhales deeply.

Frankie – Detective Kate Francis – takes a fleeting look at the dark-haired man beside her – at the top of his game, many successful cases under his belt, well thought of in the force, so very attractive. So very *married*.

The dashboard thermometer registers twenty-three degrees.

Feeling drowsy from the heat in the car and Moran's smoking, Frankie's thoughts drift back to the night before in bed with

Rory. The argument: what did she want out of life? To be the best sleuth? To settle down? To become a mother? Then Moran had called, told her to come in, that a baby boy had been found murdered in Gweedore. Frankie can still hear Rory's words ringing in her ears: "*You're thirty-five years old with your biological clock ticking. Are you telling me you want to throw it all away because a whiskey-swilling womaniser like Moran snaps his fingers?*"

Rory's jealous of course, which is why he describes Moran so negatively.

After Donegal Town, Moran turns right for the northwest coast. The road narrows.

"So what's with you and what's-his-face?" He glances over at Frankie and narrowly misses a collision with a sheep.

Frankie draws in her breath. "His name is Rory."

Stony fields whizz by. Ditches. A grotto with a painted virgin.

"So ... Rory. What's the story there? You two still together or what?"

Frankie stares out the window at mountains drenched in mist. "We're talking." The truth is, she's not sure anymore if they are or not. Last night felt like an ultimatum.

Her boss reaches over and touches her hair. "A good-looking woman like you shouldn't be on her own." He withdraws his hand slowly, slides it down over her shoulder like a caress. "A woman like you needs a man in her life."

Frankie feels a shiver of pleasure. After the aggravation of last night's conflict with Rory, it feels tempting to give in to the flirtation. But she's been here before with Moran – just that one time but still! – and remembers her resolve never to give in to his overtures again. She's acutely aware that she is of an age where she has to stay focused on her goals, and giving in to Moran does not advance them in any way. If she was younger, if he was free … But he's not and she isn't. And then there's Rory – reliable, trustworthy Rory. Whom she loves.

Frankie looks at her watch. She reaches over and switches on the radio to catch the news headlines.

"Nothing is known yet about who the mother is, where the child is from, the circumstances of its death. However, there are rumours that the Children of Bríd may be involved. Sources say there is talk about bizarre goings-on on the island. But nothing firm has been reported. We will bring you an update as soon as more information comes in. And now for the weather. Bright and sunny in the northwest, with occasional showers …"

Moran looks at Frankie. "The *Children of Bríd*?"

"Some kind of cult that decamped from London to Annagry. The locals objected to their strange ways and they took off to Umfin Island."

"Cult? As in religious cult?"

"No, the opposite. A commune. Lots of free love and all that kind of thing." Frankie fiddles with the tuner.

Moran grins, eyes twinkling. "Okay."

I know what he's thinking but I'm not going to give it oxygen, thinks Frankie. Despite herself, however, she can't deny the thrill of innuendo, the promise of the chase.

The sky clears.

"Never heard of them," Moran says.

He takes a sharp left at the sign for Bunbeg. They turn a corner and there it is – the mountain, rising up like a colossus, dominating the whole vast empty landscape: a pyramid of quartz glinting in the early-afternoon sun. For all the world, they might have been transported back in time, entered the land of the Tuatha Dé Danaan and the Fomorians, at any moment see the giants of ancient legend suddenly leap out and tower over them, as they prepare to do battle in the fight of good versus evil.

Moran gasps.

"That's Errigal," says Frankie.

They've reached Gweedore.

* * *

Moran parks in front of the barracks, facing onto the waterfront. He gets out, stretches and squints at the building that is to be their new headquarters.

"Jaysus! This place must have been built before the Famine."

Frankie surveys the fishing boats tied at the harbour: trawlers, small convertibles with outboard engines, a rubber dinghy. A tall fisherman with a mane of white hair tugs at a rope attached to a schooner, pulling it closer to the harbour wall. Nothing has changed since she was here last. Seaweed on the pier sends out a sharp smell of brine. Iron. The suggestion of blood.

She glances at the barracks, a stone building that must be at least a century old. *Let's hope we don't have to spend too much time in this place*, she thinks. They go inside. Small grubby windows block much of the light.

Garda Sergeant Liam Patsy Brannigan heaves himself up from his desk and extends his hand to Moran, ignoring her.

"Hello, hello, Inspector. Am I glad to see you!"

Frankie sighs. She's met Brannigan's type before, men who long for the good old days when men were men, and women knew where their place was. She's hardly in the door and already battle lines have been drawn. She takes in the scene. An old, stained oak desk. A job lot of office chairs stacked behind the door. A wood-burning stove that spews out smoke in whorls. A tricolour on the nicotine-stained wall behind the sergeant's desk. A picture of the Sacred Heart hanging on the wall opposite. She steps to the left. The eyes follow, interrogating her. *What's that smell?* It takes a moment but then she gets it. A mixture of unventilated air and urea.

"This is Detective Kate Francis," Moran says, smiling at his partner. "She will be doing most of the work on the murder case.

A top investigator. The best. Solved the case of the Border Weasel."

Brannigan turns slowly towards Frankie and narrows his eyes. She watches him take her in, all five foot nine of her: a woman with the body of a martial artist and whip-hard cheekbones. Capable of breaking a man's balls, his look seems to say.

He sits heavily on the edge of his desk, riffles through documents, then looks over reading glasses at the detectives.

Bright red nose of a drinker, Frankie notes.

"Okay," he says, fixing his eyes on Moran. "As you know, an infant – or rather the *body* of an infant boy – was found in the dunes at Port Arthur Strand yesterday morning the ninth May, at approximately six a.m." He gets up and jabs a fat finger at a spot on the map pinned to the wall behind his desk. He taps the map a second time impatiently, then folds his arms over the shelf of his stomach. "A tourist out for an early morning stroll came on the body. According to aforesaid, the infant was thinly covered with sand. He would have passed by except he noticed a little hand sticking up." He runs his tongue over his front teeth. "Like a child waving, he said."

Frankie winces.

"I sent our team out there immediately to cordon off the area. According to the state pathologist, the baby's skull" – Brannigan taps his temple with a knuckle – "bears the round imprint of a blunt instrument. Cause of death, a blow to the head." He pushes two antacids out of a half-used pack, leans his head back and tosses them in his mouth. "Type of weapon used, most likely a hammer. But the imprint is small. Not your usual hammer."

"A tourist, you say?" asks Moran politely.

Politeness is not Moran's style. *What's he at?* Frankie wonders.

"Yes, from Glasgow." Brannigan turns back to consult his file, chewing the antacids. He stares at the papers, flicks through them, turns them over as if a clue lies underneath. "Anyways," he mumbles, "he's been married, divorced, no children, a regular here every summer."

"Obviously he's suspect number one until he's ruled out," says Moran, a smile playing on his lips.

"That had occurred to me, sir. We're not all thickos up here," Brannigan replies acerbically.

"Other leads? The Children of Bríd? Any links, clues they might be involved in this?"

"The Biddies are always involved."

"The Biddies?" asks Moran.

"They call themselves the Children of Bríd." He snorts. "Everyone else calls them the Biddies. But, in any case, nothing concrete. Only the usual *Dúirt bean liom go ndúirt bean léi* ... an oul' one told me what another one told her ... you know the craic. When the Biddies were in Annagry – Christ almighty! Don't get me started. But, having said that, these days, ninety per cent of our time is taken up with the effin' IRA."

"You're saying they could be involved?" asks Moran.

"They have enough blunt instruments to take out a battalion of infants."

A garda comes in.

"What is it, McGinley?" Brannigan asks.

"Sorry to interrupt, sarge," says the garda, "but the priest would like a word."

Brannigan slaps the file shut and gives it a thump. "Tell him I'll be right there."

A higher power has called, Frankie thinks.

Brannigan turns to Moran and Frankie. "You'll have a young fella at your service, an intern fresh out of training in Sligo. The brightest button in the box."

There's a guffaw from McGinley.

"Supposedly," adds Brannigan.

He rises, jerks his head for them to follow. He leads the way down a cold corridor that smells of crime. Mould, disinfectant and ancient vomit. A tunnel breeze blasts them as they step out into the yard. Frankie blinks in the glare of the sun. Several bicycles lean up against the wall, never reclaimed. Beyond that a row of old gas cylinders, orange and rusting. Frankie shudders.

"That's it," says Brannigan. "Your office."

Frankie looks where his fat finger points. Directly across from the barracks is a prefab – paint peeling, cheap fittings, rusting. One of the windows sports a long diagonal crack. She shudders again.

"A bit basic, I'm afraid," Brannigan says without irony, "but it's all we've got at the moment." He pulls a bunch of keys out of his pocket. "We've been years waiting for the new barracks, but with this recession God only knows when it'll be built. Well after my time, that's for bloody sure."

He paws at a key with thick fingers, trying to remove it from the tight spiral ring, and curses.

"I'll be leaving ye now," he says unceremoniously, handing Moran the key. "The padre waits for no man."

A gull screeches overhead. Frankie looks up. *What is that in its mouth?* Another gull lunges at it. The spat ends as soon as it's begun and the gulls fly off over the harbour. *Gulls will eat anything.*

And she thinks of a baby buried beneath the sand …

CHAPTER 3

The office is no bigger than a prisoner's cell with two small classroom tables for desks. Moran commandeers the desk by the window overlooking the harbour, leaving Frankie to take up a position facing north. This is going to be a challenge in more ways than one. Such a tiny space. Working so close together.

She opens a window.

"What do you think of Brannigan?" she asks.

Moran shrugs, lighting up.

Frankie bats the smoke away. "I don't trust him."

There is a knock on the door. McGinley's head pops round. "Sorry, sir, to disturb you."

"What is it, McGinley?"

"This is Garda O'Toole, sir." McGinley flattens his bulk

against the door to let a young man in uniform into the room. "He has been assigned to assist you."

Moran nods.

O'Toole stands awkwardly to attention in the middle of the small space. The intern is tall and slim with jet-black hair. A bit intense, thinks Frankie. Still, nice to work with a man you don't have to look down on.

McGinley leans past him to hand Moran the phone directory. "Sergeant Brannigan said you might try ringing the three county hospitals. Plus there's CARE."

Moran raises an eyebrow.

"Organization that helps unmarried mothers, sir," says McGinley. "Sarge says the mother's more than likely to be an unmarried."

"Any info on recent pregnancies in the area?" asks Frankie.

"The area is very large. The hospitals and doctors would be your best bet."

"And what about Derry?"

McGinley rolls his eyes. "We have to go through the RUC for that, sir. Six counties, sir."

Moran shakes his head in annoyance. "It's just – what? – a few miles down the road and we have to go through a bloody checkpoint to get there?"

"Couldn't agree with you more, sir," says McGinley, pleased to be afforded the chance to offer an opinion. "Bloody Brits, sir. Sergeant says he'll check Derry."

Moran nods.

"What do we know about the Children of Bríd – the Biddies?" Frankie asks McGinley.

"Bunch of weirdos out on the island." He smirks. "Big into fornication, is all I know. No electricity or tap water."

"The complete simple life, drawing water from a spring well?" asks Moran. "Reading Thoreau by lamplight?"

Frankie raises an eyebrow. *Thoreau? So Moran has read a few books in his time.*

McGinley blinks. "Been condemned from the pulpit, sir, they have."

Moran swats him away. "Thanks, McGinley."

But why would they deposit a baby on the mainland? Are the Biddies being targeted because of local bigotry, Frankie wonders.

Moran claps his hands. "Okay, let's make a list, divvy out the work. *Chop-chop!*"

He opens the drawers in the desk. They are empty. He holds his hands in the air in exasperation. Frankie opens her briefcase and pulls out a sheaf of copying paper, a few biros, a miniature chess set.

Moran nods at the set, raises an eyebrow.

Frankie shrugs her shoulders. "Helps me think." She passes him a pen and some paper.

Moran leans back in his hard chair, purses his lips and blows her a kiss. "I owe you one."

Frankie loses the battle against the smile that gathers at the corners of her mouth. She feels a shiver of excitement down her spine. *What does Moran see when he looks at her? Oh, I must stop this. Why do I care what Moran sees?*

She looks up and catches O'Toole's gaze fixed on her. He coughs, shuffles his feet.

Moran glances at him and points to a stool in the corner.

"Sit down, O'Toole, you're making me nervous."

"Very good, sir."

"Let's see, now. What have we got so far? One dead body. A baby. Murdered with a blunt instrument."

Frankie takes up the baton. "Possible suspects, the tourist who found the body, the Biddies and the Shinners."

"The Shinners?" says O'Toole.

"Shinners ... Sinn Féin ... the IRA," Moran growls. "Where have you been living this past century, O'Toole?"

"Oh, I know what 'Shinners' means, sir. I'm just wondering why they're suspects in this case."

"Because, my dear straight-out-of-college garda" – Moran shakes his head impatiently – "they are the usual suspects. In any investigation, first on the agenda are the usual suspects. They smell of guilt. And if they're not guilty of committing this crime, you can be sure as hell they're guilty of something."

"Aren't we all?" says Frankie, catching O'Toole's eye.

Moran rounds on her. "Get a grip, detective!"

She presses her lips together to stop from grinning. "I'll ring the hospitals."

"Good." Moran scans the harbour. "Of course, it's very likely that crowd out on the island don't go near a hospital for their deliveries."

"In which case, things are likely to go wrong, sir," says O'Toole earnestly.

"Except in this case we're not talking about things going wrong, dear garda, we're talking about murder. Deliberate intent." Moran knuckles the desk. "And never forget, every contact leaves a trace. They take something with them, they leave something behind."

Detection 101, Frankie thinks. God help her.

Moran slides the phone directory over to Frankie with the list of hospitals. "I'm going to the mortuary. I want to examine the body for myself. I'll get a map while I'm at it." He stands up. "You come with me, O'Toole. You might learn something." Though I doubt it, his face says.

"And maybe later you can do some research on the Biddies," Frankie says.

O'Toole beams at her as they leave.

Frankie leafs through the well-thumbed tome. She agrees with Brannigan on this one: more than likely they are looking for a single mother. Her first call is to CARE.

"Hello, my name is Detective Kate Francis," she says, keeping her voice even and low-key. She's well used to how defensive people can become if they're confronted suddenly.

No response.

"I understand you help with problem pregnancies."

"That's correct," answers the prim voice on the other end of the phone.

Guarded.

"We're investigating the death of the baby boy found at Port Arthur Strand. I'm sure you've heard about it. As part of our investigation, we're looking for information about any recent pregnancies in the area." She forces a smile. People can always hear a smile, even if they can't see it. "Can you help?"

Silence.

"Are you there?"

"Yes, I'm here."

Frankie rolls her eyes at Moran who has returned for his car keys. Roadblock, she mouths at him.

"Do you have knowledge of any woman who was recently pregnant and is no longer pregnant and doesn't have a baby to show for it?"

She waits.

Finally, the voice at the other end says, as if consulting a script long rehearsed, "I am sorry, we have no such information or knowledge. I am afraid we cannot help you."

"Thank you for your time." Frankie feels a tightness in her gut, like she's been in a power struggle. She jots a note beside CARE: *Investigate further*.

Frankie returns to her checklist. Next, she calls the Mother of the Infant Jesus Hospital in Falcarragh. Another blank. There have been no pregnant women in the community hospital in the last three months, the hospital registrar tells her.

The Holy Trinity, ditto. This leaves the Mary Immaculate Hospital in Letterkenny. She dials the number and is quickly transferred to the maternity ward.

"Matron O'Keefe speaking. Yes, we had three single pregnant women in recently ..."

Frankie suddenly feels her pulse racing.

"But who am I speaking to, please?" Suddenly suspicious.

"I'm Detective Kate Francis from the murder squad. We're investigating the death at Port Arthur." Pause. "I'd like to come and see you as soon as possible."

"Yes, of course," says the matron, open to sharing confidential client information now that Frankie has identified herself.

"Tomorrow? Two p.m.?"

* * *

Moran lifts a pointer and taps a large, tattered map that he's hung on the wall of the prefab. He takes a long pull from his cigarette, rests it on a saucer on the table in front of him.

"The name *Gweedore* or *Gee Door*, as they say in the vernacular, refers to the parish here" – he traces a circle around the area – "in the northwest of the county."

"Population 4000, give or take," pipes up O'Toole.

Moran twists to squint at him.

"I've been reading up on it, sir."

Moran turns his attention to the map again. "Most of the area inland is mountainous, and uninhabitable. Errigal" – he points – "is the county's highest mountain – dominates the whole parish. Well – *that* goes without saying!"

"The people used the mountain for their sheep and cattle at the time of the Famine, sir," offers O'Toole, "and sometimes stayed with them. But the landlord took the mountain from them and –"

"Okay, okay, O'Toole, much appreciated, but enough of the history lesson. It's geography we're interested in right now."

"And the beaches?" prompts Frankie.

"There are three of them." He taps the map with three short sharp raps like hammer-blows, to indicate the location. "Brannigan tells me they're all popular with tourists, especially Port Arthur" – taps again – "because of the dunes, the long strand, the safety for swimming."

"Obviously not so safe for infants, sir," O'Toole opines.

Moran snaps around to face the rookie, sucks air in through closed teeth. "Thanks for that, Garda O'Toole."

O'Toole blinks. "Oh, you're welcome, sir."

* * *

The narrow grassy road that winds down to Port Arthur Strand comes to an abrupt end. Frankie parks and walks to the pier. Hundreds of granite rocks, of all shapes and sizes, form a barricade between the slipway and the beach to its left. From here Frankie can see the crime scene cordoned off. She steps down onto the rocks, trying to avoid the bulbous globules of bladderwrack on the bigger stones, the luminous slimy sea moss that tuft the smaller ones. *How on earth would anyone navigate this either pregnant or with a baby in their arms?* Of course, maybe the woman – if it was a woman – could have approached from behind the dunes or along them. It hadn't occurred to her to enquire about the easiest way of getting onto the beach. She slips and steadies herself. A number of barnacles huddle in a shallow pool, clinging on to surfaces with an iron grip. With difficulty she reaches terra firma and takes off her sandals. She faces the ocean and breathes in the intoxicating smell of brine. She feels a sudden desire to get into the sea and feel the sharp icy tingle on her skin. Frankie can't remember the last time she went swimming. She isn't sure she even owns a bathing suit any more – she certainly doesn't have one with her.

The sun breaks through the clouds, a shaft of light illuminating the whole strand that curves in a long wide golden arc. There is a gradual incline up to the marram grass. The place is deserted. She could be a traveller from the Stone Age, feeling the thrill of having arrived in paradise, except for the garish orange ticker-tape. She pads in that direction. At the point where the wet sand – crisp and cool on her feet and dotted with thousands of tiny crab-holes – ends, and the fine soft sand begins, up towards the dunes, there is a distinct line, curved along the shape of the strand and crowded with small stones, bits of broken shell, predominantly razor clam and barnacle, some crab and mussel. She can see long strings of weed, some of it bunched up in a tangle, more of it spread out like dark-brown shoelaces. Beyond this line, the sand turns from deep gold to almost pristine white. Frankie scrutinises the line of shingle that forms this uneven but definite line along the beach, parallel with the sea. *This has to be the high-water mark. The sea does not reach the dunes.* She takes out her notebook and starts to write. Every detail is important at this stage of the investigation.

CHAPTER 4

The trip inland to Letterkenny takes Frankie about an hour. To her right the rolling mountains of the Poison Glen are enveloped in a light ethereal heat-mist. As she drives around by Errigal, its sugar-loaf peak dented as though from a giant-sized bite, Frankie feels again the mesmerising draw of this ancient terrain. In a thousand years' time, she thinks, we will all be just another layer in another rock formation. It puts life in perspective.

She arrives at Letterkenny. The cathedral town, as it is called, sits on the River Swilly and is the largest and most populous town in Donegal. Not unlike towns up and down the country, she thinks, starved of funds since county councils lost their powers in the late seventies, it now appears slightly down at heel. Not so the cathedral, which shows no sign of lack of resources and holds its own, magisterially, on a hill dominating the town.

Without much difficulty, Frankie finds the hospital and waits in the lobby. Punctually at two, the matron appears: a friendly woman, eager to help. She leads the detective into her office, a tiny windowless room lit by fluorescent tubing, stacked with bandages, towels, blister packs – the paraphernalia of medicine – and the smell of antiseptic. More like a storeroom than office.

Frankie introduces herself and thanks the matron for giving her time. "As I mentioned on the phone, I'm part of the team investigating the death of the Port Arthur baby."

"What a tragedy." The matron crosses herself. "Is it murder? I've heard rumours."

"We can't say for certain it's murder until we have the pathologist's report. But, meanwhile, we have to carry on with an enquiry."

The matron nods. She is of medium build, plump and has a motherly look about her. "Of course, of course."

"You said three unmarried pregnant women were attended to in the maternity ward on the seventh of May?" Frankie searches in her bag for her notebook. In vain.

Matron opens a thick file on her desk, licks her index finger and flicks through, pauses when she finds the page. "There was a Mary O'Reilly. She had a little boy. God love her, she had such a long labour. You see, the baby had breached. But she was vehemently opposed to any intervention. No way would she countenance it. She lost a lot of blood. She was also reluctant to have a transfusion." She looks up at Frankie with a sad expression in her eyes. "These young girls, you'd feel so sorry for them."

Frankie nods sympathetically, jots the name down on the back of an envelope. She waits a moment. "And the others?" she presses gently.

The matron sighs. "Then there was Trish Conway. She had a caesarean. Well, that was decided long before. She was so young, only seventeen, the poor thing, and with a very narrow pelvis. Such a sad business!"

Frankie can see how involved with these young women the matron is. "And the third woman?"

The matron shakes her head. "Murder," she murmurs to herself. "Who would murder a baby?"

Frankie allows the moment, as the matron tries to come to terms with what has happened to someone she may have known, however briefly. She has to constantly remind herself that people need time to process what they are hearing, what is being asked of them – in this case, need time to process the horror of a murder.

"You said there was a third girl?"

The matron consults her file again. "The third girl was Sarah Joyce."

Frankie writes.

"Do you know what happened to all their babies, where they are now?"

"Well, I know for sure that CARE are looking after the first two women I mentioned. They were involved with the girls from early on in their pregnancies."

"Do you have much dealings with CARE?"

"Oh, yes," the matron says. "All the Catholic hospitals work with CARE."

Indeed! Frankie would have to find out more about CARE. Clearly they had more information than she had been led to believe. Just as she suspected. For why would the matron lie?

"The third woman?" Frankie glances at the name on the envelope in her hand. "Sarah Joyce? You've not said what the outcome was for her?"

"I'm afraid the report on Sarah Joyce is inconclusive."

"Inconclusive – what does that mean?"

Matron consults the file in front of her. "She came into the maternity ward on the evening of the eighth of May …"

A few hours before the Port Arthur baby was found, Frankie notes.

"Her file says '*Scan and uterus recently emptied*'. That's all."

Frankie thanks the matron, tells her she's been very helpful. Her heart is racing.

Elated, she hurries to the hospital lobby, pulls out her walkie and calls Moran. "We have a suspect."

CHAPTER 5

Sarah Joyce wakes with a headache. She pulls the eiderdown over her head. If only she could stay here forever. She glances at the clock radio: 8am. She'll have to get a move on or she'll be late. She hauls herself out of bed, and goes for a quick wash. As she steps out into the hall, she feels something squishy underfoot.

"*Goddammit! Mother!*" she yells. "*That freakin' mutt will have to go! I mean it!*"

Mags doesn't react to Sarah's call because she's not wearing her hearing-aid. She's in the kitchen, cooking pancakes on the iron griddle over the open fire. Mags cooks pancakes every morning.

Sarah raises her voice a couple of decibels. "*Mother!*"

Her mother rushes out into the hall. She sees the mess and,

horrified, brings her hand up to her mouth. "Oh, he never does that, the poor wee thing!"

Sarah calls from the bathroom. "*He's just done it!*"

Mags hurries to the kitchen to fetch a mop and bucket of water.

Sarah retreats to the bedroom, where she can hear the sound of her mother furiously scrubbing the floor, all the while muttering to herself.

Sarah frowns in exasperation. *This is all I need this morning!* What's more, she doesn't want pancakes. She's off her food ever since ... *Oh no! I can't bear to think about that.*

She pulls her thick bright-red hair into a pony-tail. dresses quickly, ducks past her mother into the kitchen, grabs her notes from the dresser and pulls on her jacket. Hannah stares mutely from her position by the fire, but this morning Sarah has no time for her sister.

When she hears the door slam, Mags sighs, returns to the kitchen and goes outside to empty the bucket and rinse the mop.

She abandons all thought of pancakes. She lifts the little Scottish terrier up in her arms and pets its curly mop. "*Ó, Goitseo, a stór!*" she says. "*Cad a dhéanamíd leis an cailín sin?* What are we to do with that cailín?"

Hannah looks over at her mother for a moment, then resumes her silent staring into space.

* * *

Sarah drives down the old ragged boreen, through a corridor of hawthorns and blackthorns, the one in full bloom, the other past. As she turns right for Bunbeg, she glances up at Errigal, a habit she has. Errigal – once a comforting presence, something solid in her life – now stands indifferent against a gunmetal-blue sky, ominous and threatening.

She so loved this place when they moved here six years ago. As she drives past the Sinn Féin office in Dunlewy, she peeps in as she does every morning. Looking to see if Mike is there. She was seventeen when she first went out with him. The bullies at school kept well away when she was with Mike MacAllister, and she had a far easier time of it. But that was then. Now all she wants is to become invisible, to disappear. Her thoughts return to that awful night. *Don't go there*, she scolds herself, *think of something else*. But there is nothing else. Just her there in that dark place with no one to help. The smell of blood. The excruciating pain. And that tiny cry ...

Sarah blinks away tears as she swings into the car park of the school in Derrybeg.

She pushes through the front door. She can hear the noise of pupils in the playground, wired as they attempt to squeeze the last ounce out of the free time before class begins, all five hundred of them bursting with energy. She can hear the chatter coming from the staff room, teachers also stretching out the free minutes before work begins.

She goes straight to her classroom and closes the door. She takes a tablet from her bag, tosses it into her mouth, and washes it down with a slurp from the tap at the end of the room. She must cut back on the pills. But they help her get through the day – when black thoughts threaten to engulf her, they keep her afloat.

Roseanne from next door – who's been so helpful to her from the start, showing her the ropes – puts her head around the door. "Hi, Sarah, anything wild or exciting to report?"

"Nothing really." Sarah closes her bag quickly. "Just Mam … she keeps trying to stuff pancakes down my throat every morning."

Roseanne laughs. "Oh dear! The joys of living at home. *Oops!* Here comes O'Connor. See you later."

A moment later, a knock on the door and the principal, without waiting for a reply, enters. He's a short stocky man, with a balding head and a pinched look about him. Sarah never took to him. "As mean as a bag of weasels," Roseanne had said that first morning, and they'd laughed. But here he is now and she doesn't feel like laughing. Her mouth feels dry all of a sudden.

"Good morning, Sarah. Everything all right?" he asks perfunctorily.

Sarah's stomach clenches. Has she done something wrong?

"Yes, absolutely." She searches his face for clues. What has she done? "I'll have those class reports up to you this afternoon," she says nervously. Roseanne has coached her on end-of-term reports on every child.

"Yes ... yes ... yes ..." says O'Connor, absentmindedly. "Whenever ..."

Two teenagers poke their heads around the corner of the school and peer through the window into Sarah's classroom. When they spy the principal glaring at them, they run off, shrieking with nervous laughter.

Sarah waits.

O'Connor sucks air in through clenched teeth, then turning to Sarah informs her she'll have to do without Special Assistance this week and abruptly he's gone.

What? No Special Assistance again this week?

Sarah stands staring at the door. He can't do that – change the goalposts on a whim and with no proper excuse. This is not the first time she's suffered. Just because she's a temp. She paces. She should have stood up to him.

Sarah can hear the thud-thud of her students milling down the corridor on their way to class. Her breathing becomes shallow. She can't stand this! She grabs her coat, walks out of the classroom, out the back door and into her car.

She barely sees anything as she barrels back up the road to Dunlewy, steering wheel held in a vice-like grip, her heart palpitating. *When sorrows come, they come not single spies, but in battalions ...* Who said that? *When sorrows come ...*

She turns into the driveway, coming to a screeching halt in the front yard. A cow with its head over the gate rears back in alarm, the whites of its eyes showing like oxeye daisies.

Her mother, sitting with Goitseo on her lap, looks up, surprised, when Sarah bounds in.

"Don't ask," Sarah warns with a black look, before rushing to her bedroom.

She kicks off her shoes and climbs under the eiderdown. Life is impossible.

The phone rings.

"*Sarah … for you!*" her mother calls. "*From the school! Roseanne!*"

Sarah drags herself out of bed and shuffles up the hall to the phone.

"Sarah?" Her friend's voice is urgent. "What's going on? Why did you leave the school?"

"I couldn't take it anymore, Roseanne. He took away my special assistant for this week. Without any proper explanation. How does he expect me to cope without a special assistant? That one from Infants sweet-talks him and he bullies me."

"Jesus, Sarah! You can't just walk out of a school. You're only a temp … don't you realise you could lose your job over this? They can kick you right out without blinking an eye. Don't you know that?"

Sarah begins to tremble.

"Sarah, go straight to the doctor and get a cert," urges Roseanne. "Ring the secretary and tell her that you're out on doctor's orders."

Sarah pulls on her jacket and drives towards the surgery in Dunlewy. She can't stop shivering. As she nears the village, she sees him. That familiar walk. She slows. The man stops. She unwinds the window, and they exchange a few words. He opens the door and jumps into the passenger seat. Sarah swings off up the mountain path.

CHAPTER 6

Moran shoves his half-eaten meal away. "Hotel food!" He knocks back the whiskey, tips out a cigarette. "Right now, I'd kill for a Kentucky Fried," he says, flicking his lighter. "Mind if I ...?"

Frankie shrugs.

"You never smoke?" he asks her.

She ignores him.

He exhales out of the side of his mouth, clears a space in front of him and pulls a notebook and pen out of his jacket pocket. "So ... Sarah Joyce, prime lead at the moment. Joyce – that a Galway name?"

Frankie doesn't know.

"Awaiting confirmation from a Doctor Long, you say. And Brannigan is to contact the RUC to check up on possible missing infants in the Derry area. I'll interview the tourist who found the body."

"Okay. I'll check at the desk for ferry times to the island."

Moran pouts his lips to deliver a perfect smoke ring. "Oh, yes! Those Biddies."

Two elderly women wander into the dining room, shake their heads and leave. The detectives look at each other and laugh. Errigal Lodge may not be the culinary equivalent of the Gresham, but it's not bad and they're not here on holiday.

He nudges her a couple of times. "At least it's discreet."

Frankie feels a shiver of excitement but nonetheless edges away.

There'll be none of that!

* * *

The water in the harbour is still as glass and reflects an azure sky. An orange lobster-buoy bobs gently a few hundred yards from the shore with a lap-lap-lapping sound. A solitary gull swoops and dives and makes away with its prey, a perch. There is a stillness in the air. Everywhere the smell of fish and seaweed and salt. Frankie and O'Toole, dressed in civvies, wait as the fisherman hoists a tangle of green fishing-net, threaded with luminous blue bobbins, from the deck and onto the jetty. The man is strong and weathered with the clearest blue eyes, face tanned and etched with lines from years in the outdoors. They pay the fare. He helps them into the boat.

"Do you get many going to the island?" Frankie asks, as they settle into one of the wooden benches running along the inside of the boat.

The fisherman sits opposite on another bench as he waits for others to arrive. "*Och*, aye," he says, "especially since that lot took up residence there. People are curious, y'know. It's human nature."

Without warning the sky clouds over and a stiff breeze blows in off the sea. The water becomes choppy. Sensing rain, Frankie pulls her raincoat out of a duffel bag. "They're a curiosity, all right," she says as she puts it on. "Do you know much about them?"

"I have a brother lives in Annagry. He tells me the hippies just arrived one day, bought a two-storey in the town and set up home – painted the outside all the colours of the rainbow, like a two-year-old might colour a drawing book. According to the brother, they were a holy show. And pure cracked too – the goings-on, the chantin' day and night."

"That wouldn't have gone down too well?"

"No, indeed'n it didn't. Aye ... and, would you believe it, young ones from the area started saying they wanted to link up. Y'know what young ones are like. The novelty."

Frankie smiles.

"The place was overrun as well with oul' eejits from here, there and everywhere, turning up every day to join in with them too. Dropouts and the like."

"But they left Annagry in the end – the Biddies?"

"When the IRA started issuing kneecap threats and bomb warnings, well, that put the tin hat on the whole thing. Y'see, Annagry had no trouble with the IRA or any of the likes of that before."

"Why would the IRA have got involved?"

"It's a long story, but there was talk of boats coming and going from Annagry in the dead of night. The IRA suspected the lunatics in the painted house were up to some skulduggery and they were having none of it. There was only one show in town and that was themselves. Myself, I'd say it was innocent enough, but there you are."

"I'm not sure I follow," says Frankie.

"No, it's a tricky one alright. But with that lot you never know what's going on in their heads."

"You mean the IRA?"

"Aye. In any case, it did the trick. The hippies left off their own bat."

"And set up home on the island?"

"Aye." The fisherman stands to help the small crowd who've gathered at the pier onto the boat, all of whom find a place to sit. As he helps the last person in the boat, he smiles at Frankie and winks. "And it keeps me in a job ferrying all and sundry back and forth."

He unties the rope attached to an iron hook on the pier, winds it up and throws it under the front seat. He moves to the controls and pushes a handle forward. The boat lurches. The engine coughs once, catches and begins to chug evenly. He pushes the handle farther forward, and they're off, the brow of the boat casting a mantle of spray.

The sky darkens. Without warning they are pelted by hailstones, tiny pinheads that bite and sting. Frankie buttons up her raincoat and pulls up the hood. The sea rises and falls as if it is a giant organism breathing. The boat takes the swells as they come, digging its wooden prow into each one, recovering with a shudder. O'Toole, feeling queasy, rushes to the side and upends the contents of his stomach into the feverish sea. He returns to his seat, asks the ferryman how long the boat trip is going to take.

The seaman chuckles. "Just shy of thirty minutes." He's used to soft city types suffering from seasickness.

Frankie glances at O'Toole, who sits huddled into himself, his face a shade of buttermilk-white. She represses a smile. "You'll be fine," she says.

The salt spray showers them with rhythmic constancy. The strong smell of seaweed stays with them throughout. Herring gulls screech overhead. The squall clears as abruptly as it started and suddenly the sun is blazing down. Umfin comes into view in the distance. They can see the water tower clearly – a black point rising up out of the rocky strip of land.

Frankie, feeling suddenly too hot, pulls down her hood and undoes the buttons of her raincoat again. "So – you did some research?" she says to O'Toole.

O'Toole nods. "A group of feminist free thinkers formed a commune – the Children of Bríd – a cult of the pagan goddess Brigid. The Children of Bríd worship the divine feminine and are outraged by patriarchy's lowering of the status of women. Brigid is the goddess of fertility. Fertility is a big theme."

"So, I take it – no men?" Frankie smacks her forehead. "Oh, what am I thinking about! Of course they need men. They worship fertility!"

"Men are welcome to join as long as they honour the goddess."

Frankie tracks the seagulls, getting ready to duck.

"So are they linked to the world goddess movement, or what?"

"I'm not sure about that."

"What about black masses?"

"Don't think so. But for them rationality equals male equals bad, emotions equals female equals good. When they moved to the island, it was in the hope they could turn it into a utopia to re-establish the feminine to its rightful place, to reverse Eve's curse, as it were."

Interesting.

O'Toole proceeds to fill Frankie in on the role of Utopia in Plato's writings.

Oh lord, he's off again!

She's glad when the island pier comes into view.

The boat chug-chugs into the small harbour. A shingle beach stretches as far as the eye can see to the left. Behind is a hinterland of outcrop, marram grass and heather.

They step ashore.

They all trek in one direction from the pier, a quarter of a mile on an uneven road with green tufts of couch grass growing up through the tarmacadam. On either side, fields of rough grass are dotted with rocks – erratics – rocks thrown up by the sea. Small seaside plants grow everywhere in and around the rocks. Frankie identifies purple thrift, blue-green kale, fleabane with its distinctive lavender petals and yellow stamens, and here and there the ubiquitous orchid.

Finally, a group of houses comes into view, a clutch of thatched stone cottages at the side of the narrow winding road.

As they approach the village, they see a couple of young men steering four cows and a calf into a field, a dog ambling beside them. They have a distinctive alternative look, dressed in homespun and Aran-knit jumpers. Near the first house, a young woman scatters grain to a brood of red and white hens that mill around her, clucking. A half dozen or so brown hens parade around in the dust behind netting wire. Further on, a group of three young people tend to a vegetable plot: neat rows of cabbages and lettuces and the green shoots of what look like carrots, next to potato drills and a strawberry patch. Children play catch in a small field across the road, with sporadic joyful shrieks. Frankie can smell the honeysuckle and woodbine that clambers untidily up the gable end of the house. A box of miniature begonias glows on the windowsill, with creeping jenny trailing down over the edge.

This looks idyllic, thinks Frankie. *Clean air, fresh home-grown food, a beautiful landscape.* She spots an aluminium milk churn standing against the wall in the background. *Goodness, they even make their own butter here.*

O'Toole stops, crouches down to take a pebble out of his shoe. "I'd say this place goes back to Fionn MacCumhail."

"Maybe so," Frankie says. "Look, we don't want to be too obvious. You wander around. Keep your eyes and ears open. Find out what you can. Be discreet. Let's keep away from each other until we get back on the boat."

Frankie approaches the third house in the village. A deep-red climbing rose laces a trellis by the door. Frankie opens the wooden gate, goes up to the cottage and knocks. A woman in her thirties comes to the door and greets her, smiling.

Frankie smiles back. "I'm looking for Zoe McWilliams, I understand she's the leader of this settlement."

"Zoe McWilliams is away on business. Can I help?" The woman has a distinctive Scottish accent. Educated.

"I'd like to speak with the next in charge, please?"

"That's not really the way we work here. Everyone is equal.

We're against hierarchies. Are you a journalist?"

"No, no," Frankie says hurriedly. "I just wanted to know how a person might get involved."

"Oh, in that case, you're more than welcome. Come in." She extends her hand. "I'm Maggie."

"Kate." They shake hands.

Maggie opens the half-door. "Listen, I'm just on my way to Brigid's Well – why don't you join me? It's our morning ceremony. Half the group will be here. The other half attend to the household and garden tasks. We take it in turns. If you come along, you'll get a better idea of what we're about."

As Maggie gathers up some things and shoves them into a shoulder bag, Frankie glances around. The cottage interior is a kaleidoscope of colour. Rugs and posters adorn walls painted a sunshine yellow. Wood burns in an open fireplace. Plaited onions and garlic hang from the rafters and give out a pleasing aroma. There's another smell too, one Frankie recognises all too well.

Maggie leads Frankie to the well. A carnival of about a dozen or so young women and a couple of men follow.

"Our philosophy is simple," Maggie tells Frankie, as they walk along. "In our community we aim to repair the social order that puts women into a subordinate place, to restore the feminine to its rightful places, to commune with Mother Earth. We're frustrated also by the secondary role assigned to women in the Catholic Church and by the rigid and disempowering education we're given. In our morning ceremony we each express our relief to be free from oppression and give thanks to the pagan gods and Brigid in particular for releasing us from all that."

"Oh! Will I have to speak then at the ceremony?"

"Each of us says what's in our hearts. Don't worry – you'll be fine, just say what you feel. There is no wrong feeling."

When they reach the well, they form a circle around it. Frankie gazes into its depths. She can almost feel the draw of its ancient healing power.

"The water in this well is like a spa," Maggie says, "and contains amazing healing minerals like sulphur, magnesium, potassium, iron and even lithium. Pagans understood the value of the healing nutrients in these deep wells, and revered them. We will all take a healing drink by and by."

One of the men lowers an aluminium pail into the well and draws water.

They walk the short distance along a well-worn path from the well to a circle of stones that surrounds a green clearing overlooking the Atlantic. A limestone slab straddles two rocks, an altar in the centre, on which rests a smooth oval stone. In front of the altar on the ground is a large earthenware vessel, like an urn. The man empties the healing water into the urn. He places the pail to one side and joins the group. All form a ring around the altar and sit lotus-fashion, arms outstretched. They set up a low chant, a soothing hum.

Maggie goes over, lifts the stone off the altar and holds it in her left palm.

"We, the Children of Bríd – the Exalted Ones – followers of the Goddess Brigid, gather here to celebrate the feminine divine. We allow ourselves to express our innermost feelings. Feelings are never wrong. Each of us tells our truth."

She reaches into her pocket with her right hand and draws out a straw doll, which she places carefully on the altar.

"This is a reminder that Brigid was the goddess of fertility, and that Imbolg was about celebrating fertility and the feminine."

Imbolg means the lamb-quickening, thinks Frankie. '*In bolg*' meaning 'in the belly'. The straw doll is a gift to the pagan gods to grant the gift of life – a sacrifice. But in the ancient Celtic religions, wasn't it a human sacrifice that was offered to the gods?

Maggie scoops up some of the healing water and drinks. She then takes her place in the ring, sitting in lotus position. The chanting continues.

Maggie hands the stone to Frankie.

Frankie holds the stone in her palm. She notices a circular design on the stone.

But oh Lord! What am I to say? She looks at Maggie.

Maggie smiles. "Everyone says what's in their hearts. The only rule is that no speaks who is not holding the stone."

All of a sudden Frankie feels uneasy, acutely aware she's here on false pretences. She pauses a moment, takes a deep breath.

"My name is Kate. Thank you for allowing me to attend this ceremony," she says. "I broke up with my boyfriend recently and have been feeling a bit lost. Disoriented. When I heard about your group, I thought I would like to know a little bit more. That's why I'm here."

Maggie nods and gestures towards the urn.

Frankie goes over and drinks from the healing water. She feels an unusual sensation as the liquid trickles down her throat, one she can't identify, but which is very calming.

She returns to her place and hands the stone to her neighbour, a petite young woman with brown hair who expresses gratitude to the pagan gods and especially Brigid, for getting her onto the right path in her life. The next woman tells how her life has changed since she's woken up to the feminine. More women tell how much more at peace they've been since they came to the island. Each takes a healing sup from the urn after she has spoken. The chanting continues in the background, melding in with the crash of the waves against the cliff, the sound of gannets and razorbills as they forage and swoop. Frankie can smell the salt and seaweed and is struck by the symphony of smells and sounds everywhere.

Next in line is the turn of a bearded young man, with shoulder-length hair. He holds the stone in his upturned palm and stares straight ahead. Silence. Everyone waits.

Without warning, and seemingly out of nowhere, a young

billy goat leaps into the middle of the ring and snatches the straw doll from the altar. There is a sharp intake of breath, a collective gasp. Maggie dashes over, pulls the doll out of its mouth and shoos it away. The goat – bits of straw sticking out of its mouth – gallops off towards the cliffs then veers right over the brow of the hill. Maggie straightens the doll, now somewhat the worse for wear after the mauling. She places it back on the altar, dips her hand into the urn and sprinkles the purifying water over it.

A sigh of relief follows and the chanting resumes. Maggie returns to her place and nods at the young man. *Continue.*

He shakes his head and looks out to sea.

After a moment, Maggie holds out her hand for the stone. He returns it to her.

"No one should feel any pressure to talk if they are not moved to do so. It's important to feel comfortable, at ease," she says to him. "Why don't you stand in the middle of the circle and we will nurture your silence?"

The young man hesitates, then reluctantly shuffles to the centre of the ring, unsure of whether to sit or not. He decides not and stands alongside the altar, looking awkward and uncomfortable. He starts to say something.

Maggie holds up her hand. "*Stop!* The rules are the rules: you can only speak if you have the stone."

Maggie passes the stone on to the next in line.

A plump pretty woman gazes for several seconds at the man,

who has by now what appears to be a decidedly taciturn expression on his face. Without warning her face clouds over.

"You remind me of my ex-husband," she says finally.

The chant momentarily turns to a murmur like the sound of a muted roar emanating from the belly of the sea, a rumble of recognition, of discontent before reverting back to a hum.

"We weren't married six months when it started – the silent treatment," the pretty plump woman continues. "For no reason at all. There wouldn't have been an argument. Not anything I could put my finger on anyway. Everything would be going fine, I would be in a great mood then suddenly *wham!* he'd sink into a brown funk and wouldn't talk. This could go on for hours, days, weeks, months. I felt so bewildered at first. What had I done to deserve this? And the strange thing was, the more I tried to find out what was wrong, the more entrenched he became." She raises her voice. "And y'know something? the more I suffered, the more I think he was actually secretly enjoying himself." She glares at the man in front of her. "*How dare he!*" He lowers his head and shifts uneasily.

As she gets up to drink from the urn, Frankie detects a change in her demeanour. *What is it? Empowerment?*

The stone is passed along. What started as a celebration of the feminine slowly slides into a venting against patriarchy. "No more demeaning wolf-whistling," says one. "Give thanks and praise for the feel-good here." "No more groping," says another looking directly at the man in the middle, before going on to praise the goddess. "No more shaming," says yet another.

The centre of attention, one of patriarchy's few representatives on Umfin, squirms.

Then it's the turn of the second man in the group. "I give praise to the Goddess Brigid and the feminine divine," he says hurriedly, before passing the stone on.

A dark-haired young woman – a teenager, hardly more than eighteen years – empowered now by the permission to speak, raises her voice several decibels as she tells of her assault and rape. "Again and again he did it, my uncle. Night after night lying there waiting for the door to open. Three years it went on for. Three miserable years!" She wails uncontrollably. "He was just like you, silent, head down, wouldn't hurt a fly. But he was a *rapist!*" She chokes, strangling the words as she speaks. "I was only fourteen when he came into my bedroom first."

Maggie rises quickly, and goes over to the teenager. She puts her arms around her and comforts her. After a few moments she leads her over to the healing water from which the young woman takes a drink. Calmed, she returns to her position and passes the stone on.

The next to speak is a tall woman, with fiery red hair and dynamic flashing eyes, who raises her head high and says, "If you raped me, mister, if you made me pregnant, I'd rip child out of my body, and ..." she arches an eyebrow, "afterwards ..." She tails off, walks over to the man and traces a red line around his neck.

She slowly walks to the urn, scoops up some water, knocks it back and looks around at each of the group, before returning to her place and sitting.

Frankie winces. *Good god! Was that blood?*

Maggie holds her hand out for the stone.

"All feelings are good, and everyone is allowed to express themselves whatever way they are moved to. Now we must move to restore peace and calm," she says. "Let us give honour to Brigid."

All bow their heads. The chant becomes louder and continues for several minutes.

Finally Maggie says, "We will finish now. Men, you may honour the goddess by collecting firewood on the other side of the island." She nods at the men and they leave.

The women stand around in small groups and chat.

"Those stories were horrendous," Frankie says to Maggie, "but I'm just wondering about the symbolism of the straw doll in the circle? And the man? Am I missing something here?"

"No," says Maggie. "Extreme things get said. But that's the point. You get out every horrible thought that you have."

"But why do the men put up with it?"

"They like being here. They get a lot of attention." She smiles. "Lots." She claps her hands. The women gather around. "Let us join hands and dance to release feminine energy, to commune with Mother Earth." She holds out her hand to Frankie.

The women, as if on cue, hold hands. With Maggie and

Frankie, they form a circle and dance to the rhythm of the waves splashing against the cliffs. Frankie can hear the oystercatchers' piping call in the distance. The sun beams down from an azure sky. Peace and harmony are restored.

Afterwards, as she walks Frankie back to the cottage, Maggie continues where they left off. "Here we want people to express their aggression because it's then dealable-with, touchable, feelable. And it's not just a horrible feeling of something going on under the surface. In patriarchal society women are not encouraged to speak up, or express their anger at the injustices they suffer. They become troubled. Damaged. Here we allow their voices."

"But why target that young man? Was that blood the red-haired woman traced on his neck?"

"It's cyclical," says Maggie enigmatically, smiling.

Meaning yes, lunar, menstrual, thinks Frankie.

"It seemed like a threat. Was it a threat?"

Maggie smiles and shakes her head.

At the gate Frankie turns to face Maggie. She reaches into her pocket, pulls out her police badge and holds it up in front of Maggie's startled face.

"I'm Detective Kate Francis," she says, "investigating the death of the infant on Port Arthur Strand."

Maggie's eyes open wide with alarm.

"I need to ask you some questions."

Maggie recoils. Her face pales as the deception that's just taken place sinks in. This is followed by a flash of anger that she could have been so duped. Her lips tighten as she glares at Frankie. "You told me –"

Frankie raises her hand and shakes her head. That game is over. She has her detective's hat on now. "Have there been any pregnancies on the island in the past year?"

Maggie eyeballs Frankie, rage bubbling not far below the surface. "I don't have to answer questions."

"Well, I'm sorry to have to tell you but you do."

Maggie finally admits there were two pregnancies on the island in recent months.

"And where did they give birth – here or on the mainland?"

"Here, of course," Maggie snaps. "We have our own midwife. Modern medicine turns women's bodies into machines."

A collie dog came up behind Frankie, barks and jumps up on her. Frankie steps back, unsettled.

"*Down, Cleo!*" warns Maggie.

Cleo, reprimanded, slinks off.

Frankie takes in a deep breath and composes herself. "And where are the mothers and babies now?"

"They are above in the end cottages. I can take you to them if you have any doubts."

"That won't be necessary for now but I would like to speak to the midwife."

"She doesn't live on the island."

Frankie gets a name and address.

* * *

Frankie stoops to pluck a field thistle on her way back to the boat.

She's conflicted. On the one hand, she's impressed with the back-to-nature self-sufficient element of the lifestyle she's observed: the small-scale farming, the kitchen gardens, the carefree happy-looking children. But, on the other, at the very least there was a level of violence in the ritual she's just witnessed that was disturbing. And what really was the significance of the straw doll? Maggie maintained they were not violent, but if it was part of the ethos of the group to work out their emotions, was it outlandish to imagine that, in another scenario, a woman with post-partum blues might act out her feelings by bashing a baby's head in?

Maggie said there were two pregnancies, and there were two babies to show for those pregnancies. But she was hostile and guarded at the end. Was she telling the whole truth? She was understandably annoyed at having been deceived, but she didn't give the impression of someone who would consider it necessary to comply with outside interference in their utopia of self-rule.

Frankie tosses the thistle into the ditch.

The question still remained: even if Maggie was lying and there was a dead baby, how did the body end up on the mainland?

As she retraces her steps towards the harbour and the boat, she spies O'Toole ahead. He does a half-turn, catches her eye and shakes his head. Nothing to report by the looks of things. Frankie plucks another thistle. She should have asked Moran to come to the island with her instead.

CHAPTER 7

On Monday, Frankie travels to Letterkenny again, this time to meet Doctor Long.

When she arrives at the hospital, she sidesteps a small knot of nurses protesting outside the front of the building.

"*No cutbacks! We fight back!*" they chant. "*No cutbacks! We fight back!*"

Frankie makes her way to obstetrics. She's early. In the waiting room, she picks up the *Donegal Democrat*. "**Baby Boy Found Brutally Murdered on Port Arthur Strand**" runs the headline. The by-line speculates as to who the killer is. A few paragraphs of description of the tourist who alerted the gardaí, where he hails from and how he found the body. The next few paragraphs are invention, the flights of fancy of a copywriter hard pressed for information. But can she blame them? Doesn't she do the same, when profiling a suspect? Imagination. Flights of fancy. It's her job. And her intuitions often turn out to be fact.

"Detective Francis?" The tall grey-haired consultant has appeared and extends his hand. He invites her into his office and closes the door. He points to a chair and she sits.

"You are looking for information about Sarah Joyce?"

"Yes. As you know we are investigating the death of the baby boy at Port Arthur Strand," Frankie leans forward. "We understand you treated three pregnant women in May, one of whom was Sarah Joyce."

Doctor Long looks at a file already open on his desk. "I did indeed treat Sarah Joyce."

"Was it a normal birth?"

The doctor is silent for a moment. He takes his glasses off and rubs his eyes. "I said I treated her. I didn't say I delivered her baby."

"I don't understand."

"Sarah arrived at the hospital for treatment. She claimed she had a miscarriage but a scan of her womb told a different story. We believe she'd given birth."

The phone rings. Long lifts the receiver and speaks.

Frankie surveys the office. Typical doctor's surgery: filing cabinet, mobile screen, a bed with a sterile paper sheet covering it. She imagines Sarah in this room, insisting she had no baby. How did she feel? Frightened? Guilty?

"Thanks. Tell them I'll be there in five minutes."

Doctor Long places the receiver quietly back in its cradle, strokes his chin. "Sorry about that." Sighs. "It's not uncommon for a woman to come into hospital after a secret home birth and a dead baby buried somewhere. I've grown used to it."

"And Sarah Joyce?"

The consultant shakes his head.

"Do you normally consult the police in these situations?"

"There's never any need to involve the police."

They hear the noisy clatter of a trolley being wheeled along the corridor outside. The doctor glances out through the small window panel. He furrows his brow. "Overcrowding."

"Did you feel any obligation on this occasion to consult the police?" Frankie persists.

Doctor Long looks at her sharply. He gets up abruptly and walks to the window. It is raining heavily outside now, slanting rain pelting the window, a sudden downpour.

Despite the rain, the strikers are still protesting. She can still hear the chant: "*No cutbacks! We fight back!*"

Doctor Long leans to the right to get a better look, buying time. He wipes the window, shakes his head, then finally turns to face Frankie again. He sits down, holds the tips of his fingers loosely together.

Here's the church, here's the steeple ...

"Sarah Joyce stayed in hospital for three days, and then was released by me. During her stay, I asked the hospital chaplain to talk to her."

"So you didn't report to the police?"

The doctor winces. A long moment passes. He collapses the church into a prayer, fingers locked in a plea.

"You're looking for evidence regarding the death of the Port Arthur baby." He rebuilds the church again. "In my view, you're on the wrong track."

He gets up again and paces. The rain has eased. He stretches to see the strikers but there is silence from that quarter. He turns his attention to the hospital lawn.

Frankie stands. She follows his gaze. A lone mountain ash stands forlorn in the centre of the green patch, blood-red berries in embryo forming. Finally, he faces Frankie.

"I don't consider Sarah Joyce killed that baby on the strand. As I said before, I think you're on the wrong track. Send someone out and you'll probably find her baby closer to home. It was most likely a stillbirth. I ask no questions. These sad women have suffered enough."

* * *

Back at Errigal Lodge, Frankie rings the barracks.

Within an hour of her phone call, Garda Dinny McGinley is sent to bring Sarah Joyce in for questioning.

CHAPTER 8

Sarah sits in the detention room in Bunbeg harbour. She stares across the deal table at the two bucket-seats facing her. She shivers and wraps her cardigan tightly around herself. *It's summer – why does it feel so cold?* A solitary cupboard stands to attention with its back pressed against the wall. Through the window she can see a local fisherman dragging his nets down to the pier to set up for the night's fishing. She knows all about late-night catches of herring – many a time she helped her Uncle Pat haul in the fish. She can visualise the lobster pots strewn out on the pier, the fluorescent orange nets, and the intoxicating smell of seaweed. *It will have been a high tide because of the full moon last night. Or is it vice versa?*

She looks around the large high-ceilinged room. *What a dump!* Mike used to say it was a relic from the days of empire:

"The RIC here to put manners on us peasants." Mike. Often they had passed this place on their way down to the pier when they first started dating. Often she had wondered what it was like inside. And now look at her!

Oh God, oh God. Will they find out? What if they find out? What is to become of me?

The door opens and two gardaí come in. Or are they detectives? One is a stocky middle-aged man. The other a thirty-something blonde with hair tied back in a ponytail, electric-blue eyes that would bore a hole through your brain, and very high cheekbones. Sarah shivers.

* * *

Moran sits and places a tape recorder in front of him. Frankie opens the window. The sash falls like a guillotine. She looks for something to prop it up, finds a wood offcut – shaped like a pawn chess piece – in the press, and carefully lowers the window onto it. She sits on the old radiator. *This may take a while*, she thinks.

Moran switches the recorder on.

"It's Tuesday, the 16th of May, nineteen eighty-nine. Time: eleven a.m."

He swivels the recorder at an angle towards Sarah, sits back, hands clasped and resting on the table. He waits.

Sarah glances up at Moran, then down.

Moran starts the interview. "We know you had a baby delivered recently."

A red flush starts at Sarah's throat and rises all the way up to her face. Her cheek muscles flex. Frankie notices a nervous tic playing on her upper lip.

"We want to ask you where the infant is now?" Moran continues.

No response.

"As you know, we are investigating the murder of the baby found on Port Arthur on May the ninth," he adds. "You're advised that anything you say will be recorded and can be used in evidence."

Sarah meets Moran's eyes for the first time and glares at him.

The radiator is digging into Frankie's sit-bones and she changes position. The dirty oak floorboards creak underfoot. Sarah shoots a glance over at Frankie, then resumes her previous pose, head down.

"You don't deny you had a baby recently?"

Seagulls screech in reply. But nothing from Sarah. Moran looks at Frankie. She comes and sits beside him and leans in towards Sarah, forcing eye contact.

"Sarah, your gynaecologist confirms that you did have a baby. He has scans to prove it. So why don't you tell us what happened to the child?"

Two fat tears roll down Sarah's face.

"Where is your baby now?" Frankie presses.

Sarah lifts a fist and wipes the tears from her face, feels in her jacket pocket for a tissue, then searches in the second pocket in vain. She puts the back of her hand to her nose, wipes and sniffs loudly, then mutely bows her head.

Moran and Frankie exchange looks.

"If you continue to refuse to cooperate," Moran says. "I am afraid we are going to have to charge you with the murder of the Port Arthur Strand baby."

A stifled sob.

"We have evidence that you recently gave birth to a child," Moran repeats. "You give no satisfactory report of where that child is. Meanwhile a baby has been found murdered on Port Arthur Strand. I put it to you, Sarah Joyce, that you are the mother of the Port Arthur Strand baby, that you brutally murdered the child on the eighth of May and buried the child in the dunes."

Sarah looks straight at Moran for the first time. Her eyes are red and blazing with anger and misery.

"I didn't do it. Do you hear? I didn't do it. That Strand baby was not mine!"

"Then where is your baby, Sarah? Tell us that."

Frankie leans forward and asks quietly, "Who is the father, Sarah? Is he involved in any of this?"

Sarah shakes her head, clenching her teeth, like an animal trapped in a cage. "A two-timing bastard, that's who!"

"Who's a two-timing bastard?"

Sarah frowns, presses her lips together and shakes her head.

Frankie sighs. One step forward, two steps back. She leans back. "You do admit you gave birth to a child?"

They wait.

"We know you did, Sarah, so it'll make things a lot easier for you if you admit it now and not waste any more of our time. We have the gynaecologist to back us up."

Sarah starts to sob. She rocks back and forth, crying uncontrollably for a while.

She looks up. "Yes, I did have a baby!" she blurts out. "I'm sorry ... oh, God help me!" She slumps onto the table, her head cradled in her arms.

Moran turns off the recorder. "We'll take a break."

Frankie and Moran leave the room.

* * *

Frankie places a box of tissues on the table and assumes her position by the window. She glances at the wood offcut that's about to drop and carefully secures it. Moran switches on the recorder and leans towards Sarah who shrinks back. She appears hollowed out, like a paper bag that has been blown up and punched.

"You say you didn't give birth to the Strand baby," Moran begins. "If that's the case, can you explain where the child is that you gave birth to?"

Sarah's eyes well up. A tear gathers slowly and shoots down

her cheek. She gives it a swipe with the back of her hand. Another tear wells up. And another. Nothing can stop the flow. Frankie goes over and slides the box of tissues towards her. Without looking up, Sarah pulls a wad out of the box and scrubs her eyes. She blows her nose noisily, then stuffs the tissues into her pocket.

Frankie sits down, leans towards the young woman and asks quietly, "Where is your baby, Sarah?"

Sarah, convulsed, weeps uncontrollably.

Moran switches off and the detectives leave the room.

Outside he opens a pack of cigarettes. "Okay, enough of the rolling punch. What has it unearthed so far?" With great concentration he pulls a cigarette out, taps it on the box and inserts it between his lips.

"Sarah's body language is all wrong," says Frankie. "Yes, she's ashamed. Yes, she's guilty of something. But murder?"

Moran flicks a lighter into flame, ignites the cigarette.

Frankie leans back out of the airstream. "She's admits she had a child but denies she murdered the Strand baby."

"Then where *is* the child she gave birth to if it's not the Strand baby?"

The corridor smells of damp and decay. Of secrets. Of the many bad things that have unfolded within these walls.

At length, Frankie gives voice to what they are probably both thinking. "Are we talking about two babies?"

"Let's get a search warrant," says Moran as he stubs out his cigarette.

* * *

A flock of reporters clamour for news outside the station. Frankie tries to side-step the crowd but is accosted by no fewer than five microphones. Cameras click.

"We heard you've been interviewing Sarah Joyce in relation to the murder of the Strand baby. Is she the killer?"

"How did she do away with her baby?"

"It's rumoured the child had received multiple stab wounds?"

"Did Mike MacAllister have a role in the murder?"

Frankie barks: *We have nothing to report as yet.*

* * *

McGinley drives Moran, Frankie and O'Toole to the Joyce home near Dunlewy. They pass the River Clady, flowing through the wild moorland.

"The Clady is great for sea trout in August. Grilse too from May to September," says O'Toole. And in case anyone is in any doubt, adds, "By the way, grilse is a salmon that has returned to fresh water after a single winter at sea."

"We know all that already!" McGinley snaps.

"I didn't," says Frankie.

They drive past the hydroelectric station at the head of the river, then the old Cúirt Hotel. "Once home of Lord George Hill," says O'Toole, "the landlord who bought up half of Gweedore a century or so before, whose legacy still casts a long shadow."

Frankie sighs.

"This place is full of secrets," O'Toole continues. "I've been clueing up. This isn't the first murder to have happened in this locality. There was the infamous murder of a landlord in the nineteenth century ..."

Frankie zones out. *He might be a bright thing, this young garda, but does he ever shut up?*

"Famous for being infamous," remarks Moran drily, looking out the window.

O'Toole, not one for irony, reels on. "Hungry tenants brutally killed the landlord, who sucked them dry."

McGinley squints at him through the rear-view. "That was a century ago," he says. "Anyway, it wasn't the landlord was killed, 'twas his agent."

O'Toole babbles on like the River Clady in full flow. "And now a hundred years on a very different kind of murder. The Irish killing their own. *Ye gods!*"

McGinley scowls at him through the rear-view mirror.

Errigal comes into view now. The rookie takes a detour into mythology. "Errigal was named after the Fir Bolg, who hailed from Greece, and worshipped Errigal as they had Mount Olympus. Name comes from the Latin *orare* which means *to pray* and the Greek *ekklesia* which means *church*. It's supposed to be one of the oldest place-names in Ireland."

"Is that a fact now," says Moran.

"Oh, it is indeed, sir."

All murder investigations follow a similar path, Frankie reflects. *You start at the end, work backwards and only when the mystery is solved and all the pieces fit do you get the full story. The sequence. The truth. But at the start, all the secrets and lies.*

They finally come to Inchacarragh, a tiny village near Dunlewy. They veer off the main road and up a lane, much in need of repair, rough grass pushing up through the centre. Thick hedgerows flank both sides of the lane. Hawthorn in full flower: white florets with pinkish tips, blackthorn past flowering, elderflower with its pungent white bloom sprays. The isolated cottage comes into view at the end of the lane, its roof in need of rethatching, an extension visible at the side.

They park outside the gate and walk to the door. A small clump of purple aquilegia shares space in an unkempt border with dandelions and daisies. Frankie can see the thick lace curtain inside move. McGinley raps on the window. Slowly the latch is lifted and the door opens a fraction. Two dark eyes peer out at them.

"An Garda Síochána," says McGinley, flashing the official warrant. "Mags, we have a warrant to search your premises."

"*You have what?*" shouts Mags. "*Ye'll have to speak up! I can't hear ye!*" She closes the door an inch or two.

"*I said,*" says McGinley, raising the volume a few decibels, "*we* have a warrant to search your house!" He has his hand firmly on the door to stop it closing further.

"*Go away out of that with ye!*" shouts Mags, pushing the door shut.

McGinley blocks it from closing and marches through.

Mags backs away. "Oh, God oh God, what has the world come to? Is it not enough ye've incarcerated me poor daughter, but now you want to go pushing an old woman about in her own home!"

"Now, Mags," says McGinley, "stop that."

"Don't you 'Now Mags' me, you little whelp! I remember you when you were in nappies."

McGinley chuckles. "Ah now, Mags', I don't know who you're thinking of, but you never saw me in nappies and you know yourself we have to do our duty. There was a baby murdered, as you well know."

"I know nothing."

Frankie takes in the woman standing stubbornly in their way, her lined face, her stoop. *This woman is ancient. How can she be Sarah Joyce's mother?*

O'Toole arrives at the door, carrying a couple of spades.

Moran nods at McGinley. "You two start in the back garden, we'll do the house."

O'Toole hands a spade to McGinley. They march through the living area and out the back door to the garden, Mags on their heels.

Frankie glances around. A creel of turf stands near the big open hearth that occupies one whole wall in the living room, stained black from years of smoke. An iron crane pivots down over the fire to the left side. An adjustable pot-hanger is hooked into the arm of the crane, from which a black kettle hangs suspended over the flames. On the wall opposite a red light burns beneath an image of the Sacred Heart. Beside the fireplace is a wall cupboard, on which are displayed willow-pattern plates, cups and saucers behind a glass door. On a shelf above, two china dogs – black Scottish terriers – act as bookends, with an old-fashioned mantel clock in between as centrepiece. An oilcloth covers an oak table that stands by the narrow sash window, surrounded by old straight-backed chairs. On the table a heavy glass sugar bowl and an aluminium teapot.

Suddenly Frankie notices a woman – dressed entirely in black, rendering her almost invisible – sitting still by the fire. She can be no more than forty although the first impression is of a much older woman: overweight, hair grey, shoulders slumped.

"Who are you?" asks Frankie.

The woman looks straight ahead, solidly occupying the wooden seat built into the side of the hearth, apparently neither seeing nor hearing.

"Leave her be, the *créatúr*." Mags has come back into the house and stands scowling at Frankie. "She's not doing anybody any harm."

Frankie gives the woman by the fire a smile and wanders into the tiny kitchen, off which is a door leading to the extension with a bathroom and two bedrooms. She opens the door into the first. Brightly coloured tops hang from a hook on the back of the door. On the wall are posters of popular singers: Prince, the Bangles, Madonna. This must be Sarah's room. She is about to explore further when suddenly she hears a commotion outside.

Frankie swiftly retraces her steps out through the kitchen, and into the back garden.

The whole area comprises about a half-acre, by Frankie's estimation. At the very back is a row of tall straggly trees – most likely Leylandii – that frame the space. The rest of the garden is a hodgepodge of plants and trees, testament to the enthusiasm of the amateur gardener rather than someone knowledgeable about plants and their cultivation. A buddleia, that butterfly magnet, stands in the middle of the grass area – you couldn't call it a lawn. Frankie spots a painted lady and a monarch as she makes her way to where the others are, partly concealed at the end of the garden.

Moran and O'Toole are both hovering over McGinley, who is just visible behind a large willow, bent over, spade in hand, peering into a hole at the bottom of the plot. Lupins and hollyhocks lie splayed on the ground around where he's been digging.

"Ruinin' me feckin' flowers," Mags grumbles as she hovers, worrying the tea towel in her hands, swatting bees.

"We've found something," McGinley announces triumphantly, scraping away at the hard soil.

Mags, Frankie, and Moran form a circle around him.

McGinley sets aside the spade, kneels on the grass and flings clumps of soil out of the hole, the better to see what he's found. He leans down, lifts it out, holds it at arm's length and stares at it, frowning in disgust. "A friggin' chamber pot." He drops the offending article back into the hole.

O'Toole chuckles, puts his hand over his mouth, his body quivering.

"*Oul' eejit*," Mags mutters, shaking her head and shuffling off to the house.

"Keep digging," orders Moran.

He and Frankie walk around the rough half-acre, searching for signs of recently opened ground. The plot is a wild cacophony of flowers and weeds jostling for space. Perfect lilies grow alongside nettles. Camelia and poison ivy entwine in a lovers' embrace. The world turned upside down.

A paroxysm of sneezing takes hold of Moran.

"Histamine," says Frankie, pulling aside honeysuckle to get into another nook of the garden.

"What?"

"Pollen."

"*Oh, Jesus, Mary and Joseph!*" McGinley shouts from the bottom of the garden. "*We've found it!*"

Frankie stiffens. She yanks away the catchweed bedstraw that clings to her hands and clothes, and retraces her steps.

McGinley makes a low growl that might be a curse.

CHAPTER 9

"I always know by the eyes if someone is guilty, the way they look down or away – just a little push more and you'll have a confession." Brannigan on his soapbox.

The murder team are assembled in the incident room for the briefing. A baby girl has been found buried in the back garden of Sarah Joyce's family home. Cause of death? Possibly strangulation. The state pathologist has been called in for a second time. Can this be another homicide? Sarah Joyce is still in custody.

Brannigan pauses for a moment, self-satisfied, then clenches his stomach and grimaces, opens a drawer, searching in vain. "Sarah Joyce," he continues, "was nineteen years old on her last birthday. Born on twenty-third of May, nineteen sixty-nine."

A birthday next week, four days before mine, thinks Frankie.

"Attended the Dominicans until nineteen eighty-two." He hands McGinley the file. "You fill in, Dinny."

McGinley straightens up, clears his throat and addresses the assembly. "By all accounts, she was a bright child. But her behaviour got out of control for a while with the result that at age nine she was sent to St Anne's for a period."

And St Anne's would be? Frankie wonders.

On cue, O'Toole announces: "St Anne's is a special unit for disturbed children, attached to Letterkenny General. A relative of mine went there."

"Figures," said Brannigan sourly.

O'Toole blinks. "A distant relative."

McGinley glances at Brannigan for permission to continue. The sergeant gazes silently at his stomach.

McGinley continues. "We don't know if it did her any good, but anyway she settled back into primary school. She attended the convent secondary for the next four years. Some trouble there too, by all accounts."

"Relationships?" asks Moran.

"She hung around with Mike MacAllister for a while." He curls his lip. "So-called volunteer."

"One wilder than the other," mutters Brannigan, unwilling and unable to stay out of the conversation.

"Is she an IRA sympathiser?" asks Frankie.

"Whatever she is, it was at that punk's house we arrested the bould Sarah. And," Brannigan, recovered from his gastric bout, is riding high again, "she wasn't the only thing that fella was hiding."

Moran frowns.

"We found MacAllister in possession."

"Of what – guns? Weapons?" Moran asks.

"Drugs."

Frankie scrutinises Brannigan's face. Where's this going? Why haven't they arrested MacAllister if he's been found in possession?

But Brannigan is preoccupied, looking for antacids again while the assembly waits. He pulls out drawer after drawer.

Moran goes out for a smoke. Frankie joins him. She looks at the River Clady, the warm colour of tea, rushing headlong into the sea. The usual busyness of a harbour: fishermen fixing nets, cargo being hauled on and off boats, sea birds squealing and bickering over the spoils of the harbour detritus.

"Do you notice the way McGinley hops to attention whenever Brannigan opens his mouth?" she says.

Moran shrugs. "C'mon, let's get this over with."

* * *

The detectives sit opposite Sarah in the detention room. Sarah looks down.

"We found a baby in your back garden, Sarah," Frankie says.

"Strangled," Moran adds.

A small explosion erupts from Sarah, like something held down deep in her belly that fires its way to the surface. She gulps for air.

Moran taps the table. "We know the child is yours and the sooner you admit to it the better."

The young woman before them utters a stifled sob, misery etched on her face.

Frankie leans across the table. She holds Sarah's eyes. "That baby we found in the back garden of your house in Inchacarragh was your baby, right?"

Sarah sobs. "I didn't ... oh God, I didn't kill her, it was an accident ... I didn't ... I'd never have killed her."

Frankie presses on. "But it is your child?"

Sarah cries silently, tears running down her cheeks.

Can this woman really be acting?

"The child we found in the garden yesterday is yours? Isn't it, Sarah?" Frankie says.

Sarah nods her head slowly, rests her head on her arms and continues to weep.

"And the Strand baby?"

Sarah wipes her eyes with the sleeve of her jumper. She shakes her head vehemently. "*No. No. No.*"

"No, what, Sarah?"

Sarah's eyes are red and bloodshot from crying. "That other baby isn't mine." She slumps.

There's something about the way she said that, Frankie thinks. *She knows something. There's something she's not telling.*

She slides the tissues over to Sarah.

"Do you know whose baby it is?" she asks.

The detectives wait.

The clock ticks like a metronome tapping out the seconds. *Tick. Tock. Tick. Tock.*

Still they wait.

"All right, I did do it!" Sarah snaps finally. "I'm to blame. Is that what you want to hear? Are you happy now? I did do it."

"What did you do, Sarah?" asks Frankie quietly.

Sarah eyeballs the detective. "I killed it." She holds up her hands, looks at them, twists them around as if wringing out a cloth, and says, "With my bare hands I killed it."

"With your bare hands?"

"Yes. With my bare hands." Sarah's face is crimson. Her eyes have a strange manic fire burning in them.

"Are you saying you strangled the Strand baby?"

"Yes." Sarah is exhausted, deflated, indifferent.

"Can you describe to us exactly what happened."

"I don't know. I don't remember. I killed it, that's all. What more do you need to know?"

"You're saying you killed the Strand baby?"

"Yes – yes – yes – I'm guilty. Guilty as charged, m'lord." A hollow laugh. "Or should that be – guilty as sin?" She looks from one detective to the other as if trying to crack the riddle. "That's it – guilty as sin."

Moran looks sideways at Frankie, shakes his head and frowns. "Sarah, we'll need you to sign a statement."

Sarah's head slumps onto the table.

Frankie reaches her hand out towards her. "Sarah?"

"I'm sorry," Sarah mumbles.

"What did you say?"

"I'm so sorry. So sorry. I'm just a bad person."

* * *

"Twenty pounds? Christ," Brannigan says into the phone and wipes away spittle that's gathered at the corners of his mouth. "Where exactly?" He glances at Moran and Frankie, waves them to sit down, covers the mouthpiece. "IRA bomb found near Castlefinn," he tells them. *"Okay, you know the drill!"* he barks into the phone. *"Get cracking!"* He jams the receiver down on its cradle. "Bloody Shinners." But he does not look at all unhappy.

"She's admitted it," says Moran.

Brannigan gapes at the detective. "What?"

Moran lights a cigarette. "Both. She's admitted she is the killer of both the garden baby *and* the Strand baby."

84

"What? She had twins?"

"There are some contradictions in her statement," said Moran, "but we have an admission."

Frankie frowns. *Contradictions, indeed. Why did she say she killed it with her bare hands?*

Brannigan thumps the table. "*Jesus H Christ!* It's true what they say – God doesn't shut a door but he opens a window!"

McGinley puts his head around the door. "The curate is here, boss. About the burial."

Involuntarily, Brannigan crosses himself. "Christ, I almost forgot."

Father Roche sweeps into the room, like a man with an entire kingdom at his disposal. King of Souls, Master of Consciences. It's been a while since Frankie's been in the presence of clergy, witnessed their sense of importance, of entitlement.

Roche is a large man, and holds himself tall. He seems to occupy the whole room. The gardaí genuflect before him, or as good as. *Jesus wept!*

Brannigan pulls out a chair for the curate. "Good of you to come, Father. Detectives Anthony Moran and Kate Francis."

Roche's gaze pans the room, latching on to the newcomers. "Hello, hello," he beams. He lifts his coattails magisterially, which fan out behind him as he sits. He leans back, settles himself comfortably, like a man used to pleasure, to living in the sensual moment: a man of the world as well as of heaven.

In a way this appeals to Frankie – better than those with their heads in the ether.

Roche spreads his arm along the back of the chair next to him, his fingers creeping towards Frankie. She edges away.

"But this is a terrible business, a terrible business. Has Sarah ... confessed?" He lifts his palm upwards, offering the question to the Lord.

Moran stubs out his cigarette. "For legal reasons we can't ..."

"Of course, of course," says Roche, joining his hands as if to lead them all in a decade of the rosary.

"So, Father" – Brannigan strikes a match, applies the flame to the half-burnt contents of his pipe – "you're here about the burial, pending results from forensics."

"The burial, yes."

"What's the protocol?"

Father Brendan Roche fixes his gaze on a dirty splodge on the far wall, under the picture of the Sacred Heart. "Oh dear ... the unfortunate unbaptised."

* * *

Frankie and Moran return to the detention room. Sarah is sitting, shoulders hunched, just as they left her. Moran opens his folder and produces an A4 sheet. He scans the document, reads Sarah's short statement out loud and then slides it over to her.

"I have drawn this up for you to sign." He holds out a pen.

Sarah doesn't move or make any effort to take the pen. Moran thrusts it further in her direction. She lifts the pen and holds it in her hands for a moment, looks at the tip as if seeing a pen for the first time in her life. After a moment, she puts it down on the table beside the statement. The detectives wait. The old schoolhouse wall clock chimes the hour.

"Sarah ..."

Sarah jerks out of her reverie. She glances at the confession sheet, folds her arms and sits back in her seat. She taps out a beat on the wooden floor with her foot, draws her lips into a defiant line. "I'm not signing that."

"You've already admitted to the crime. You'll only prolong the agony by being stubborn."

"I'm not signing it."

"We found the body of an infant in your back garden ..."

Sarah bows her head.

"And you've confessed to killing the baby at Port Arthur Strand. So why not sign the statement?"

"Because I didn't kill that baby at Port Arthur Strand."

CHAPTER 10

The sky darkens. Rain streams down the window of the prefab like tears. Frankie switches on the light.

Moran faces Frankie, McGinley and O'Toole. "Okay. Let's see. What have we got?" He raises a thumb. *One*: a baby boy has been found dead on Port Arthur Strand. Murder weapon – a ball-peen hammer – according to the autopsy."

McGinley appears puzzled. "A ball-peen?"

"O'Toole, you've done the research. Explain."

"A ball-peen is a hammer that comes in all sizes, but the type commonly used in jewellery-making, although small, with a good hard strike, especially in just the right spot at the temple, has the potential to—"

"Yes, yes," Moran says, cutting him short, impatient to move on. Index finger and thumb. "*Two*: a second baby, a girl, is found in the garden of Sarah Joyce's home in Dunlewy. Cause of death inconclusive. Possibly strangulation. Possibly not. We have yet to establish if we are talking about murder here too. *Three*," – he raises his middle finger – "Sarah Joyce confirms she is the mother of the baby found at her home. She remains in detention. *Four*: we have the Biddies, more work to be done there. But, as yet, we've no firm suspect for the baby murdered on the strand. We await forensic tests to confirm its blood group."

"What about Derry?" asks Frankie. "Were we able to check Derry for information on recent pregnancies?"

"Ruled out," says Moran.

Frankie raises an eyebrow. "So Brannigan was able to get access to the hospitals in Derry?"

"Yep! Influence in high places."

Moran throws his biro down on the desk. He laces his fingers, flexing them inwards. There is a loud click as the joints crack. "Okay, folks. Where do we go from here? Ideas, ideas?"

Not much so far, thinks Frankie. One murdered baby. Another baby dead, awaiting confirmation about how it died. A woman who confesses to the murder and then withdraws her confession.

O'Toole scratches his head. "I'm a little confused here. We know that Sarah is the mother of the garden baby because she's admitted it. But if we're saying she might be the killer of the

Strand baby, does that mean we're saying she's also the mother?"

"We'll keep an open mind on all probabilities until we have hard facts," Moran says. "We should try and establish who the father of Sarah's baby is. That might be a lead. Meantime, we need to check Sarah's workplace, her home and education etc. What she liked to do in her spare time. What she likes to read. Everything about her. She is, after all, still Exhibit A."

Frankie grimaces. "I'll do that."

* * *

From the car park of Derrybeg Community School, Frankie has a view of Port Arthur Strand as it stretches in a golden arc. The tide is out. The sea is a silver strip between the azure cloudless sky and the immaculate white sand. *What a glorious vista!* No sooner does this thought enter her head than it's replaced with the dark reality of what happened in the dunes just ten days before. She shivers. *Murder in paradise.*

She hurries up the concrete path to the school.

The smell of bananas and milk hits her as soon as the pushes through the heavy pneumatic front door: the smack of schools. She can hear screams from the school yard: the eleven o'clock break. Memories: *Race you to the end of the pitch!* As she makes her way up the corridor, the sounds from outside subside and are replaced by the muted adult chatter from the staffroom and the clink of cups. Frankie peers at door labels, searching for the secretary's office. Too late she sees the figure in front of her hurrying by with a bundle of books. They collide, books scatter, folders fall.

"Sorry. Sorry. It was my fault."

"No, it was mine."

Both apologising for not paying attention.

Then the double take.

"Roseanne? Roseanne Doherty? Oh, my God!"

"Kate Francis!"

The two women stand, broad grins on their faces.

Roseanne jabs an index finger at Frankie. "Looking great."

They examine each other, the years collapsing like a concertina. The memories of their college days flooding back. Each placing a template of what the other was back then onto the person before them now, fifteen years later.

Frankie stoops to pick up the fallen books. "I thought you were teaching in Dublin?"

"Past tense. But what on earth are you ... Oh Lord. Of course. You're here about that case?"

"Yes, on my way to talk to the Head."

Roseanne rolls her eyes. Still pretty. Still wearing the long hippy skirts she always wore at college. Thick hair, the colour of corn, long and luxurious. No longer slim. "Good luck with that." She points. "His office is second door on the right."

Frankie smiles at her friend. "Roseanne, would you be free to meet up later?"

"Absolutely. I live about a quarter of a mile down the Harbour Road from Bunbeg Cross. Dúnaras – used to be the family home. You'll see the sign. You can't miss it."

O'Connor's office is just across from the staffroom. Frankie instinctively holds one cupped hand to her nose to mask the unmistakable smell of disinfectant from the toilet across the corridor. She knocks.

"Come in."

Frankie introduces herself. "Detective Kate Francis from the dedicated murder squad investigating the death of a baby at Port Arthur Strand."

The principal, a man in his late fifties, shakes her hand limply. He is a portly man of medium build, with thinning hair and a jaded look about him. He points to a chair in front of his desk as he sits down in his own swivel, his back to an interior window that opens onto reception. The window is clumsily sellotaped over with heavy black sugar paper. Was that not against regulations? Anything could go on in this little office and no one would be any the wiser. *Stop that, Frankie – O'Connor is not the one under suspicion.*

Frankie involuntarily addresses the faded sugar-paper barricading the principal in from his secretary: *What is he hiding?* She shakes her head again.

"As I mentioned on the phone to your secretary, I'm here to discuss Sarah Joyce."

"Ah. Sarah Joyce."

Everything about him is stiff: his gait, his manner, his demeanour. *He's tired, of his work, his life too probably. I certainly wouldn't fancy working for this guy.*

"Yes, in connection with the investigation into the Strand baby death. Just a few general questions, if that's okay?"

O'Connor yawns.

"For example, what was Sarah like as a teacher?"

O'Connor takes in a deep breath that sounds like a hiss. Getting information out of him is going to be like pulling teeth from a seagull.

"Fair enough as a teacher, I suppose. But not much of a team player." He pushes his lips out like a duck's bill and shakes his head brusquely. "No, definitely not a team player."

"Could you explain what you mean by that?"

O'Connor waves his hand in the air as if the information is out there floating around, so why is he being bothered with having to provide it? He frowns.

Frankie waits.

He narrows his eyes. "Too much into herself, too much up her own backside, if you'll pardon the vernacular." There is the hint of a sly smirk.

Frankie flinches. Her sympathies lie with Sarah Joyce.

"Are you saying she didn't do her job well?"

O'Connor bites down into his lower lip and worries it in irritation. "She didn't fit in, thought she was above taking orders."

Oh dear! Let's try another tack, get some information. "Did you notice a change in behaviour in recent weeks, anything that would have alerted you to something being wrong, anything that might make you take note?" *For example the obvious, that she was pregnant!*

"Well, she took off without a by-your-leave last week and I haven't seen her since. Left me with a class minus a teacher which is a major pain in the butt. And not even an excuse. That's what I call irresponsible, to say the least."

There's a knock on the door.

"*Who is it?*" barks O'Connor.

"Sorry, Mr O'Connor," says the secretary, "but Father Roche has just called about the celebration next week."

Celebration?

"Tell him I'm on my way." O'Connor turns to Frankie. "Sorry, I have to go. In any case, I've told you all I know."

Which isn't very much, thinks Frankie. *And what's the celebration?* She puts away her notebook, stands to go.

"Did you know Sarah was pregnant?"

He didn't. But his curiosity is piqued. "So is she the prime suspect then?" he asks, with an expression approaching a leer.

"Obviously we can't divulge details at this stage."

"Obviously."

At the door, Frankie turns to O'Connor. "Is there anything else you are aware of that might be of help to us in this investigation? Any talk among staff, anything at all?"

O'Connor shrugs, shakes his head, opens the door, practically pushes her out.

* * *

"*Unconfirmed reports say that a second baby has been found dead in Gweedore in the back garden of Sarah Joyce's home in Inchacarragh, a townland fifteen miles from where the first baby was found hammered to death. The cause of death of this second infant is allegedly strangulation, but this has yet to be confirmed. There is huge international interest in this case, given the nature of the crime. In our other news, in Tiananmen Square, 1 million gather as part of a pro-democracy protest against the Chinese Government ...*"

Frankie flicks from station to station. The press has taken up position in Inchacarragh – the village is groaning under the attention. Hospitality is turning into a thriving business. Two small cafés have turned their back yards into tea gardens to cater for the influx of journalists and photographers with zoom lens who make their way to the town. Four young people have been employed as waiters. Locals are kept busy supplying sandwiches, cakes, scones.

Frankie switches off and drives the short distance from Errigal Hotel over to her friend's house. As she turns into the gravelled driveway of the home Roseanne inherited from her parents, Frankie takes in the well-kept front lawn, with its golden centrepiece, a laburnum in full bloom, heavy with trailing yellow tendrils. Hydrangeas, in colours of white, deep-pink and blue grace the border. Here and there are pots with begonias in salmon and creamy white. She parks, struggling against feelings of envy. Here is her friend, settled with a nice house, a lovely garden, a partner, and soon a baby, no doubt. She could have all this too, if she could make up her mind about whether to sink into domesticity or to continue her rise in the service. Getting that balance between what you need and what you want is so difficult. The trouble is she wants both ... She sighs.

"*Hi!*" she calls in through the open door.

Roseanne appears and they embrace.

Frankie appraises her. "You look happy. Content."

Roseanne is wearing a loose exotic house robe that accentuates rather than disguises a body that's thickened over the years. She shakes her head and smiles at her friend. "And you – look at you. You make me sick. Thin as a whippet. Those high cheekbones. Not to mention delicate legs!"

They laugh at the reference to an incident, when a youngster trashed Frankie with his worst insult, "And you … with your delicate legs!" The circumstances they'd long forgotten. Just the punchline stuck.

Roseanne leads her down the hall and into the kitchen where an island in the centre is set for tea. A freshly baked rhubarb tart resting on a glass Pyrex plate gives off the delicious smell of home baking.

Lord, will I ever be able to bake a rhubarb tart? Or is life too short? She'd read a book once called *Superwoman* in which the author came up with the famous catchphrase: *"Life is too short to stuff a mushroom."* It was a paean to liberated working women, and it had resonated with Frankie. Now she's not so sure: domesticity has its appeals too.

Roseanne pours boiling water into a teapot on the counter and sets it on a copper stand on the island. They sit up and reminisce about the old days and their lives since. *How have things been for you? And you?*

Roseanne slices the tart and serves Frankie a wedge.

"What about Rory? My God, you two were joined at the hip at college. Then I heard it was off. Are you back together or what?"

Frankie shrugs as she helps herself to whipped cream. "On and off. I invited him over for a meal the other evening. We listened to music, the old favourites, Leonard Cohen …"

"Ah yes – 'Suzanne'…"

"'Hey, That's No Way to Say Goodbye' …"

"'So Long, Marianne'…"

"Needless to say we ended up ..."

"In the sack." Roseanne laughs. "As one does."

Frankie sighs. "He finds my long hours impossible. We keep breaking up over that."

"It's a bummer alright." Roseanne pours tea into a rough-hewn earthenware mug and passes it to Frankie. "But, as I remember, you were undecided at one point whether to continue with arts, follow your dream to be a writer, or go into the force. What decided you in the end?"

"Something my father said stuck a chord: 'You have to stand up to live,' he said, 'before you can sit down to write.'"

"That's a good one. I like that. A smart man, your dad." She pours tea into the second mug, adds milk.

"Talking of which – actually, I need to ask you something, Roseanne. I'm building a profile of Sarah Joyce?"

Roseanne shakes her head. "Poor Sarah! What a mess."

"You worked with her? How did you find her?"

"Sarah's the salt of the earth. Only problem is she never knows what's good for her. She's way too honest –"

"Honest?"

"Too trusting. Naïve, you might say. Although she was a student at the school, I only got to know her last year when she joined the staff." Roseanne nurses her mug in both hands and sips. "She didn't get the points she needed for university. She was very disappointed about that."

Frankie nods. "I understand she got a job as a temporary teacher?"

"She did. And then she got accepted for training in Limerick. She was over the moon about that, especially after the previous let-down. There was a very good chance she'd be made permanent in the school.'"

"She'd got a foot in, isn't that what they say?"

"That's right. But trouble is, temps don't have the same rights as permanent teachers."

"She had to watch her Ps and Qs."

"Exactly. I had to remind her of how insecure her position was when she left the school after an argument with the Principal. Just before her arrest, in fact." Roseanne shakes her head. "My God, to think all I was worried about then was that she might lose her job at the school. Now look at her ... It's tragic. Sarah is not a killer. No way."

Both are silent for a moment.

"The thing that puzzles me is," says Frankie, "how could her pregnancy have gone undetected in a school? I mean, did the school know she was pregnant? I asked O'Connor already ..." Roseanne rolls her eyes – "but he said he didn't know. Surely someone must have suspected?"

Roseanne shrugs. "The pregnancy wasn't obvious for ages. She wore these long loose cardigans for the last few months. It's actually common enough in first pregnancies for the woman not to show much."

"But at the very end, surely...?"

"Well, yes, there was some talk at the end, nods and whispers, but it was never brought out in the open. It was like people were a bit embarrassed. Since Sarah acted as though nothing was going on, everyone else took the same attitude. It's a sad fact, but pregnancy outside marriage is still looked on as shameful, or at least the pregnant woman fears it is."

"But you, as her friend, must surely have asked her about it?"

"I did. More than once. I was concerned about her. But there was no budging her. She refused to talk about it, would immediately change the subject."

"And then afterwards, when she arrived in school with no bump, what did you think happened the baby?"

"I assumed she had arranged to put it up for adoption. It's what we all thought."

The doorbell rings. Roseanne rises.

"That's the plumber. Sorry. The bloody sink is blocked. Again." Roseanne grimaces as she goes to answer the door. "Manus is useless at things like that."

Frankie can't resist a smile. So Manus is useless: not so perfect after all. Left on her own, Frankie has an opportunity to look around as she finishes her tart. On the wall, photographs of family in brass frames side by side with images of yogi in impossible positions. Roseanne was always into meditation and eastern philosophy. Zen Buddhism was really popular back in their college days. It certainly had its appeal. Frankie was drawn to Zen art but somehow couldn't bring herself to embrace another life system, having thrown off the shackles of the one she'd grown up with. But she doesn't deny it: meditation is certainly useful. "You're too intense," Rory often levels at her, "Chill out." *Pot kettle black* always comes to mind.

A large tabby saunters into the room. He skirts around Frankie, wrapping his thick furry tail around her legs, caressing, before hopping up onto the windowsill, where he sits, sphinx-like, in a pose of complete Zen relaxation, pondering the problems of the universe,.

Roseanne returns. "'Twill be great to get that thing fixed. No more drip-drip at night. Well, hello, Toby."

Both women gaze fondly at Toby who stares out the window at a blackbird in a tug-of-war with a worm.

"What do you know about Sarah's ex?" asks Frankie.

"Mike?" Roseanne narrows her eyes. "Oh, that's been over for a good while, two years at least, I'd say."

"He's an IRA volunteer, right?"

Roseanne nods. "I taught him. Hard to think of him as an IRA volunteer."

"And have they been in touch since? Sarah and Mike? I mean, since they broke off their relationship?"

"Not that I'm aware of. No. Not together-together anyway, if you know what I mean. I think Sarah would have told me."

Is Roseanne showing uncertainty? Wariness? Frankie can feel her jaw tighten as she struggles, conflicted between friendship and duty.

Toby abandons his perch on the windowsill and exits the kitchen through the cat-flap in the back door.

"Did Sarah have other lovers?"

Roseanne blinks, clears her throat, fidgets. "Sorry, I'll just see how the plumber is doing. Back in a minute." And she's off again.

There's something amiss. Why did she seem edgy when asked about lovers? I mean, she practically bolted off. Frankie's skin crawls at the thought of giving credence to Brannigan's theory of the 'loose woman'. Her eyes follow Toby who has wandered out to the back and now prowls the flower border sniffing for clues.

Roseanne returns.

"Lovers?"

Roseanne takes in a deep breath. *She's uncomfortable. Why? What does she know that she's not telling?* Frankie locks onto Roseanne with a steady gaze and waits.

"As far as I know, Sarah only ever went out with one man. Or should I say 'boy'. And that was Mike MacAllister – he was seventeen at the time. But ..." Roseanne looks out the window as if collecting her thoughts or trying to decide how she will frame what she has to say. "I don't know if I should mention this. I mean, Sarah told me in confidence and I feel a little ... y'know, like maybe it's a betrayal ..." She pauses for a moment. "There was this teacher, Derek O'Brien, who Sarah had a big crush on when she was in her Leaving Cert year. A music teacher. Terrific at his job. Well, all the girls had a crush on him. Extremely good-looking, late twenties, well-built, dark and ... you know yourself."

"And this music teacher, is he from the locality?"

Roseanne shakes her head.

Frankie observes her friend closely. She's clearly struggling with herself. Frankie watches the little muscles at the side of her lips twitch. *What's going on here? What is she hiding?*

"So where does he live, this music teacher that all the girls had a crush on? And you said *had*, like it's in the past tense? This could be important, as part of the investigation."

"The thing is ..." Roseanne, lowers her voice, a habit she developed back in college days when they wanted to exchange stories of the previous night's adventures during symposia, "... he's gone."

"Gone?"

"No longer at the school."

"What? Was he sacked? Did he resign? You make it sound like there was something up. Was there something up?"

Roseanne looks conflicted, as if she's about to wash the school's dirty linen in public. "The truth is he left very suddenly. Just handed in his notice. And disappeared."

"When did this happen?"

"A week last Monday."

The eighth of May. My god!

"For no reason?" Frankie asks. "Didn't anyone ask why?"

"No one knows why. He was very popular with the students. With the staff. With everyone. He was a nice guy. The women thought he was great. No one had any inkling he was unhappy in the place. Just upped and left. Very strange."

Very strange indeed. A popular young music teacher Sarah had a crush on leaves the area at the precise time a new-born baby is found dead, murdered on Port Arthur Strand and a baby is found dead in Sarah's back garden. A coincidence? Or something more sinister? And Roseanne wouldn't have mentioned it if she hadn't pressed her? Why?

Another thought struck her. Why didn't O'Connor think to mention this when she interviewed him?

* * *

From Bunbeg village, Frankie drives the mile down the narrow road to the Beach Hotel on Magheraclogher Strand, where Moran has arranged to meet her.

The tide is out. The channel forms a sleek narrow ribbon of dark blue between the flat expanse of amber sand and the islands. She will have to check if the strands along this stretch of coast are connected.

The Beach Hotel, a solid, pale-grey rectangle, sits high on the dunes overlooking the shore, its featureless windows peering sightlessly over the strand. How on earth did they get permission to build a hotel here, on such a location? As she parks, Frankie glances at the shipwreck lying on its side in the middle of the beach.

In the dining room, she finds Moran at a window-seat table. He has already ordered a bottle of Rioja. He tips out a cigarette.

"Well? What do you think?"

"More Brutalist than Bauhaus," Frankie says as she settles into a chair opposite him. "From the outside anyway."

"You what?"

"Y'know – *North by Northwest*?"

Moran stares blankly at her.

"With Cary Grant? No?"

Moran shrugs and lights up.

"You must know it. It's one of the most iconic films of the fifties. Hitchcock at his best. With the final scenes set in a Frank Lloyd Wright style modernist house supposedly on Mount Rushmore. That's the point I was making. This place is no Frank Lloyd Wright lookalike."

Moran looks at her appraisingly. "Ah, so on top of everything else – great looks, great body –"

Frankie shakes her head in mock annoyance.

" – we're also an architecture and film buff!"

"This looks like nothing so much as a giant Lego construction."

Moran chuckles. He taps the table with his index finger.

"Brutalist or not – the important question is, should we decamp from here?"

"Depends on the food, I suppose," says Frankie.

A well-dressed woman comes into the dining room

Moran winks at Frankie. "Here's Lucy. The manageress. Lovely woman. We're already acquainted. And just listen to the accent!"

Lucy approaches their table, high heels clicking like castanets on the terracotta-tiled floor.

A woman in her forties, she has an hourglass figure, short fair hair brushed back off her face, green eyes and a very smooth complexion. She is indeed lovely.

"Hello. Can I get you something to drink?" she asks Frankie with a soft Donegal lilt.

"I'll have a bottle of still water, thanks," Frankie says. "And the herring." Lucy writes down the order. "Great location you have here. Lovely beach."

Lucy smiles. "Magheraclogher Strand is very popular with tourists. Families especially love it here, because the kids have such expanse of sand to play with, and there's swimming when the tide is in. It really has everything."

"Is it possible to get from one beach to the other?" asks Frankie. "I'm just wondering if it's possible to move from one to the other without going back up to the road?"

"No, unfortunately, it's not possible," says Lucy. "It's very rough and rocky in between, dangerous even. And by the way, the channel is treacherous too if the tide is out. People can be a bit starry-eyed about Gweedore." She pronounces it 'gee door'. "You need to be careful around the sea here."

Moran beams at her.

Frankie nods at the boat on the beach. "And the shipwreck?"

"Oh, it wasn't a shipwreck. That's *Bád Eddie* – 'Eddie's boat' in English. Its real name was *Cara na Mara* – Friend of the Sea. Eddie Gillespie had it towed in to shore here in 1977 for repairs but somehow it just got left here. It's a bit of an eyesore, really, but tourists love it, so I suppose we shouldn't complain if it brings customers our way."

"I'll have the chicken," Moran says.

Lucy makes a note, smiles at him and leaves.

Moran lifts the bottle of wine to pour some into Frankie's glass. She shakes her head. He pours one for himself, still smiling.

"So? Find anything out at the school?"

"Not a team player, according to the curmudgeon, but ...I did find out something..." Frankie raises her index finger in a gesture of triumph. "It seems that a music teacher that Sarah had a crush on a couple of years ago, has suddenly left the school. Just upped and vamoosed. No reason."

"Another possible suspect?"

"Wait for it ... he left on the eighth of May. The precise time a murdered infant was found on Port Arthur Strand. It can hardly be a coincidence."

"Wow. But strange coincidences do occur."

"We need to find out the reason for him leaving so suddenly."

"Back over to O'Connor."

"That'll be fun."

The food arrives. Moran cuts a piece off his Chicken Maryland. He chews. "Okay, not the Shelbourne, but better than that other place, and the lovely Lucy makes up for any culinary shortcomings." He sticks his fork into the broccoli. "*Al dente.*" He smiles at Frankie. His cheeks dimple when he does that, she notices, not for the first time.

Frankie glances at her herring – glassy eyes staring back at her – then at the wreck of the old ship lying forlorn and dead on the strand. She should have ordered the chicken.

CHAPTER 11

From Dublin to Frankfurt, from Helsinki to Singapore, the brutal death of an infant grabs the global imagination. And then the second baby! Editors, with a keen eye for a scoop, free up budgets and discharge reporters to the north-western tip of a little island at the far side of Europe. Where is Ireland anyway, a journalist from CBC wonders? An outpost of Scotland? Of mainland Europe? No, believe it or not, it's an island. A republic to boot. Amazing!

Frankie monitors it all.

The focus switches to Gweedore and its fabulous beaches, its magnificent mountain, Errigal. "**Death in Paradise**", runs a headline.

The focus turns to Sarah Joyce.

Sarah Joyce Lived on the Wild Side. *Global News.*

Walking on the Wild Side! *The Daily Press*.

Slapper! *The Telegraph*.

Spéirbhean Glic! *Celtic Journal*.

Fräulein Joyce ist Nicht ein Gute Mensch! *Bild*.

Sarah was wild as a teenager, uncontrollable. She was promiscuous, man-crazy, a femme fatale, it was a wonder she got her Leaving Cert at all.

Pat Mullarkey, from the *Irish Journal*, paints a different picture. **Women's oppression is alive and well,** she writes. **Innocent until proven guilty**. She refers to the socialists who march outside the hospital, in support of the nurses striking for better pay and conditions. Women in solidarity with women, she writes. Hers is a lone voice amid the shrill cacophony denouncing Sarah Joyce as the scarlet woman.

The Church remains silent, writes Mullarkey.

* * *

"So, the piano man – get any more info?" asks Moran.

Frankie fans herself with a couple of A4 sheets. She looks at the temperature gauge: twenty-seven degrees. The prefab is a baking tin.

A sparrow flies through the open window. It flutters and wavers in panic. Twirls in a figure of eight, creating turbulence in the small stuffy room.

Moran leans back as it swoops past. "*Jesus wept!*"

Frankie feels pity for the poor frightened bird.

O'Toole makes a lunge at the bird, which swirls away from him.

The head detective gets up quietly, tiptoes over to the tiny bird. "Easy does it." He swoops down over it, cupping his hands. But the sparrow glides off.

Frankie opens the door. "Why don't we just leave it be? It will find its own way."

Defeated, the men sit.

"Well? The piano man?" asks Moran, whooshing the demented sparrow away.

"He's moved back to his hometown, Galway."

O'Toole keeps his eyes firmly fixed on the bird, by now frantic in its attempts to escape. "What piano man?"

"A teacher who worked alongside Sarah," Frankie tells him. "Who she once had a crush on, and who recently left the school for no apparent reason."

The sparrow flies out the door.

Moran punches the air and kicks the door shut.

Frankie wipes her forehead, sighs, glances sideways at the door, tempted to open it again to let in some air.

"But ... but ... are you saying she still had a crush on him while she was teaching alongside him?" asks O'Toole.

"No, not when she was teaching. Before that, when she was a

pupil. But then Mike MacAllister came into her radar, at which point she switched her affections."

"The new nail that pushes out the old," says Moran.

Frankie stares at Moran. *What?*

O'Toole frowns. "So if she's not had a thing for the music teacher since then, why is he a suspect?"

"He's suspect because he left mysteriously just after a baby was found brutally murdered on Port Arthur Strand. He left on the eighth of May. " Moran squashes his cigarette out in the overflowing ashtray, releasing stale cigarette fumes into the air. "Let's move on it this afternoon." He stands and stretches. "What is it from here to Galway – a three-hour journey?"

Frankie opens the door a fraction. "More like four and a half hours. Three hours from Donegal town."

She makes a phone call to get an address.

* * *

That afternoon, Frankie and Moran hit the road south to Galway.

"I don't trust Brannigan," says Frankie.

"Thick as a plank."

"More cute hoor than thick, my guess."

"*Jays*, you're cursing," Moran says, smiling at her. "Is he a native? Hard to make out from the accent."

"Cavan, he told me. Stationed here in the late seventies."

"So, a blow-in like ourselves."

"McGinley too."

"Then there's O'Toole."

"*The whole world is queer, except thee and me ...*"

"Oh, Lord," says Frankie, "you can't say that."

"*And even thee's a little queer,*" – Moran glances sideways at Frankie – "God be with the good old days when we could say what we liked."

She can't resist grinning back.

* * *

They book into the Imperial Hotel in Galway city centre. They have a meal in the nearby restaurant. Afterwards they take a walk around Eyre Square, past the nineteenth-century Great Southern Hotel, the famous Bank of Ireland – "*A listed heritage building,*" they read on the plaque. They stop to have a look at the Pádraic Ó Conaire statue.

"He was a modernist," says Frankie.

"Thought that fella wrote in the Irish?" says Moran.

"He did. I mean he was a modernist in Irish fiction."

Blood-red streaks splash across the turquoise and yellow canvas that is the sky as the day closes in. *Red sky at night, shepherd's delight ...*

"Enough culture for one day," says Moran. "We have a long

day ahead of us tomorrow. Let's have a nightcap before we retire."

Two beers later, as they leave the bar, Moran puts his arm around Frankie, pulls her in and kisses her full on the mouth. For one brief moment Frankie succumbs, before pulling away. No, she's not going there. She's been there once before and she's not going there again. Nevertheless, as she closes her bedroom door, she's aware her heart is racing, she can feel the taste of his mouth on her lips. Can smell the tobacco, at once repulsive and alluring. She takes three deep breaths and banishes thought of going to his room.

* * *

Next day they trek down Williamsgate Street, Shop Street and onto High Street. According to Roseanne, the best place to look for him would be most likely Flannery's. He used to talk about Flannery's pub a lot, seemed like it was a favourite haunt.

As they walk through the medieval town, in the 'City of Tribes', memories flood back. It was in Galway that Frankie met Rory. She was twenty and totally carefree. She can still remember that lightness, can conjure up the joie de vivre she felt back then, when the world was full of promise, when her future stretched out before her like a ream of shimmering eastern silk. When did the lightness disappear? Still only thirty-four now, and she feels like she carries the weight of the world on her shoulders. Does she really have so much baggage? Is it that as we get older we accumulate hurts and disappointments and, if we don't deal with them as they come along, they gather and build up, until eventually they distil into dread?

"So where is this pub?" asks Moran.

Frankie shakes herself back into the present. The past is done, she reminds herself. "She just said Flannery's."

They pause at the Wolfe Tone Bridge and watch a couple of kayaks rowing against the flow of the River Corrib – one of the fastest-moving rivers in Ireland, Rory once told her – attempting to make it under the bridge, failing, hovering over by the Bridge Mills, the seething frothing river at high tide, charging like a ravenous animal, a mesmerising challenge for young kayakers.

The detectives move on.

Moran stops a couple of passers-by but no one seems to know where Flannery's bar is. Something isn't adding up. Did Roseanne get it wrong? Or did she send them on a wild goose chase? But why would she do that?

A soft Atlantic drizzle has settled in by the time they stumble on the little pub tucked away up a side alley, facing onto the canal that feeds the river: Flannery's. They peer in through the window.

"Christ, you'd miss this if you weren't sharp," says Moran.

They scrutinise the many notices in the window: an ad for Guinness, an upcoming concert, a public meeting on Cuts to

Health. And plonked right in the centre a large multicoloured poster – in tones of pinks, purples and orange – advertising the current festival. The detectives stare at it, then at each other in slow comprehension.

Moran groans. "Oh, for fuck's sake! He dances with the left foot."

Why didn't Roseanne tell Frankie? Was it because Frankie was police? Or could it have been she didn't know? Or, on the other hand, if Roseanne knew O'Brien was gay then she also knew he wasn't having an affair with Sarah. Strange and stranger. She would have to challenge Roseanne on that one.

They push their way into the dark interior. Strobe lighting illuminates first one face then another through the smoke-filled air of the disco bar. At the far end a small area has been set aside for dancing. A DJ, seated on a dais, orchestrates the music, Freddie Mercury's spine tingling "*I Want It All*", a song Frankie loves. The clientele are mostly men, of no particular age group. Couples dance slowly on the dance area.

The smoke gets to Frankie and momentarily she's overcome with a sudden spasm of coughing. It passes. The detectives approach the bar. One of the patrons offers Frankie his stool. Moran finds another, drags it over to the counter and plonks himself beside her.

Frankie catches the barman's eye and orders a pint and a half of Guinness. The young man, attractive in a goth sort of way, a

David Bowie lookalike, complete with make-up and gold chains around his neck, removes dirty glasses from in front of them, wipes the countertop. *Wow! Galway has certainly changed since I was here last*, thinks Frankie. *Or is it just that I'm getting old?*

The young barman pulls the beers carefully up to almost the top and waits.

"We're looking for Derek O'Brien," Frankie says.

He lifts the almost full pint and, holding it at an angle, taps it to the brim. "Derek O'Brien?" He shakes his head. "Sorry." He repeats the process with the half pint and places the drinks in front of the detectives.

"I'll get these," Moran says. He hands the barman a fiver, lifts the Guinness to his lips, takes a sip and sighs. "A perfect black and white." He wipes his upper lip with the back of his hand.

Frankie holds out a photo to the barman who squints at the creased image.

"Oh, yeah, that guy? Sure. I know him ..."

Frankie's heart skips a beat.

"That's him over there. In the alcove."

Both detectives turn to face the alcove but the light is so low it's impossible to see. They rise in tandem and walk over. Frankie recognises O'Brien from the image – medium-sized and well-built with thick black hair slicked back – engaged in an intense conversation with another man.

Moran flashes his badge and breaks into the conversation. "Are you Derek O'Brien?"

Taken by surprise, O'Brien looks up at the two detectives blocking the entrance to the booth where he was a moment ago enjoying a quiet drink with his friend. Alarm spreads over his face like a cloud on a summer's day.

"Yes. Why?"

"We'd like to ask you a few questions."

"In relation to what?" demands O'Brien, suddenly defensive, aggressive.

O'Brien's friend stands. "See ya, Decko," he says as he lifts his drink and moves to the bar.

Moran and Frankie slide into the bench facing O'Brien.

"We're investigating the murder at Port Arthur Strand in Gweedore." says Frankie. "You are aware of the investigation?"

The man opposite them nods, abandoning the aggressive pose.

"Until recently, you were a teacher in the community school in Derrybeg? Right?" Moran says.

Sweat beads and gathers on O'Brien's forehead. You can practically smell the fear. He puts his closed fingers up to his brow and slides them across, in a futile attempt to stop the stream.

He's clearly terrified, thinks Frankie. *Why? What has he to hide?*

Moran lights up, leans his head back as he exhales, screws up his eyes as the smoke stings. "Why did you leave so suddenly?"

"I got a job here."

"Where exactly?"

O'Brien shifts on the bench. "In St Joseph's Patrician College."

Moran presses. "And what, may I ask, was the reason for your leaving? You already had a job, which by all accounts you liked. You got on well with the pupils from what we hear."

O'Brien blinks. He glances over at the bar but he gets no inspiration from that quarter.

Why don't we just cut to the chase, thinks Frankie. *It's obvious why he might be frightened, and not hard to guess why he might have left. But we need to hear it from him: he needs to spill it out.* "Is there something you want to tell us? Some reason you might have felt compelled to leave."

O'Brien draws a deep breath and cups his mouth and chin with his hand. His shoulders slump and the rims of his eyes redden. "I left the school," he says, "because one of the teachers found out I was gay and gave me an ultimatum." He struggles to control his feelings.

Frankie hopes he's not going to start crying.

"She told me that if I didn't leave by the Easter holidays ... she would out me."

They've just had a wasted journey.

"Who is this 'she'?" Moran asks.

"Dolores O'Hara."

"The vice-principal?"

"Yes. She's a member of a very right-wing Catholic organisation. I've don't know how she found out, but that outfit has its tentacles everywhere."

Frankie is aware of one organisation in particular that has a strict code on sex and sexual orientation, especially homosexuality which is an abomination in their book. "I think I know which organisation you're referring to."

O'Brien takes in a deep breath as he regains composure. "You see, in a small close-knit community like that ... there was a great danger ..." He stops. "I begged for more time until I got another job."

"What about O'Connor, what had he to say about all this?" And why didn't he mention O'Brien when she interviewed him, Frankie wonders.

"He didn't know I'd been threatened. At least he never approached me about that. I simply told O'Connor I had to go home to care for my mother – I told him she was seriously ill – and left before they kicked me out."

Frankie meets his eye. "You made that story up?"

"I could well have been sacked if I'd stayed.

"And is that what you told the other teachers too? Or did you simply leave without telling any of them anything? I mean, how many of the teachers knew you were gay?"

"Only the one who threatened me, as far as I know. As I said, the only one I spoke to before I left was O'Connor."

So Roseanne didn't know he was gay.

Moran gets tough. "You are aware that homosexuality is a criminal offence?"

O'Brien looks at him defiantly but says nothing.

They might as well get on with it. "Where were you on the night of the eighth of May?" Frankie asks.

"I was here in Galway for that weekend." O'Brien glances in the direction of his friend who has taken up position at the bar, keeping a close eye on proceedings. "With Peter."

Frankie rises and goes over to the bar to check out the alibi.

Yes, they were together on that date.

She nods at Moran, who waves the piano man away. The interview is over. O'Brien joins his friend and they both leave the bar hurriedly. Frankie returns to the booth.

Moran beckons to the barman. "After that great work, we might as well recharge the batteries before heading off."

Frankie sighs. "He's clearly telling the truth."

"Yep. By rights we should press criminal charges." Moran asks the barman to bring them two rounds of ham and cheese and two more drinks. "But I suppose after the European findings, it's only a matter of time before the law's overturned." He shrugs. "Anyways, we've got a more pressing job to do."

* * *

Brannigan taps the contents of his pipe onto the table. Using an old envelope, he scoops the ash into the wastebasket. A plume of dust shoots up into the sultry midday air. He fills his pipe carefully with freshly shredded tobacco and lights up. Several staccato puffs later and a red glow appears.

"You know, your wan cracked the case of the Border Weasel?" Brannigan says, bringing his lips over his teeth in a mirthless grin.

McGinley stands by the barracks door, cigarette held behind his back, as if afraid of a reprimand from the headmaster should he be caught smoking. "Is it Detective Francis you mean, sir?"

"Thinks she's a better detective than me, no doubt."

"Ah, for the sake of Jaysus, sir! A woman!"

Brannigan removes a shred of tobacco from between his teeth. "So, remind me again exactly what you found at MacAllister's?"

"Well, when we entered the punk's premises, there was Sarah Joyce, brazen as you like, lying on the sofa. We showed our warrant, told her she was under arrest."

"Yes, yes," says Brannigan, frowning, "we know all that. Frig's sake. Get a move on, godammit. I want to know about the cannabis, how much there was, et cetera and so on."

"We did a thorough search as per orders. At first, sir, nothing except all the rubbish MacAllister's accumulated ... the mess, sir, you wouldn't believe,"

"Speed it up, McGinley, you're giving me piles."

"When we went to the extension out the back, indeed more

like a byre or cow shed, didn't we find pots and pots of weed, sir?" He takes a last quick pull of his cigarette, throws it on the floor and hurriedly stubs it out with the toe of his boot. "A herb, he called it, by the name of Mary Jane. Thinks we're friggin thick. Like we never heard of Mary Jane before!" he scoffs, rolling his eyes. "An entire room full of the stuff. You'd smell it a mile off."

Brannigan coughs – a rasping smoker's cough. "Hash, you say?"

"Yep, that's what we found."

Brannigan narrows his eyes. "What Sarah Joyce was doing out there, if they're supposedly no longer together, is anyone's guess. Odds on he's the father of that slaughtered child." He lifts his pipe and sucks and puffs slowly. "But there's an even bigger picture here."

"There is indeed, boss."

"There could be a salary raise in it for you too." He squints at his deputy. "So, are you with me in this, McGinley?"

"Oh, God, absolutely! Screw the runt."

"So we scare the bejaysus out of MacAllister, tell him he'll be in jail forever if he doesn't cooperate." Brannigan laughs. "If he does – then no charges. Simple."

"As you say, boss. Simple."

"And we'll keep herself from getting a whiff of it, okay?"

"Aye, sir. What about himself?"

"Fat-arse gobshite, full of hot air. It was herself nailed the Weasel – she's the one to watch."

* * *

Moran drives on the return journey back to Bunbeg.

Frankie wipes her forehead with a tissue. The sun glares down and the car feels stuffy: they're in a glasshouse. She yawns. Smoke always makes her feel lethargic. She winds down the window to let in a refreshing blast of fresh air and breathes deeply.

"Here's what I think is a possible scenario. Sarah didn't kill the Strand baby. She suffered a breakdown – after all, she is of a nervous disposition ..."

Moran winds down his window and leans his elbow out. "Okay ..."

Frankie shivers suddenly with the cross-air flow and closes her window. "She killed her own new-born child by intent or accident ..."

"We don't know that yet," says Moran.

"Then – in her confusion and terrible distress – she assumed the dead baby on the strand must be her own ..."

"But in the interview she said she *didn't* kill the Strand baby ..."

"Afterwards, yes, she retracted. But initially ..." says Frankie.

Moran comes to a narrow bend, slows down as a large truck rounds on them with inches to spare between the two vehicles.

Frankie's stomach lurches.

Silence settles for a moment.

Moran leans back in his seat, stretches and does a neck roll, sticks a cassette into the dash recorder. He presses the start button and nods his head in time to the beat of "A Kind of Blue".

"*Nah*," he says finally. "Doesn't add up."

After they pass through Donegal Town, Moran presses the accelerator and speeds along the near-empty road for the next hour until they reach Bunbeg. Frankie tries not to look at the speedometer. He's almost certainly above the 55mph speed limit. She's glad when they arrive back at the hotel.

* * *

Back in her bedroom, Frankie flops into the armchair beside the coffee table where she has her chess set up. She picks up the queen and addresses the alabaster royal. "We're no further on than when we came to Gweedore – what is it now? – almost a fortnight ago?" she says. "Nothing adds up. Two babies dead. Nothing to link the mother of the garden baby to the Strand baby except coincidence that both babies were born around the same time. But there's no *evidence*. I might be brilliant but at times I can be bloody thick too." Frankie replaces the chess piece. "You don't know what I'm talking about, Your Majesty, do you?"

She throws herself onto the bed and kicks off her shoes. Glances at the phone. She reaches out to pick up the receiver, stops, and lies back on the pillow. The ceiling is a network of cracks. She can hear a motorbike revving outside her window, can almost smell the diesel. Then the sound stops abruptly. She sits up again, lifts the receiver and dials. It rings. His voice.

"Hello, Rory." Frankie can feel her heart racing, her palms clammy. She twists the telephone cord around her finger. "I was just wondering if ..." She picks at a loose thread in the counterpane as she speaks and pulls. The thin material puckers and she stops. "Oh ... a trip to Barcelona?" She bites her lip. "Well, have a good time. Ring me when you get back."

CHAPTER 12

Sarah Joyce paces. One foot in front of the other. From wall to door measures eight feet. She puts her fingers to her nose to block the stale stink of fish. How long are they going to keep her incarcerated in here? How long will she be able to stick it? Back to the wall and turn. *One, two, three, four, five* ... She stops and glances at the window above the low bunk bed. She climbs onto the bed and peers out. The window is grimy with years of sand blasting against it. A long diagonal crack adds to the difficulty. Plus the bars. She can just about make out a back yard with a prefab in one corner. Rusted bicycles lean against an opposite wall like a battalion of old soldiers, retired and useless. Seagulls squeal in the harbour. The deadness in the cell is broken with the sound of keys jangling. The cell door opens. A trainee garda enters with food on an aluminium tray: a bowl of soup and two slices of white bread smeared with margarine. He avoids eye contact, leaves the tray down quickly and departs.

Sarah leaps off the bed. "*Come back, let me out of here!*" Too late. Her heart is racing. She *must* get out of here. But the garda is already turning the key in the lock from the outside. Sarah hammers the door with her fists. She puts her hands up to her head and pulls at her hair. She'll go mad in this place. She must do something. She runs over to the food, lifts the bowl and hurls it against the wall. The dish bounces and pings off the floor like a tuning fork before settling upside down. A lumpy yellow stream, like vomit, courses its way down the wall and drips onto the stone slabs. Sarah bangs the door again, a hollow echo her only reply.

Hours seem to pass, but they might be minutes.

The garda lets the prison doctor into the cell and stands with his back to the closed door. The doctor approaches Sarah, who lies on the bed, spent.

"I'm going to give you a little injection, dear, to calm you down – it will help you relax."

Sarah closes her eyes, disempowered, worn-out and listless. The doctor picks up a hypodermic needle and fills it from a phial, taps the syringe to loosen the bubble. He puts the needle down on a steel plate and rolls Sarah's left sleeve up. Sarah makes no effort to resist as he injects the drug into a vein in her arm. He withdraws the needle, places it carefully into its case and packs up his things. He and the garda leave the cell.

Shortly afterwards, the door opens again. The garda and two orderlies in white coats lift the drowsy Sarah onto the stretcher, strap her down, and wheel the gurney through the station corridor, out to the waiting police ambulance.

* * *

Brannigan pours tea into a stained mug.

"The way I see it is this. Well, we'll say, this could be a very likely scenario."

He scoops up two heaped spoons of sugar, dumps them into the tarry beverage. A splash of milk, some of which lands on the table, and inches its way slowly towards a folder, like a slug on a mission. O'Toole moves the file a fraction. McGinley stands to attention by the door, face blank, waiting for Brannigan to expound on his theory. Overhead, a fly buzzes, circling.

Frankie looks coolly at Brannigan.

"The way I see it" – Brannigan takes a slurp of his tea – "Sarah Joyce is well known to have been wild. A wild thing. Sure, wasn't she hanging around with that young waster from Bloody Foreland, MacAllister, when she was barely seventeen? And they don't come much wilder than that young bucko. Then there's that other fella we're just after hearing about – O'Brien – now by my way of thinking, someone immoral the likes of that could well get up to anything."

"What's are you talking about?" says Frankie. "We've just told you O'Brien has an alibi."

"Well, if it's not O'Brien, it could be some other fella that we know nothing about yet.'

The sergeant plonks the mug down – another splash – and grips his stomach. He sucks air in through his teeth, thumbs out two tablets from a blister pack, tosses one into his mouth and flings the pack back in the drawer. He chews the antacid savagely until the spasm passes.

"Where was I?" he barks.

"You were saying, sir," says McGinley, "that Sarah Joyce was a wild thing," adding in a moment of inspiration, "a slapper."

Brannigan, not well pleased at being upstaged, scowls at McGinley who retreats into invisibility again.

"Oh yes, I have my train of thought now. Okay. We've established she walks on the wild side. So here's the likely story." He pops another tablet into his mouth. "Here's the story … well, a possible story, I'm not saying this is what actually happened. But it could have. Me bould Sarah, being a wild thing, and used to many romances, has a fling with loverboy number one at, we'll say, ten o clock. Now, being a goer, and in a good mood, what's to stop her going up the road, hooking up with lover boy number two, having a bit of a how's your father, know what I mean," – guffaws – "then home for a rest?"

McGinley looks puzzled.

Frankie has had enough. She doesn't intend wasting her Saturday morning listening to this sort of stuff. *When is that pathologist going to come back with the blood results?*

"What's to stop those two dalliances from bearing fruit at the same time?" announces Brannigan, locking eyes with Frankie. Daring her.

"But, sir, I thought a woman could only ..."

"You thought, McGinley? What exactly did you think?" Brannigan demands of the flustered McGinley. "What are your precise thoughts on the matter?"

McGinley decides on reflection that critiquing Brannigan's theory might not be a sound career move.

"No, it is possible," affirms O'Toole, who knows everything.

Brannigan scans the assembly. "Do any of you doubt the possibility that Sarah Joyce, having dallied with two men could nine months later have borne twins? *Huh?*"

McGinley doesn't doubt the possibility.

Frankie gestures to O'Toole to follow her.

Brannigan locks eyes with her even as she gets up to leave. "And that having borne bastard twins out of wedlock, she kills both, buries one in the garden – this she admits – and in order to confuse things takes the other out to Port Arthur and buries it there."

Oh God in heaven, thinks Frankie, *this is preposterous – next thing, he'll be saying it was a virgin birth!*

She retreats to her quarters, O'Toole in tow.

Frankie rounds on the intern. "So – twins by two different men?"

"Yes, it's possible."

Frankie sighs and waves her hand for him to get on with it.

O'Toole, delighted to oblige, straightens up to his full height. "Well, Greek mythology is full of it. Hercules, for example. The story goes that Hercules's mother Alcmene, refused to have sex with her new husband, Amphitryon, until he had avenged her eight brothers who had been killed by a neighbouring king. So Amphitryon duly went to wage a war against the king. While he was away, Zeus, who fancied Alcmene, impersonated Amphitryon, assured her that the avenging was done and proceeded to have sex with her all night. The following evening, the real Amphitryon turned up, and now he had sex with Alcmene all night. And nine months later twins were born – with two different fathers."

"You're not presenting Greek mythology as evidence surely?"

O'Toole looks offended. "Of course not. But you did ask me."

"I thought you knew of such cases in the real world!"

"Well, yes, of course. It's called 'heteropaternal superfecundation'. It's often seen among animals where breeding isn't controlled – as in the case of stray cats and dogs. As for humans, it's not so easily observed but, for example, in 1982, twins were born with two different skin colours as a result of it. It's extremely rare, of course."

Frankie shakes her head in exasperation. "Okay, but why are we even talking about this outlandish notion of Brannigan's? She could have had twins, yes, but why should they have had two fathers?"

O'Toole frowns. "Indeed – and the question I have is this ... if Sarah had given birth to two babies – how could she have immediately buried one in the garden, then driven a mile to Dunlewy, seven to Bunbeg and a further three miles over the road to Lunniagh, and down to Port Arthur to bury the second in the sand?"

"Exactly," says Frankie.

Moran puts his head around the door. "Ex-Biddy lined up for interview this afternoon." He raises an eyebrow. "The fun never stops."

* * *

Frankie is certain the young man facing them in the interview room is the same who stood in the centre of the ring on the island a week ago. The same Aran jumper, the same long hair and beard, the same hangdog expression. He registers no surprise that Frankie is now in Garda uniform, nor indeed does he show any sign of recognition.

"She said that that all men were good for was sex and chopping wood," he says.

Moran opens a packet of cigarettes, withdraws one and sticks it into the corner of his mouth, searches in his pockets for a lighter. "So she said men were good for sex – go on."

"It was wicked, so it was," the young man grumbles. "You couldn't be yourself. They'd throw you into the Atlantic, naked, if you held on to conventional ways."

"Naked, is it?" says Moran, playing him.

"If you were so unhappy with the group, what brought you there in the first place? You surely weren't kidnapped?" asks Frankie.

"I did like it at first, I mean the idea is a good one – living the natural life, growing your own food, getting away from the rat race. In theory it's all good."

"And honouring the goddess? Celebrating the feminine?" Moran says.

The man shrugs.

"Anyway, lots of women," Moran says.

The renegade scowls. "Too many women."

"But in practice?" Frankie prompts.

He shakes his head as if he can't find words to adequately describe the experience on the island.

"What was it about the Children of Bríd that you didn't like?"

"Everything. It was all terrible, so it was."

"In what way terrible?"

The man shrugs. "Too much about bloody feelings. You were supposed to get rid of your pain by letting it all out. Then you could get put in the middle of a ring for no reason and be humiliated, everyone yelling at you. Psychological totalitarianism is what it was."

"Why didn't you just leave?"

"Once, when I threatened to leave, she took my boots and burnt them – in some damn fool fire-worship ceremony – to stop me making another attempt. She was a complete control freak, so she was."

Moran smirks. "By 'she', I take it you mean Zoe McWilliams?"

"Or Maggie?" asks Frankie.

The man doesn't answer.

"If you're saying you were a prisoner there, how did you escape?" asks Moran.

"I waited by the quayside till the ferryman delivered a boatload of visitors and begged him for a ride to the mainland."

All very interesting, thinks Frankie, but not exactly germane to their inquiry. "Were there any babies born there recently," she asks.

The man frowns as if a baby is a concept he's unfamiliar with. "She said men were a load of weak shits who wanted their nappies changed."

Frankie sighs. "Can you tell us how many of the women – if any – were pregnant in the past year?"

He shakes his head.

Moran squints at the young man. "What? There were no pregnancies on Umfin with all the shenanigans going on or you just didn't notice?"

The escapee looks down as if thinking very hard. "There was three, yeah. I think it was three."

Three? Maggie said two.

"And how many babies were actually born? Think hard. This is important."

He shakes his head. "All I know is, the Burtonport lassie was pregnant when she left the island. Yeah – she was lucky to get away too."

Frankie's stomach does a somersault. Maggie said there were two women pregnant with two babies to show. Now they're hearing of a third pregnant woman, who left the island. This is dynamite. "When was that?"

The man shrugs.

"In the past month?"

"Yeah, I think so. Not long ago anyway."

"How did she leave?"

"Same way as I did, I suppose. She must've asked the boatman."

"Was she a blow-in?"

"Her name is Lara Richardson. She joined the commune and then, like myself, tired of the whole thing."

Frankie's heart is racing.

They let him go.

Frankie opens a window. "We have a name."

"Let's find her."

CHAPTER 13

Sarah wakes. Clean white sheets. Clean white walls. A solitary crucifix faces the bed. The overwhelming smell of antiseptic. Where the hell is this? Her head is full of cotton wool. She presses the bell on the locker beside her bed.

A female medic appears.

"Where am I?"

The doctor picks up the chart at the end of the bed and, without looking up, writes. "You're in the unit."

Sarah blinks, struggles to sit up. "The unit? What unit? Where?"

The young doctor flips one of the A4 sheets on the chart over and writes on the next page.

Sarah stares at her, trying to comprehend, trying to get her attention. She can hear a trolley trundling down the corridor:

the sounds of hospital. Someone calls out. Something. If only she could get her head straight. She makes an effort to focus. "You mean the madhouse?"

The registrar, writing done, looks at Sarah. "It's a unit, not a house, mad or otherwise ..."

"But where? Where? Am I in Ballinasloe?"

"You're in Letterkenny General. Psychiatric ward."

"*Oh God. Oh God.*"

"And if there's anyone mad in here, it's me" – the young doctor laughs – "with all the work I have to do."

Sarah, intense, miserable, frightened, is unable to appreciate the banter.

"But, to look on the bright side, you have a visitor."

Roseanne appears bearing a big bunch of yellow roses. She goes over to Sarah and gives her a hug. Sarah, eyes welling, looks vacantly at the blooms.

"How are you, hon?" asks Roseanne.

Sarah blinks. "Is there a guard outside?"

Her friend nods. "How are you bearing up?"

Sarah twists a sheet in her hands, wringing the pain out of them. "I want out of here, Roseanne – what am I in here for anyway? Am I mad or what?"

A nurse pops her head around the door. "The curate's on his way." She spots the flowers and whisks them off the bed. "He wants to know – are you receiving Holy Communion?"

"No, I'm not receiving!" Sarah snaps.

"I'll put these in some water." The nurse shoots off like a bullet out of a Kalashnikov, roses in hand.

"Friggin' Church!"

Roseanne touches Sarah's hand. "Take it easy, love, just hospital routine."

A knock. The door opens slowly. Father Brendan Roche stands for a moment framing the entrance. Both women turn to face him. He comes in and closes the door quietly. The young women look at this man who has heard it all in the confessional, has seen it all in his daily rounds, a man to whom all the weary foibles of the human condition are known, who is used to handling fraught situations. He turns his attention first to Sarah, then Roseanne.

Roseanne gets up. "Oh, listen, I should be off."

Sarah reaches out and holds her arm in a tight grip. "No. Stay!"

Roseanne sits back into the chair, ill at ease.

Father Roche moves closer. "How are you, my dear?"

Sarah frowns, worrying the sheets. She winds them around her clenched fingers. Round and round. She bows her head. Her red hair falls forward, like a veil, covering her face. She feels a knot in her stomach.

Roche stands at the end of the bed. "So sorry to hear you are unwell."

Sarah shrinks back. Her head is throbbing.

Roche looks at Sarah steadily for several moments. Finally her says, "I'll pray for you, my dear." He draws his hand over the end of the coverlet, in a gesture almost like a caress, nods at Roseanne and leaves.

Sarah chews her thumbnail. Tears well up. She reaches down and pulls a wad of tissues from the box on the locker and blows her nose. "The bloody Church is never there when you want it."

A noisy clatter as a caterer opens the door. She slides a tray of food onto the locker.

Roseanne touches Sarah's shoulder. "No point in banging your head against a brick wall, love. And sure, poor oul' Roche, he's not the worst."

Sarah scowls at the crucifix.

CHAPTER 14

Black clouds scud across the sky, threatening rain, as Frankie drives for the second time to the Joyce household. At Inchacarragh, a small knot of journalists, desperate for nuggets of information, stand in front of the sign in large bold print that spells: **TRESPASSERS WILL BE PROSECUTED. KEEP OUT.** A photographer holds a large camera, with zoom lens, at the ready.

O'Toole hops out and opens the gate amid an avalanche of questions. McGinley drives through. O'Toole closes the gate hurriedly, climbs back in the car and they make towards the small cottage. Frankie glances at the fuchsia bush growing near the front door. Little ballerinas in red and purple.

Frankie knocks on the door. She can hear a flurry from inside, the rattle of chains, a key turning in the lock; but the door remains fast shut.

A thin high voice calls out from inside. "*Who's there?*"

"It's Detective Kate Francis. Can you open up, please, Mrs Joyce?"

The door opens a crack. Frankie speaks in a low voice. "Mrs Joyce, we'd like to take you to Bunbeg station for some questioning."

Alarm spreads over Mags' face. "What for? I've not done anything."

She closes the door a fraction but Frankie nudges her foot into the opening. Mags, losing the battle against the younger woman, shakes her head defiantly, and marches back into the living room, the detectives in her wake. Her tiny Scottish terrier takes up position beside the old woman and growls.

Smoke whorls and twists, black against the stained hearth wall. Frankie's eyes sting. She blinks away involuntary tears, then coughs. It's hard to breathe. Hannah, Mags' daughter, is sitting by the open fire.

"And don't you lot go giving me daughter Hannah there any aggravation," says Mags.

Hannah gives Frankie a look, slow and expressionless, like something dead or long ago defeated. Mags however, undefeated, stands, arms folded, a barricade of belligerence. Frankie notes she's wearing one of those long floral pinnies, very popular in the sixties, a type of apron that resembles a housecoat, but without sleeves, that crosses over in the front and gives complete protection.

"I'm not going nowhere," she says. "You've taken my little girl into custody under false pretences. Not only that, but now where is she but in the madhouse?" Her eyes narrow. "Oh, I hope you have someone dear to you have something bad happen to them and then you'll know. May your children end up with the pox! May you end your days alone in the world!"

A worm curls inside Frankie's stomach. Jesus! This woman knows how to twist the knife. By Frankie's reckoning she must be going on eighty, which means she would have been sixty when she gave birth to Sarah. How on earth can she be Sarah's mother?

"We're taking you in, Mrs Joyce," Frankie says firmly, "for questioning." They would bring the daughter in later.

"Not content with incarcerating my poor innocent girl, now ye want to incarcerate a poor auld defenceless woman, and me crippled with arthritis into the bargain." She glares at Frankie. "You should be ashamed of yourself, and you a woman. Well, I have news for you, this here critter ain't going nowhere. And that's my final word on the matter." She turns and looks out the window, trying to pretend they aren't there.

The Scottish terrier barks at Frankie.

The mutt looks harmless enough but nevertheless Frankie flinches. Once bitten twice shy, as the saying goes. It was a long ago time in her youth but she's never forgotten the helpless terror of being attacked by a hungry dog as she cycled home from school.

She takes a step back.

Mags sits on a chair, lifts the dog onto her knee and strokes him. "D'yeh see what they're doing to us, Goitseo?"

Goitseo? Ah yes. Clever.

"They're crucifying us, that's what." The mutt melts, gazing up at his mistress with two big brown marbles.

Frankie nods at O'Toole.

The trainee garda goes up to Mags and takes her firmly by the arm. Goitseo hops onto the floor. "Now, Missus, you've got to come with us."

"You can't make me." She puts her hands on the wooden arms of the armchair and holds tight with thin veined bony hands.

O'Toole puts his two broad arms around her shoulders and effortlessly lifts her out of the chair like he was lifting a child.

"*Okay!* Okay. Jesus, Mary and suffering Joseph, take your hands off me! Do you have to rough me up?" She rises. "I'm not going anywhere without Goitseo, and that's my last word on it." She removes her housecoat and, taking her coat down from its hook, pulls it on. Then she puts her hat on and grabs her handbag, lifts the dog again and moves towards the door, muttering to herself. "Sure Hannah here would let him starve, the poor wee thing."

Hannah looks at her mother, without expression.

"Not that she'd mean to, the *créatúr,*" Mags adds.

They leave the house in procession, O'Toole, Mags, Frankie. McGinley opens the car door, places his hand on Mags' head to ease her in.

Mags straightens bolt upright suddenly, banging her head. "*Ouch!*" She rubs her head, as she struggles to escape from McGinley's grip. "For God's sake! Let go of me. I forgot my key."

"Can't your wan inside let you in?"

"For your information, mister, her name's Hannah."

"Okay, can't Hannah let you in?"

"Hannah, is it? Are you joking?" Mags laughs. "Sure that one'll not answer the door to anyone, not even her own mother."

"Is she alright?" asks O'Toole, puzzled. "Hannah?"

"Of course she's alright!" snaps Mags, glaring at the rookie.

O'Toole looks at Frankie, who frowns at him. "Ah sure, you'd know she's alright," he says to Mags, in an effort to right the situation.

McGinley rolls his eyes. Frankie nods.

They all march back to the house. Hannah slowly turns her head to look at the parade as they re-enter, her face blank. The terrier whimpers.

Mags gets her keys and out they troop. She bundles herself and Goitseo into the back seat with O'Toole. McGinley drives.

Mags fidgets as she tries to get comfortable and lifts Goitseo onto her knee. She opens her bag. Pulls out a long grey hanky and wipes Goitseo's eyes. Once the car starts, the mutt lifts up his head and lets out an almighty howl. He paws the window, struggling to get out. Mags pulls him back onto her lap. "*Shush, shush, mo pheata*, don't mind these eejits."

Goitseo jumps free up onto the back window and claws the glass. O'Toole grabs him. Goitseo bites his hand. O'Toole groans. "*Fuck!*" He flings him onto Mags' knee. The terrier bares his teeth and growls. He wriggles free from Mags' lap.

Frankie sighs. The grinding detail of police work. They don't prepare you for the foibles of humanity in training school – nor mutts with attitude.

Suddenly a roar from O'Toole in the back seat. "*Friggin hell!*" Frankie swings around. "What?"

O'Toole is gingerly edging himself away from a hot stream on the leatherette where Goitseo has just relieved himself. He throws his hands in the air. The car smells of dog-piss. A bright red spot has appeared high on his cheeks. Frankie rummages in the car pocket for a cloth. She finds a chamois in the glove department and tosses it back to O'Toole, who scowls and wipes furiously.

"God, he never does that!" exclaims Mags. A little smile plays at the corner of her mouth.

Dirty looks are exchanged.

They eventually arrive at Bunbeg harbour. McGinley parks and they pile into the station. O'Toole rushes to the bathroom to clean up after Goitseo's performance in the car. McGinley escorts Mags to the interview room.

* * *

An hour later Moran and Frankie start the interview. Mags sits huddled at the table, working a pair of rosary beads. She stabs them with a dirty look. "What have ye done to Goitseo?"

"Gutcha?" Moran frowns.

"She means her dog." Frankie looks the old woman before her. She has spirit, that's for sure. "He's being well looked after, Mrs Joyce. The sooner we get this over with, the sooner you'll get back to your dog."

"What can you tell us about Sarah's pregnancy and labour?" asks Moran.

"You've already tortured that poor girl for information, what are ye on to me about?"

"As you well know, Mrs Joyce – for you were there yourself when we found the remains in your garden on the sixteenth of May – a baby was buried there." Frankie leans forward. "So you know about Sarah's pregnancy."

"I know nothing."

"Whose baby do you think we found in your garden?"

Mags works her beads with gnarled fingers, for a moment lost in prayer.

"I would remind you, Mrs Joyce, of the serious consequences of withholding information," Moran warns.

"Sarah has already admitted that this is her baby." Frankie leans back. "Can you tell us what you knew about her pregnancy and confinement?"

Mags folds her hands across her stomach, beads twined around her fingers, and slumps. The detectives wait.

Mags shakes her head. "One was surely enough," she says at last, almost talking to herself. "Why did she have to go and get another?"

Frankie feels her heart beat faster. It's as if the atmosphere in the room has been shot through with a bolt of electricity. Is the case about to break, she wonders.

Moran leans forward. "What did you just say?"

Mags crinkles her eyes, staring into space.

"Are you saying, Mrs Joyce, that Sarah had two babies?" Frankie asks.

Mags frowns in concentration. She brings her long bony hand up to her face and over her eyes as if to shield herself from something unpleasant. She sighs. "Two babies, yes."

Frankie hardly dares breathe. Is this it? Have they cracked it? Was it twins?

"When did she have these children?" Moran presses.

Mags drops her hand to her lap and yawns. She remains like that, like she's in a trance, pale-blue eyes staring.

"Mrs Joyce?"

The old woman jerks out of her reverie and gapes at her inquisitors. She looks around. Stands up. With difficulty peers under the table.

"Sit down, please, Mrs Joyce," orders Frankie.

"Where's Goitseo?"

"Forget about the dog, he's not in any harm," Moran states, anxious to keep up the momentum. "You say Sarah had two children. Where is the second child? What happened to it? Was it a boy or a girl?"

Mags sits back, brows knitted in concentration. "It was a girl ..."

"When did she have that other baby, Mrs Joyce?"

"About a year ago ... I think ... or maybe ... am I wrong?" Mags scratches her head. "Or was it more?" She gives a low laugh. "God! The memory I have!"

"And where is that infant now?" demands Moran.

Mags shrugs. "Oh, the Lord only knows."

"So let me get this straight, Mrs Joyce!" barks Moran. "You're saying your daughter Sarah had two babies?"

Mags looks up at him, startled. "What?" She looks around the room. "*Dia ár sábháil!* Ye are doing me head in! Where's me little dog?"

Frankie sighs. "Concentrate please, Mrs Joyce. Goitseo is safe."

"How many babies did Sarah have?" asks Moran.

Mags glares at him. "She had one baby, I told you that already. Let me out of here."

* * *

The detectives take a break. They walk down to the river.

Frankie breathes fresh air into her lungs. Moran pops a cigarette into the side of his mouth and strikes a match. He looks at Frankie questioningly. "The question is: is she daft or just pretending?"

"First she says Sarah had more than one baby. Then she backtracks and says she had only one baby. You're right – the question is – is she reliable?"

"With a dog called Gutcha anything is possible," mumbles Moran.

"*Goitseo*, as you well know of course, from the fourteen years you spent learning the Irish language at school, is an abbreviation of '*Gabh anseo*'."

"Which means 'Come here' *as Gaeilge*." Moran rolls his eyes. "*Goitseo!* Of course I knew."

Frankie can't help chuckling as she leaves Moran to finish his cigarette and goes in to consult with Brannigan.

"What's the story with Mags?" Frankie asks him. "She can't be Sarah's real mother, surely?"

Brannigan opens the drawer and takes out a pack of antacids. He peers into the used pack. Only one left. She knows by now he needs two. He rummages around in the drawer and sighs with relief when he finds what he's looking for and teases open the new pack, tossing the tablets into his mouth. He closes his eyes as he chews, leans back in the chair, tilted on two legs, and strokes his stomach.

Frankie listens to the seagulls screeching outside as she waits. A haul of herring?

"Mags is not Sarah's real mother," Brannigan says, "although everyone pretends she is." He throws the antacid pack back into the drawer. "Hannah is the mother."

Ah, that explains things, Frankie thinks. "Hannah seems … strange."

"That's probably because of the fact she was raped when she was nineteen. Sarah is the result."

Frankie winces. "Good lord! Who assaulted her?"

Brannigan shakes his head. "Some blackguard who hightailed it off to Scotland."

Moran comes into the office.

"Hannah is Sarah's real mother," Frankie tells him.

"Right. And does that throw any light on anything?"

The door opens. The postman hands a delivery to Brannigan who riffles through the bundle of envelopes, before slapping them down on the desk.

"Where was I?"

"We were talking about Hannah."

"Oh yes, what happened was – Mags' daughter is up the pole and when the baby is born, doesn't she try to smother the child?"

What? Hannah tried to kill her own baby! "Why weren't we told this before?" Frankie asks angrily. Hannah should have been a prime suspect from day one.

Brannigan sucks air in through clenched teeth. He's not going to be reprimanded by a woman. He breaks a match in half and spears a tooth with the pointed end before continuing, ignoring the question. "As I said she *tried* but, as luck would have it, she was stopped in time, just as she was trying to drown herself."

"*She tried to kill her own baby!* She has to be a prime suspect," Frankie says. "Why weren't we given this information?" And then the thought – could it be that Mags is confusing the fact that Hannah had an unwanted baby, then Sarah had a baby under similar circumstances?

Brannigan shrugs. "She's been depressed ever since. Drugged to the eyeballs, by all accounts. And Mags herself is … a bit" – he puts his forefinger to his temple and twists – "y'know yourself."

Frankie and Moran exchange looks.

"This is a no-brainer. Let's bring Hannah in," says Moran.

CHAPTER 15

McGinley and O'Toole arrive at Bunbeg station first thing in the morning, with Hannah, Mags and Goitseo in tow. Everyone piles out of the police car and into the front office. Commotion reigns as Frankie and Moran arrive on the scene for the interview. Goitseo has just broken free and is barking at Brannigan.

The sergeant aims a kick with his boot. "Get that frigger out of here," he growls. "Whose bright idea was it to bring that animal back in?"

"Hell's Gates!" Mags scolds as she rushes over to rescue Goitseo, who has started to whimper.

"Sorry, sir," says McGinley, and nods in the direction of Hannah. "Your woman wouldn't budge without the mother, and the mother says she goes nowhere without the dog."

Hannah stands still and expressionless by the door,

"Ye're a pair of fuckin' jam jars, that's what ye are!" Brannigan hisses through clenched teeth. "As if we didn't have our fill of that mangy mutt first time around." He flings his arm in the direction of the door. "*Get him out of my sight!*"

McGinley looks at O'Toole and then back at Brannigan. "We could tie it up, sir?"

O'Toole eyes the dog and, remembering his own recent ordeal, involuntarily shakes his head and steps back.

Mags lifts Goitseo up in her arms. "*Ná bac leis an amadán sin, a thaisce* – he's nothing but a bad article!"

McGinley steers Mags to the door. Mags elbows him sharply out of her way and marches out ahead. Hannah makes to follow her mother, but Moran puts his hand out, detaining her.

"*Hannah, a stór!*" Mags calls back through the door. "You have to go into the room with those people. They'll ask you a few questions. Don't let them upset you. I'll be back in for you in a minute – I'm just going out for a biteen of fresh air, to get away from that bad blackguard supposedly running the show in there."

Frankie and Moran usher Hannah through to the high-ceilinged interview room where they questioned her daughter only a week before. Hannah shuffles forward slowly and takes up position with her back to the wall. She is dressed entirely in black as if in mourning: black dress, black stockings, black laced-up boots. By Frankie's reckoning she can't be much more than forty, but being overweight has the effect of making her appear older than her years. Her hair is long and tied back tightly in a bun, reminiscent of how old women wore their hair decades before. Loose strands of grey hair escape.

Frankie indicates for her to sit down. The woman doesn't budge. "Please sit down, Hannah," Frankie says firmly and leads her to the interviewee's chair. "The sooner we start, the sooner you can get back home."

Under duress, Hannah plumps heavily into the seat. The detectives sit opposite.

Moran switches on the tape recorder. "It's Tuesday, the 23rd May, nineteen eighty-nine. Time: 9.30am."

Frankie looks at the woman facing her. "You know why we've detained you, Hannah?"

Hannah folds her hands on her lap and stares straight ahead, blanking the detectives.

"We must ask you some questions and you must answer them. It's not a choice. You have to answer them."

There is no reaction from the woman opposite them. Her face shows no expression. It's as if she hasn't heard a word.

"Where were you on the night of the eighth of May this year?"

No reply.

"You must answer the question, Hannah."

Still no reply.

"Can you tell us what you know about what happened on that night?"

The clock on the wall indifferently registers the time passing.

An hour later and they are no further on. They might as well be talking to the spider weaving a web in the corner near the ceiling, for all the response they're getting from Sarah's mother.

A shaft of sunlight pours through the window, illuminating Hannah's face. Her skin is smooth and wrinkle-free. Up close, the resemblance to Sarah is striking. It's clear she was once beautiful. Frankie reflects on the life this woman must have led since she gave birth twenty years ago. She reflects on the shame that was attached to women becoming pregnant outside marriage all though the century. Independent Ireland handed moral control over to the Catholic Church, whose main focus was controlling women and their bodies, punishing those who broke the moral code. Once she became pregnant without a ring on her finger, Hannah fell victim to that morality.

Frankie feels sorry for Hannah, but she has a job to do.

She examines the woman in front of her. She tried to kill her own baby but couldn't do it. She hardly seems mobile now. Is it likely she had anything to do with the recent murder? Has she any knowledge of it? Does she know how many babies Sarah had? How can they get her to talk?

"When were you last in Port Arthur Strand?" Frankie asks.

The ticking clock is the only answer.

Moran leans across the table. "Listen, Miss Hannah! You can continue with the silent act as much as you want but, just so you know, we have all day and you'll be here all day, tomorrow too, and the day after, if you don't start talking."

Hannah doesn't flinch.

This is hopeless, thinks Frankie. Why is the woman so expressionless? Is she deaf? Or dumb? What's wrong with her? No one has suggested she cannot hear or speak. She is clearly medicated, but medication doesn't hinder speech. So, if there's nothing wrong with her, why is she not responding to anything that's being said to her? Why is she choosing not to speak? Frankie remembers how Hannah responded to Mags back at their house in Inchacarragh, albeit non-verbally. But it was an indication she's not comatose. *Oh lord* ...

"Let's take a break," she says abruptly.

They go outside.

Moran lights up. "Not much joy there. Like squeezing blood out of the proverbial." He takes a long drag of his cigarette. "This is a waste of time. Let's check in with Head Office."

Frankie shakes her head. "No, wait! I think I get it. I don't know why I didn't think of it before." She nods in the direction of Mags who is sitting on a low wall by the river with Goitseo on her lap. "It's just a hunch but I want to have a word with Mags."

Moran attempts to blow a smoke ring, but the brisk breeze swirls it away. "Get what?"

But Frankie is already on her way over to Mags. "Back in a minute."

She sits on the wall beside the old woman. Mags turns her back, settles Goitseo more closely on her lap, and looks out at the river in fast flow. Frankie takes a moment too to look at the dun-coloured water with its creamy frills of foam, rushing headlong to the sea, its gurgling sound mesmerising. Close to the surface are a myriad insects, and a small shoal of trout ripple the surface. She thinks on the teeming energy that must populate the depths and remembers Rory telling her once that his father often fished a little further up the river for trout. O'Toole, who knows everything, tells her angling is not allowed between the hydroelectric dam and the bridge, so the question arises: was Rory's father fishing illegally?

Frankie turns her attention to Mags. "Why won't Hannah talk?"

Mags wriggles her shoulders in irritation, annoyed at the question. She frowns.

"Mrs Joyce, please answer."

"*Arrah!* Why don't ye leave the poor creature alone. Tormentin' her. As if she hasn't been through enough in her life already."

"It's because of what's she's been through herself, that we need her to talk. I know she responds to you, Mrs Joyce, for I've seen her, so I know she can hear."

"Of course she can hear. It's that she doesn't speak. Only the very odd time. So ye are wasting your time, barking up the wrong tree."

So she does speak! Maybe just the odd time, but that means she's not dumb. She can both hear and speak. The question is when did she stop speaking? And why?

"When did she stop speaking, Mrs Joyce?

Mags sucks her lips in to a thin line and presses them together. She's said enough. More than enough. She's saying no more. Not another word are they going to squeeze out of Mags Joyce, so help her God! She hugs Goitseo in close to her.

Frankie waits. Bides her time. Let's the situation breathe. Further up the pier she can see a ferryman helping visitors into his boat for a trip out to Gola, one of the islands, derelict since the nineteen sixties, she's told, and a draw for tourists fascinated to see houses abandoned with artifacts still in situ, as if the owners just went out for a walk.

"Was it after Sarah was born?"

From Mags' reaction Frankie senses she's hit a nerve. "Mrs Joyce, this is very important. The sooner we get to the truth the sooner you and Hannah can go home. Was Hannah like this before Sarah was born? Was she always like this or did it happen after the birth of her daughter?"

Mags ignores Frankie. Addresses Goitseo instead. "Ah Goitseo, them and their oul' questions, raking over the past.

159

Stirring things up. Why can't they leave well enough alone?"

She's not going to make any more progress here, but Frankie has observed enough in the old woman's body language for her to think she's on the right path. She rejoins Moran.

"Well?" her boss demands.

"I'm just working on a theory here – when I was at secondary school, there was a girl in my class – a bright girl who did well in her lessons – who never spoke."

Moran frowns. "And this is relevant because …?"

"Hear me out. It wasn't that she couldn't, but she elected not to. As a result of a trauma she'd suffered when she was very young, for a long time afterwards she refused to speak. This was the first time I'd ever heard the term 'elective mutism.'"

"Come again?"

"*Elective mutism*. It's when someone chooses not to talk."

"What! She's choosing not to talk?" Moran harrumphs. "Well, we'll make her talk."

"No, that won't work."

"What then? You mean good cop bad cop?"

"Not that either. There's usually a reason, well, almost always there's a reason, some trauma or other. At college when we studied the phenomenon in psychology as part of our training –"

"You did?" Moran raises his eyebrows.

"Yes, after your time."

Moran makes a face.

"Well, when we studied it, I remembered that girl at school. And since then, I encountered it only once. That Clocherhead rape case – you remember it – when the young woman at the centre of the investigation was so traumatised with what had happened to her, she refused to talk to anyone, especially any male detective. And I was called in."

Moran stubs out his cigarette. "Yes, I remember that case, but I wasn't involved nor was I aware of that detail."

"If Hannah is an elective mute, and my guess is that she is, then we need to employ a different method of interrogation, a different approach to getting her to cooperate."

Moran shrugs. "Well, since you're the expert on this ... "

"I'm no expert, but I'll take over, if that's okay."

Moran nods. "To hell with it – let's get this over with."

They go inside.

Hannah is seated as still as when they left her. She makes no sign or acknowledgement of their renewed presence. It's as if they don't exist. Despite appearances, Frankie is now certain this woman is not comatose. If her theory is correct Hannah is choosing not to speak.

This is not going to be easy. She's not had much practice at this and she could get it wrong. She looks at Hannah for several moments, trying to make eye contact with her.

Frankie breathes deeply. "Hannah, is Patrick Hilary the president of Ireland?"

Moran looks sideways at his co-detective.

Hannah face furrows ever so slightly, as if she too is puzzled.

I've got her attention, thinks Frankie. She leans forward. "Hannah, you don't have to speak, but I want you to nod or shake your head in reply to my questions. Is Patrick Hilary the president of Ireland – yes, or no?"

Hannah stays absolutely still. Her eyes are now on Frankie, but she makes no move.

"Is Ireland an island?" Frankie tries another tack.

Still no response from Hannah.

"Would you die if you ate a bar of chocolate?"

Hannah frowns.

Frankie's heart is racing. That's a no, she's certain of it.

"Is Mags your mother?"

Hannah is engaged now, although still not responding to the questions.

"Is Sarah your daughter? Can you please nod your head if she is?"

Hannah's face clouds. She shifts in the chair, moves her shoulders as if in discomfort.

Moran leans forward. They can hear Goitseo barking outside. Either Mags is on her way back into the front office or someone has disturbed them by the river. Hannah inclines her head slightly in the direction of the window, straining to hear.

"Sarah?" prompts Frankie. "Is she your daughter?"

Hannah looks back at Frankie then down at her hands.

Both detectives have their eyes fixed on this countrywoman who never talks.

"Is Sarah your daughter?"

The clock-tick becomes a metronome, beating out a *will she won't she, will she won't she.*

And then, without warning, it happens. Hannah nods slowly. Frankie can hardly believe it. They've broken through the barrier. She presses ahead, afraid to lose the momentum.

"Did Sarah have a baby girl who lived?"

Hannah shakes her head. She's responding.

"Did Sarah have a baby girl who died?"

The body language indicates yes.

Frankie's heart is thumping in her chest. She can feel the palms of her hands sweaty. Her mouth is dry. She takes a deep breath. She has got to get this next one right.

"Hannah, I want you to think very carefully before you answer my last question." She leans forward and maintains direct eye contact with Hannah. "Did Sarah give birth to another baby – a boy?"

Hannah stares at Frankie, eyes wide.

"I need you to answer this question, Hannah. This is very important. Did Sarah give birth to two babies?"

Very slowly Hannah shakes her head and keeps on shaking it as if to fumigate such a thought.

* * *

Frankie and Moran take a break and retire to their office. The prefab is stuffy. Frankie opens a window to let in some fresh air. She can smell fish from the harbour. Seagulls squeal. A fisherman shouts out to someone.

Moran throws himself into his chair. "So, where are we now?"

Frankie sits on the end of her desk. She feels ebullient. "I think we made progress. Definitely. Hannah seemed adamant that Sarah did not have two babies. Which corroborates what Mags said."

"Yes, but if I remember correctly, the bould Mags first of all told us Sarah *did* have two babies, and then afterwards decided she had only one after all. How much credence can we give either of those two geniuses?"

"Hannah was very definite. She shook her head when I asked whether or not Sarah had two babies."

Moran taps his foot off the floor, unconvinced. "But couldn't it be, given her state of mind, she is just repeating the family story?"

Frankie disagrees. "From what I know of elective mutism, I would give credence to what Hannah was saying, albeit not saying it with words. When I asked whether Sarah had two babies or not, she shook her head repeatedly. That was a definite no. I would put money on it. I believe she's telling the truth."

Moran takes out a cigarette and lights up. "What about signing a statement? Would she be capable of doing that?"

Frankie inches away from the drift of smoke, and stands by the window. "I don't see why not. She lived a normal life for twenty years, went to school, did well enough by all accounts. Her condition is emotional, not mental. I see no reason why she wouldn't be able to sign a statement if that's what we need her to do."

* * *

Sarah glares at the crucifix over the door. *Where were you when I needed you, all alone out in that field? Where were you when my baby daughter took her first and last breath out on the freezing early-morning grass? And where are you now when they are torturing me?*

She gets out of bed and rummages in the bedside locker. Drab, dirty fragments. Memories. Where are they? Where did she put them? She pulls off the elastic band and runs her hands through her hair, trying to sift through the fog in her head. She reaches deep down into the pockets of her dressing gown. Nothing. Slides her hand under the mattrass and pulls out wrapped paper tissue which she opens carefully. Two tablets fall out. She hesitates a moment before tossing both pills into her mouth and swallowing hard. What matter if she takes one or two? Or three? Or the whole lot?

CHAPTER 16

Frankie wakes late. Of all mornings! The pathologist's report! She manages a quick cup of tea before driving down to the barracks. It's a tight squeeze between Moran's and Brannigan's car – the latter parked awkwardly at an angle, wouldn't you know! She knows she should reverse, try and tuck in a bit tighter, but what the hell! She leaves it, jutting out onto the road: might as well be killed for a sheep as a lamb. As she locks the car, she spies two old local men, the one hanging out over a half door, the other leaning against the wall smoking a pipe. Both watching her. Taking in her bad parking, no doubt.

She should question them sometime, they might know something, might have snippets of local information.

She runs up the path to the barracks. All heads turn as she

enters. Her attempts to close the clanky door as quietly as possible fail: she might as well be ringing the Angelus bells from the cathedral in Armagh. She mouths an apology to Brannigan who scowls at her and then nods at the tall spare man with a shock of white hair – Dr Johnston – to continue. The doctor rests his glasses on the tip of his nose, peers out at the assembly, in the manner of an absentminded don, and clears his throat.

"Okay," he starts, "as you all know, I'm here to give the results of the blood tests in the case of the murdered baby on Port Arthur Strand. In addition, I have the results in relation to the baby found in the back garden of the Joyce home in Inchacarragh."

He lifts his folder, pulls out a document and peers at it.

Frankie feels a shiver down her spine. Now – the moment of truth, of revelation. She thinks of the young woman incarcerated in the psychiatric unit in Letterkenny, unaware that her fate lies between the covers of a manila folder. Will it prove Sarah Joyce is a murderer?

Johnston touches the nosepiece of his glasses gingerly, pressing in. "The garden baby is blood type O," – he nudges his glasses a little further up his nose – "a fact coincident with Sarah Joyce's blood type, also O."

Okay, okay. What about the Strand baby? Frankie realises she is holding her breath.

Johnston places the document into the folder. He picks up another, puts his glasses on again, holds the paper back a little, adjusting his focus. "The Strand baby is blood type A." He puts that sheet back in the folder and sits down.

But what does that mean? Frankie wonders.

The old school clock hung high up on the stained barracks wall chimes the hour. *Dong. Dong. Dong. Dong.* A shaft of sunlight breaks through and picks out myriad dust mites dancing like mad demons searching for a place to settle. The Sacred Heart looks down mercifully from his frame on the wall. No one says a word. *Dong. Dong. Dong. Dong. Dong. Dong.*

"Is it possible that Sarah Joyce is the mother of the Strand baby?" Frankie asks.

Suddenly a sharp loud bang from outside, the sound of a collision.

Oh Jesus, my car, thinks Frankie. *I bet it's my car.*

A room full of gardaí and no one moves.

"She could be." Dr Johnston strokes his chin. "She could be. But only, and I repeat – *only* – if the father is blood type A." He holds his glasses by one stem, gently twirling. "If the father is not blood type A, then Sarah Joyce is not the mother of the Strand baby."

* * *

Relieved to find her car intact, Frankie joins Moran and in silence they make their way back to the prefab. It's raining heavily. The temperature has dropped, and Moran fumbles to unlock the prefab door. Frankie covers her head with her jacket and addresses Moran's back as he opens the door.

"If I didn't remind myself, I'd think this was March, not May. But then" – she shivers – "in the circumstances it's hard not to feel chilled."

Moran doesn't appear to hear. She follows him inside and turns on the two-bar heater. Moran throws himself into his chair and lifts his feet up onto the desk.

"Well, well, well. The plot thickens, as the bard who comes up with all the best cliches would say. Blood type O by two and blood type A by one. But two into one won't go."

Frankie warms her hands. "I'm O."

"You're O?" Moran looks puzzled. "And this is significant because …?"

Frankie shrugs. "O is the commonest blood type. It proves nothing much."

O'Toole enters. He hands a mug of tea to Moran who accepts and sips, grimacing as the acrid taste hits his palette, his mouth a wide E as he recovers from the toxic hit. Frankie declines the second mug and O'Toole has it himself.

"Blood types," says Moran. "Someone talk to me about them."

O'Toole starts up on the principle that if there is a lacuna in information, he's the man to fill it. "Blood type is a classification of blood, based on the presence or absence of antibodies and inherited antigenic substances …"

Moran glares at him. The intern presses his lips together, showing the whites of his eyes.

Frankie adjusts the level on the heater and moves to her desk. "The facts: the garden baby is blood type O – the Strand baby blood type A." She swivels a biro in her hand, thumb to index to middle finger, back to thumb. She notices a biro stain on her palm, drops the biro and rubs at her hand. *Out damn spot.* She rubs again, gives up, and pulls her cardigan sleeve down over her fist.

Moran looks out the window, stretches to see something. "That trawler's cutting it very tight."

Frankie follows his gaze. A forty-foot hooker has pulled up to the pier. The tide is high and the boat bobs at an unsafe angle with the wharf.

"If the skipper isn't careful he'll scrape the hull," Moran says absentmindedly. "So now the question is: who is the father?"

Frankie looks at Moran. So he's thinking what I'm thinking. "We need to know who the father is to further this case."

"But Sarah's not saying."

Moran cranes his neck to see what's going on outside. The hooker is tilting at a forty-five-degree angle. Too low. "Damn fool. That man's going to be in trouble."

"Who?"

"Doesn't matter ..."

Frankie frowns. Is he listening at all? She leans back, folds her arms and waits until she has her boss's full attention. Moran shrugs his shoulders by way of apology and turns his back to the window.

"We know the Strand baby was killed with the use of a blunt instrument," he says. "Mike MacAllister would certainly know all about blunt instruments."

McGinley walks in, hands Moran the pathologist's file and leaves.

"The gardaí found Sarah Joyce in his house when they went with a warrant for her arrest," says Frankie. "I'll take a trip over to Bloody Foreland to interview MacAllister first thing in the morning. He could know something."

Moran raises an eyebrow. "Bloody Foreland?"

"'*Bloody*' comes from the sunset casting a reddish hue upon the cliffs." O'Toole is back in his element.

Moran rounds on him. "Are you the *Encyclopaedia Britannica* or what?" He points to the door and waves at the young garda to leave. "Lara Richardson's address in Burtonport: *go find!*"

"It's a new police rule," he says with heavy irony when the intern leaves. "Hire a teenager while they know everything."

Frankie smiles. "A hyperopic personality."

"You what?"

"Farsighted but can't see what's under his nose."

"Still … we now know what Bloody Foreland means."

"Rory had already told me that."

At the mention of Frankie's ex-boyfriend, Moran bends over the typewriter and starts to tap with one finger.

Suddenly, there's a hubbub on the wharf. The boat has come to grief.

* * *

The drive to Bloody Foreland takes a half hour from Bunbeg. The sea lashes the craggy shore. On the horizon Frankie can see the islands floating in the Atlantic, surrounded by thousands of foaming white horses fringing the waves: Gola, Inishmaan, Inisheer.

Suddenly the heavens open. A quick squall and the sun is bursting through the clouds again.

Between the twisty narrow road and the sea, cottages dot the rough landscape, in a sprawling, meandering sort of way. Modern holiday bungalows, testament to the many sons and daughters making good in exile and returning to the home turf. Other houses just as they were in the time of the Famine. A harsher time back then, she thinks, but just as bloody. More so, if truth was told: mothers dying, fathers dying, babies dying. Nature is a harsh reaper in the affairs of women and men. Frankie sees a sign for *Carraig an Aifrinn* – Mass Rock – in the grassy verge. She knows tourists will flock to see this relic of Irish history, and the uninitiated will be surprised to find themselves looking at nothing more than a large granite boulder, an erratic washed in from the sea, unable to fathom its significance in times long past.

An old man whooshes a donkey along the road. Frankie slows

to a stop and lowers the window. The man turns and peers in at the detective.

"I'm looking for Mike MacAllister."

The local looks at her for a moment, screwing up his eyes, apparently trying to figure out who she might be, whether he should recognise her or not, gives the unmarked Garda car the once over.

"Ah yes," he says finally, "that'd be Mike Dan Tom."

Frankie knows from Rory about the practice they have in Donegal of addressing each other by kinship names. So, Mike Dan Tom is in reality Mike, son of Dan whose father is Tom MacAllister.

Great, this will speed things up – she won't have to spend ages going up and down boreens. The man – has to be a fisherman, judging by the Aran sweater, the suntanned face with the white halo on the forehead where the cap blocks the sun – wipes his hands on his homespun breeches, tells her to drive down that boreen up yonder, take a left, then a right and straight on, and there you'll have her – first house on the right. He smiles broadly, happy to be of service.

Frankie drives down the boreen, turns left, then right and straight on, as instructed. But then – nothing. Back to the map. After many more twists and turns, Frankie finds the house. Her informant hadn't been completely wrong, he just forgot one important turn or maybe thought she would guess it. She feels a sense of something – what? – that he took her for an habitué?

Frankie pulls into the driveway and steps out onto the gravel. An old broken-down Fiat is parked at the side of the cottage. A shovel and rake lean against the wall. On the gable end of the cottage she notices graffiti painted in large black capitals.

FAMILY DISPUTE ON HERE. KEEP OUT.

Charming, she thinks.

She walks up to the front door, painted green and flaking . What does she know about Mike MacAllister, other than that he was the main suspect's boyfriend when she was seventeen? That the gardaí found Sarah Joyce in his house at the time of her arrest. That he's an IRA volunteer.

She raps the door and waits. The curtains are drawn. She raps again. Finally, the sound of movement inside. The door opens and Mike MacAllister stands in front of her, tall, very thin and gaunt-looking. He is unshaven, clothes rumpled and dishevelled, still in his socks. This guy is not long out of bed. It's two in the afternoon, for God's sake.

Oh, troubled youth!

Frankie flashes her badge. "Detective Kate Francis from the murder squad, investigating the death at Port Arthur Strand."

MacAllister winces, reluctantly opens the door wider to let Frankie in. He shuffles ahead of her and stands behind a red velveteen settee that takes up most of the living room, his hands gripping its back. He looks more doped than guilty or afraid.

Frankie closes the door and glances around. A single naked

light bulb throws a dim yellowish hue over the space. She sees clothes scattered on the floor, the settee, an overturned cane chair. A bundle of newspapers are piled high on a sideboard in the corner. And that all-too-recognisable smell again. Like earth or metal, or burnt popcorn. No, not popcorn.

The young man scowls. "I don't know what you want to talk to me for. Me and her split up two years ago. I don't see her now."

"But Sarah Joyce was here when the gardaí arrested her on a charge of murdering the Strand baby."

"It was a fluke she was here." His mouth twists. "I'd gone to Dunlewy to meet up with my cousin, along comes Sarah in that banger of hers, practically mows me down, she does. Begs me to let her kip here for the night." MacAllister runs his hand over his head and scratches the back of his neck. "I didn't know about any of that other stuff."

Frankie sighs. Getting information out of MacAllister is not going to be easy. A case of whatever you say, say nothing; and keep on saying it. She knows the republican maxim.

Frankie nods at him to sit down. He collapses onto the sofa, long gangly legs sprawled out in front of him. She sits on the other end and takes out her notebook.

"Let's start at the beginning, shall we? When did you two meet?"

MacAllister huffs. "A few years ago. I can't remember."

"How long were you in a relationship?"

Mike frowns, reluctant to open up. Frankie waits.

"We were together about two years. I don't remember exactly how long. Probably two years."

"What did you do together?"

Mike shakes his head. "I dunno. This and that. The usual things."

"What? Did you go to discos? Parties? Meet up with friends?"

Mike shrugs. "We hung out. That's it."

How can she get more out of this young curmudgeon? "Did you know that Sarah Joyce was pregnant?"

"No!" MacAllister snaps. "Like I said already, we haven't been together for a while."

"So you had no idea she was expecting a baby?"

"What would I know about pregnancies? Or babies?"

"And yet the gardaí found Sarah here, days after she gave birth?"

"I told you already. I didn't know she was coming."

Frankie raises an eyebrow.

"Why do you keep asking?" MacAllister stares at the threadbare carpet. "She practically ran me down in Dunlewy ... begged me to put her up."

He's shifty, that's for sure. But is he lying?

"Where were you on the night of the eighth of May, the night the Strand baby was murdered?"

A wave of fear passes over McAllister's face. He blinks. "I was with my cousin in Hiudái Beag's pub in Bunbeg that night, getting hammered." he says. He looks directly at Frankie. "I spent the night at his gaff in Knockerstoler. I can prove it."

Frankie writes in her notebook. And so will we, she thinks.

"When did you and Sarah break up?"

"I told you. Two years ago or so I think, I can't remember exactly."

"Why did you break up?"

"She has a terrible temper," he says, rage bubbling just below the surface.

"And you haven't?" Frankie says. MacAllister scowls. "So you haven't been together for two years?"

"No."

"Except you were together, when the gardaí came searching and found Sarah here."

"I told you already, that wasn't my idea.".

All the while he's speaking, MacAllister keeps stabbing the carpet with his toe. "Anyway, I have an alibi for that night," he mutters.

Which we will check out, Frankie thinks. But even if he has, still the nagging doubt. Something is not adding up. Why did Sarah choose to come here to stay with McAllister if they hadn't been together for two years?

Frankie toys with her notebook, deliberately saying nothing, hoping to crack MacAllister's nerve. Sarah was found here by the gardaí two nights after she gave birth. She'd just had the trauma of childbirth. There were problems at school. Why was Mike the one she chose to come to for shelter when things were going so badly wrong? Or was it as he said – just chance that she came on him walking by Dunlewy? What were the odds? And why did he agree? It suggests that there is more to this than he is telling. It suggests they still have a relationship.

MacAllister fidgets with the zip of his hoodie, still saying nothing.

As she drives back to Bunbeg, Frankie wonders: *Is Mike the father of Sarah's baby? Of both babies? Could he be the killer?*

CHAPTER 17

The Angelus chimes out from the small television mounted on the wall. A still of Raphael's *Madonna and Child* fills the frame for one minute as the bell rings, summoning the faithful to prayer – all over Gweedore, Donegal, Ireland, the one Holy Apostolic Roman Catholic world, umbilical cord stretching to the Vatican, representing a tradition going back centuries, solid as the rock it was built on.

In St Peter's ward, Mike lounges on a chair facing the TV, legs spread out. He scowls at the TV. "Friggin' Angelus! Did you know we get the news a full sixty seconds after Derry because of that bloody thing?"

Sarah blinks. She is sitting up in bed, propped up on a pillow. "What?"

Mike shakes his head, dismissing the subject. He draws his hand over his skull, pulls his hair back from his forehead, and looks at her. "They said you ...?"

She rubs her eyes as if trying to erase something. "Was it you who left them? The pills?"

"You asked me."

"I asked you? God! My brain is a complete fog." She sighs. "When did I ask you?"

"I called in on Sunday, d'you not remember?" He frowns. "Mind you, you were a bit out of it. You didn't try to ...?" He shakes his head. "Nah, you didn't!"

Sarah shrugs. "I don't remember." She picks up the book on her lap, opens it, flicks through quickly and puts it down again. "Did you bring this?"

Mike, glancing furtively over his shoulder, reaches into his jacket pocket, holds out a small packet. "Here's some more, if you want them – although maybe ..."

Sarah shakes her head. "No, better not. I'm medicated enough as it is. But thanks, anyway." She looks sideways at him. "You growing your hair again?"

Mike coughs and clears his throat, as if calling forth the courage to say something important. "Listen, you gotta tell them I'm not the father,"

Sarah draws back. "Of course you're not the father."

"But you gotta tell them."

"I told you, you're not the father."

Mike taps the floor with his boot, his knee jerking up and down as if in time to some rhythm in his head. "Yeh, *I* know that. *You* know that. But *they* don't know that. On top of all the other shit, I'm a fuckin' suspect."

Sarah frowns. "How could you be?"

A trolley trundles noisily on the other side of the door. Sarah peers out through the glass panel, then back at Mike. "They can't charge you without proof. What proof have they?"

"Since when did those fuckers need proof of anything? You should know that! They're crucifying me."

A woman in a blue uniform comes in and lifts Sarah's dinner tray off the table. "You didn't eat much, love … everything all right?"

Sarah smiles wanly. "Yes, thanks."

The woman nods at the card displayed on Sarah's locker. "And it's your big day an' all. Happy Birthday! Lord! I remember twenty." The woman glances, eyes narrowed, at the dour youth spread-eagled on the armchair before leaving with the tray.

Mike scratches his head. "Oh, God! Yes … sorry, I forgot … Happy Birthday!"

Sarah's eyes moisten.

Mike shifts uncomfortably. Softens. "How are you anyway?"

Sarah searches in her dressing-gown pocket, finds a tissue and blows her nose. "They have me doped to the eyeballs."

Mike nods. "Yeah, you look kinda rough."

"Thanks." Sarah slides down on the bed and closes her eyes. She puts her hand on the book in her lap. "Thanks for the book. Not sure I'm up to reading ... but thanks anyway."

"Shows nothing has changed in five years. Effin' pigs never change their spots."

"Pigs don't have spots," Sarah says and yawns.

Mike tugs a big toe poking out from under the blanket, a couple of times. He gets up, scraping his chair, and pushes it back to the wall. At the door he turns.

"You'll tell them?" He waits.

Sarah opens her eyes, attempts a smile.

"Yeah, I'll tell them."

* * *

Roseanne places a cake on the bedside locker just as the signature tune for *Coronation Street* strikes up.

Sarah opens her eyes, hoists herself up and stretches. "Oh, hello, Roseanne."

Roseanne gives her a hug. "Happy Birthday, hon."

"Thanks."

Roseanne nods in the direction of the TV. "Do you want to watch this?"

Sarah shakes her head.

Roseanne turns the sound down. Smiles at Sarah. "Twenty today."

Sarah shrugs and sighs. "I thought Mam would have come up by now. And Hannah."

"Oh – didn't you know?" Roseanne puts her hand over her mouth, apprehensive at having to deliver the bad news. "Hannah was brought in for questioning. She's probably a bit shook after it."

"What!" Sarah frowns. When?"

"Yesterday, I think. Seems there has been pressure on Bunbeg to get the case resolved. Mags went to the barracks with Hannah. And of course Goitseo had to be brought along too, you know yourself. I believe it was pure carnival. But, all the same, poor Hannah!"

Sarah chews her thumbnail. "Like they were going to get anywhere with Hannah! And why would they put her through that, God's sake?" She pulls herself up in the bed, gives one of the pillows a few punches and puts it back underneath her head, before settling back. She looks intently at Roseanne. The moment hangs. Then she says, "You know Hannah is my real mother? Everyone pretends it's Mags, but it's really Hannah."

Roseanne nods slowly, conscious of the importance of what Sarah has just told her, anxious to react sensitively. She clears her throat. "Yes. Everyone knows. I wasn't sure if you did. You've always referred to Mags as your mother."

"I was brought up to believe she was my mother, and I think

183

of her as my mother, but I figured out a long time ago that Hannah was my real mother."

"Poor thing! She's not been well for so long." An alarm goes off somewhere, a shrill intrusion. Someone turns it off. Roseanne points to the cake. "Anyway, it's your birthday. Today we celebrate your being born twenty years ago."

Sarah takes an elastic band off her wrist, sweeps her hair up into a pony-tail, and twists the band around the hair. "Y'know, they wore me out me with all their questions over the past few weeks. *Questions, questions, questions.* But the one they most tormented me with was: *Who is the father? Who is the father?* It was relentless. *Who is the father?* And, now, you know what?" She stretches her arms back, grips the ponytail with both hands, pulls to tighten it. Hands still back on her head gripping her ponytail, she looks out the window into the distance and, as if addressing the universe, says, "All I can think about is: who is *my* real father?" She looks at Roseanne. "I mean, I have a right to know."

Roseanne blinks, anxious not to say the wrong thing. "Would you ever ask Hannah?"

Sarah leans back on the pillow. "Hannah doesn't talk. To anyone. Ever."

"What about Mags then?"

"If she knows. If she'll tell me."

Roseanne stands. "Let's see if I can find something to cut this cake with. Tomorrow will be time enough for investigations."

CHAPTER 18

Moran stands by the open door. Brannigan and Dinny McGinley are seated, hunched over the desk. The odour of ham sandwiches, the debris of lunch-packs, vies with the acrid smell of tobacco. Brannigan leans back.

"It's not as farfetched as it seems, y'know," he announces and lifts his pipe.

"What's that, boss?" asks McGinley.

"My twin baby theory." He pats tobacco firmly into his pipe. "It's not as farfetched as it seems."

Frankie looks up from the filing cabinet.

McGinley leans forward, eager for information. Women's bodies have always been a mystery to him; indeed, truth be told, women's bodies could be an embarrassment at times.

O'Toole frowns.

Brannigan strikes a match and lights up, takes a few puffs.

Stomach cancer, thinks Frankie, down the line. Maybe not so far down the line. Or throat. One or the other. Possibly both, you'd never know.

Brannigan narrows his eyes. "The thing is, the blood sample taken from the Port Arthur baby's lung tissue, which has been used for blood-grouping purposes, was contaminated. Therefore," he says, eyeballing the assembly one by one, and pausing before dropping the bombshell, "the A-grouping could be wrong."

Frankie does a double take. *What?* This is surely crazy? Whoever heard of contamination changing blood types? Anyone with even a smidgeon of knowledge of biology knows DNA takes millennia to morph and change by the tiniest of mutations.

"Contamination cannot change blood type O to blood type A," she says.

Brannigan, on red alert for the weasel question, wags a finger. "*Ah, hah!* That's where you're wrong, Detective Francis. That's where you're absolutely wrong. We contacted an expert in Derry who says ..." He pauses.

"What does the expert say, sarge?" McGinley prompts.

"The expert says, contamination could not change blood group O to blood group A. However," – the sergeant addresses Frankie directly – "however ... immersion could."

He folds his arms triumphantly and waits for all to digest this new piece of information.

Frankie looks from Moran to Brannigan. "This is nonsense. I don't believe it. Where's the proof?"

Brannigan smirks smugly "I'm glad you asked that question, Detective Francis. Very glad. A very important thing is proof."

Frankie knows he's playing her, feels vexed for allowing herself to get riled.

"Here's the proof." Brannigan clears his throat, pipe in hand, stretched out. "The pathologist has read of tests done on two halves of the same female corpse, each half pulled out of the Foyle at two different times."

McGinley crosses himself. "Oh, the Lord save us and bless us!"

Brannigan lifts the pipe to his mouth, takes several small puffs to spark the tobacco into life, keeps his eye on it until a small red glow spreads out from the centre. He removes the pipe, holds it in mid-air again.

"The top half gave one blood-group reading. The bottom half gave a different reading entirely."

* * *

Frankie opens a window in the prefab. "It's bloody ridiculous, I never heard such a farfetched idea in my life: blood types changing. It defies logic. Head Office are breathing down our necks, the press are looking for answers, and that moron," she looks at Moran – "sorry! That idiot is wasting our time with his garbage."

Moran tips out a cigarette. "They have the precedent. Derry."

Frankie raises her palms. "It's hardly believable. I'd like to research that data."

She turns to O'Toole.

"Done!" says the rookie, on cue.

"Anyway," says Moran, lighting up. "We've got work to do."

"Sir," O'Toole says, "it's probably a stupid question ..."

"Probably." Moran sighs. "Go on, spit it out, anyway."

"According to my research, infanticide of babies under 12 months was no longer a capital offence in Ireland after 1949, as applied to the mother ..."

Frankie nods. "On the supposition she hadn't fully recovered from the effect of giving birth and might be mentally disturbed."

"So?" says Moran.

"Well, it seems that for decades dead babies have been found the length and breadth of this country, and yet apart from a few column inches in the newspapers, there's nothing more said about all those other cases."

"Get to the point, O'Toole."

"Well, sir, I'm just wondering why some babies' deaths are investigated – like this one at Port Arthur and that other case five years ago in Kerry – while so many others are not?"

"The manner of their deaths is the point," retorts Moran. "The violence and use of force."

"It's a good question, O'Toole," says Frankie. "And the other thing to ponder is why so many women feel the need to abandon their babies? Do we not value pregnancy and birth in this country?"

"*Whoa!* Get a grip, detective. Is this a philosophy symposium or what!" says Moran. "Methinks we might be in danger of losing the plot here. Which reminds me – *chop-chop!* There's work to be done. I've arranged to meet the island midwife later this evening, to see if the number of births on Umfin tallies with the number of pregnancies over the past nine months."

* * *

Frankie drives over the road and takes the long narrow beach road down to the pier at Port Arthur. She wants to measure the distance from the tide mark to the dunes one more time, to double check in the light of Brannigan's talk of immersion. She parks at the pier and this time finds the proper path down to the beach. Cumulus clouds meander across a cerulean blue sky and where the sun breaks through their tops seem like brilliant white tufts. The sharp Atlantic breeze whips at her jacket. She zips it up against the chill. She's reminded of the tale her father used tell her as a child, one of Aesop's fables. The Wind and Sun were in competition to see which of them was stronger, which of them could get the traveller to remove his cloak. The Wind, despite all its efforts, failed. The harder he blew the more the traveller wrapped his cloak round him. Then the Sun came out and shone in all its glory upon the traveller, who soon found it too hot to walk with his outer garment on. The moral of the story? Persuasion is more effective than force.

The answer may be obvious, staring her right in the face. She just doesn't see it. Thinking of the story reminds her of her father. Since her parents broke up she doesn't see him so often. She feels protective of her mother, and angry with her father about what happened. But she misses him. They're alike. It would be so nice to be able to talk to him about the case; he had such great insight.

Soft sand blows into her face. She blinks against the grit stabbing her eyes, and half closes them as a shield against the white grain, legacy of centuries of erosion. Listening to the charge of the waves rolling onto the beach, retreating, then careering back in again, closing in, brings home once again the fragility of human life. How insignificant we are in the grand scheme of things. In decades to come all this drama will have faded. The anguish Sarah Joyce is feeling now will have lost its power, Brannigan will be long gone, the killer will have been found or not, she will have continued on in the force or not, have had a child or not.

She takes off her sandals and kicks the sand before her as she makes her way over to the fateful dune. She measures the distance between the sea, now at high tide, and the dune where the baby was found – a distance of twenty feet. Once again, as on that first previous trip, she notes the high-water mark. There is a definite demarcation between the darkish sand that has been immersed in the water, even for the briefest of periods, and the soft powdery white sand that the sea never touches. The dune where the baby was found, in a cocoon of marram grass, like a cradle, is further back still. She will ask Dr Johnston, but Frankie is convinced the Strand baby was never immersed in water. She's also convinced that Sarah Joyce is neither the mother nor the killer of the Strand baby. What Brannigan's agenda is in pursuing that line is another matter.

Without warning, the sky clouds over and fat drops of rain start to plop onto her head. She pulls up the hood of her jacket, hurries to the car and back to barracks.

* * *

"We can't ignore them," McGinley is saying to O'Toole when she walks in, "One day soon we could see them marching down O'Connell Street heading for the Dáil."

Frankie sighs. Still on about the IRA.

"Is Donegal a big republican stronghold then?" asks O'Toole.

"Is Errigal a mountain?" McGinley retorts.

Frankie nods at O'Toole and they head back to the prefab.

"We focus on the Strand baby," she says firmly.

"What if there's an overlap? What if the IRA *are* involved in the murder of the Strand baby?"

"And their motive would be exactly?"

O'Toole shrugs. "I dunno. Revenge killing?"

Frankie unlocks the prefab. "Don't be daft! Garda O'Toole, it's 1989 and what the IRA are hell-bent on is taking out Brits, not Irish infants."

"It could be a British infant," bats back O'Toole, unwilling to give up.

Frankie frowns, momentarily irritated at being upstaged. But O'Toole's right. The strand baby *could* be British or from the North, or goodness knows where.

A blast of heat hits them as they enter. Frankie hurries over to open the window. A strong smell of old fish and seaweed battle in the still air. She puts her cupped hand to her nose.

Moran appears, waving a file in the air. "The expert report. She did four tests to be sure, to be sure. The blood type of the Strand baby is definitely A. The garden baby is blood type O, as is Sarah Joyce."

"So Brannigan is talking utter garbage!" said Frankie. "Or barefaced lies?"

"Yes, one or the other."

He tosses the file onto his desk and stands in the middle of the cabin, facing them, arms folded. "Which leaves Brannigan with possible twin babies, but us, unfortunately, with Sweet Fanny Adams."

"What about Lara Richardson?" Frankie asks O'Toole. "Do we have an address yet?"

"We do."

"We do?" She grabs her car keys. "What are we waiting for? Let's go."

* * *

Brannigan and McGinley have just arrived at Bloody Foreland to put the thumbscrews on Mike MacAllister. The trio stand in a circle in the living room. The youth feels trapped and kicks the threadbare carpet with the toe of his boot.

"I've already answered her questions."

"By 'her' I take it you mean Detective Garda Francis?"

Mike frowns and keeps kicking.

"Well, there'll be plenty more questions if you don't cooperate."

MacAllister squirms. He glowers at Brannigan, who returns the compliment, re-engaging, like lovers who cannot move on or let go.

"I'm a writer," MacAllister mutters. "I want to be left in peace to write."

Brannigan laughs, a deep guttural mirthless growl. "You'll be writer-in-residence in Castlereagh jail if you don't cooperate,

Sunny Jim. You are aware that possession of drugs is a criminal offence?"

MacAllister's head snaps up in alarm. What? He thought they were here about the murder. He blinks, runs his hand through his hair as he considers his options.

"You could face … what?" Brannigan looks sideways at McGinley with narrowed eyes. "Five, ten years minimum?" He bares his teeth in a faux wide leer. "But, sure, then you probably wouldn't mind that, you being a writer and all."

Mike MacAllister agrees to cooperate.

* * *

The drive south to the fishing port of Burtonport takes Frankie and O'Toole less than half an hour. En route they pass the wild rugged rocky terrain of the Rosses district through Crolly, Annagry, Kincasslagh. As they near the fishing port they can see the islands: Inishfree, Aran and Inishmacadurn floating in the near distance. Fishing boats and trawlers crowd the small harbour. Again the strong smell of seaweed, the screech of seagulls, the sharp sea breeze.

"I've just been reading about a new cult that have just settled here," says O'Toole.

Frankie does a double take. "What? Another one?"

"They're called the Silver Sisterhood. They believe God is a woman."

Frankie laughs. "Ah, that's all right then. Must be something in the air here that draws them."

She parks near the pier. They get out and look around.

O'Toole notices a plaque on the harbour wall and reads. "It says here a French military force landed in that island there – Inishmacadurn, the one beside Umfin, the island we visited two weeks ago – during the 1798 rebellion. Led by Napper Tandy, in a failed attempt to assist the rebels." He shakes his head. "Everything that could go wrong during that rebellion, went wrong."

"Indeed," says Frankie. "What happened here two hundred years ago is, of course, of huge significance, but the question of the moment is the whereabouts of Lara Richardson? Harbour Row, you said?"

O'Toole glances at the slip of paper in his hand, nods, looks around. He points. They're right beside it – Harbour Row, a row of whitewashed cottages facing the harbour pier. They find the address they're looking for at the end of the row.

Frankie knocks. A woman in her forties answers. She has rollers in her hair and is clearly surprised and a bit put out to have unexpected visitors.

Frankie smiles. "Hello, My name is Kate Francis. I'm looking for Lara Richardson. Have I come to the right house?"

O'Toole blinks. He's done the research. Of course it's the right house.

"Yes, that's us," the woman says, a puzzled look on her face as she tries to make out who these two handsome strangers are.

"*Who is it?*" calls a female voice from inside.

The woman opens the door wider as she leans back. "Someone looking for you, Lara."

An inside door opens onto the hall and young woman appears. O'Toole's eyes light up. The young woman is strikingly pretty – petite, with long auburn hair and a creamy complexion. In her arms she cradles a tiny infant, who is wrapped in a multicolour crochet shawl. The child is not much more than a month old.

CHAPTER 19

Frankie wakes early. She dons her tracksuit and runners. She wants to see for herself if there isn't a way to get from one strand to the other. Plus she needs some exercise.

Frankie runs at a steady pace a mile down the narrow boreen. A light breeze blows into her face, very pleasant and cooling. Gallen Strand is smaller than the other two, but still has the stretch of white-gold sand, the deep-blue sea topped with white horses. The water is choppier, here – a haven for surfers, she's told. There are not too many surfers here at this hour, something she's grateful for. Right now, Frankie wants solitude. She falls into a steady jog, settles into its rhythm. As endorphins course through her body, she begins to feel relaxed. She hopes that by freeing up her mind, the pieces of the mystery will begin to fit into place. She believes in eureka moments, allowing that fathomless iceberg – the subconscious – to sift through all the data and throw up solutions. So far it hasn't thrown up anything much. Unfortunately.

Frankie goes through a mental inventory of the suspects so far. The tourist – Moran did the interview and he's cleared. The Biddies – their midwife established that babies born on the island did indeed tally with pregnancies. Lara Richardson left in the ferry to go back home to her mother and had her baby two days after the Strand baby was found murdered. The music teacher – gay. Mike MacAllister has an alibi, but something's not adding up there, plus O'Toole has unearthed that the IRA have thrown him out of the organization. The question is: why? Then there's Sarah, of course.

They have no good leads in the murder case.

She comes to the end of the beach, steps carefully over the shingle and scrambles up onto the grass embankment above. She can see a strip of sand further north – that might or might not be Port Arthur – but enormous rocks and boulders block her way. She is about to retrace her steps when she notices something moving in the long sward, something bulky, white, alive. She approaches cautiously. A seagull, lying on its side, wounded, its right wing hanging at a strange angle – most likely the result of a spat with a crow or some other bird – flaps its good wing helplessly when it sees her. She stands for several moments staring at the bird staring back at her. She feels sorry for it, knows it will surely die if it's left there. But all she can do is tell them back at the hotel to ring the ornithological society, if there is one in these parts. Not for the first time, it strikes her how, underneath the appearance of serenity and peace, nature is indeed '*red in tooth and claw*'.

She climbs back down to the beach and over to her car. She feels strangely unsettled after seeing the dying bird. With an effort, she forces herself to focus on the day's schedule: a visit to the local curate Father Roche. She needs to deepen Sarah Joyce's profile. In these parts, the priest usually has his finger on the pulse. And who knows, maybe he will be able to throw some light on lovers. Who better to know what goes on in a place than the priest who has an ear to the throbbing heart of the locality? Not that she expects him to divulge what someone says in the confessional but, you never know, she might glean something.

* * *

After breakfast, she drives to Derrybeg, past the supermarket on the left, over the bridge and down the steep slope to the old church. Frankie gazes at the massive building settled in a nook gouged out of granite: a dark gothic structure, the centre of the community since the foundation of the state and long before. The church seems to inhabit a dark cave. It's strange, Frankie thinks, churches usually loom from the highest point in a locality, so why not this one? Maybe a throwback to hedge schools and the need for surreptitious prayer, confession, the whispering of secrets in a treacherous world.

Frankie feels cold all of a sudden.

She parks in the gravelly area in front of the church. She's long since given up practising her religion, but still she can feel the pull, the overwhelming ecclesiastical power, and invisible line of gravity from every corner of Christendom to the palace in Rome, anxious lest even one of its flock strays. She's had this conversation many times with Rory. An apostate, that's what you are, he'd say. Even so, you are always, and will always be, defined in relation to the Church. Once in, you never leave, they never *let* you leave. *Long ago, you know, you'd have been burnt as a witch a single woman with no faith.* She shudders.

The thought brings to mind her trip to Barcelona last year with Rory, and the image of a witch trial they viewed, since engraved on her consciousness. Picture the scene: a dungeon with a grill on the open arched window, three clerics sit at a cloth-covered table under a stone arch, a foot-high silver crucifix rests on the table in front of them. One of the men has a quill in his hand and is writing in a ledger; another, bearded and well dressed, a royal perhaps, has his hands clasped in front of him; a third, a monk, sits, face cupped in his hands. A fourth man stands to the extreme right of the picture and operates a wooden pulley structure: a trestle with rope wound around the cross bar. The rope stretches from the pulley to a beam in one of the many stone arches. Suspended from the rope is a young woman, arms crossed behind her back, a toehold her only support. Her body – completely naked – hangs in space, head falling forward, supported by this one touch. If the man at the pulley turns the handle, the woman swings into mid-air, her weight drops onto her arms and her shoulders are dislocated. The four fully clothed men gaze at the "witch" suspended before them.

Once you see an image like that you can never unsee it. It lodges in the brain like a worm, or some kind of warning. Of what though? The Church doesn't wield that kind of power in the twentieth century. Or does it?

Frankie shudders again. *Pull yourself together! Enough of this macabre thinking!*

She walks over to the river – more a fast-moving stream – that appears to flow right under the foundation of the church. She peers over the low stone wall. A clump of mauve valerian, in all its papal glory, thrusts out from one of the crevices. The June sun reflects blue in the meandering rivulet. As she listens to the gurgling water and breathes in the scent of wild garlic also pushing out from a niche in the wall, she allows the moment's transcendence, for nature to flood her senses, to relish the oneness with all living things, and dissolve the previous dark train of thought.

To access the main entrance, she has to pass by the towering dank granite wall to her left. At the rear of the church she finds a row of steps, also of granite, that lead up to the priest's house. As she psyches herself to meet Father Roche, Frankie feels adrenalin rushing through her veins. She can't quite put her finger on what, but there's something about this man that intrigues her.

Frankie rings the bell and waits. Rings again. Still no response. She sees a parishioner about to go down the steps and approaches him, learns that Father Roche resides in Bunbeg now, ever since the structural problem.

Frankie follows the man's directions, takes the mile from Derrybeg to Bunbeg and parks in the pebbled driveway in front of the bungalow that's now the priest's temporary home. From where she has parked, she can see right into the living room. Nobody draws net curtains in this locality, Frankie notices. She wonders if this is due to the spirit of discretion of Gweedore people, who wouldn't stoop to spying on the lives of others, or perhaps to an equal northern certainty that they wouldn't do anything that was worth spying on.

Father Roche answers the door in person, welcoming, flamboyant. "Come in, come in," he beams, extending his hand. "We've met already, Detective Francis. May I call you Frankie? Everyone else seems to."

The smooth familiarity.

She smiles, shakes his hand and steps into the spacious hall, floored in parquet, covered with a large expensive-looking Persian rug of deep carmine. The hall is furnished with a semi-circular mahogany table above which hangs a large bevelled oval mirror. Large expensively framed museum prints adorn the walls. How can a curate in a parish in Gweedore afford all this, she wonders?

"What a glorious day!" Roche has a line-free round face, with brown eyes not unlike a spaniel's. He wears a grey shirt, sleeves rolled up, under a black waistcoat. His fine black hair, silver in parts, is slightly long at the back. He doesn't wear a dog collar, she observes.

He leads her into the front room, which doubles as a study. The room is full of books, oak shelves weighed down under them. You could easily imagine the walls one day caving in. Frankie glances at the title of the book face down on the armrest of the fireside armchair: *Ten Men Dead* by David Beresford. This man is a republican.

"I've just been to the old church in Derrybeg. Is it my imagination, or does that river run right under the church?"

Roche waves a finger. "Your observation is absolutely correct. The church was built straddling two sides of the river. It flows under the floor of the church."

"Goodness! Isn't there a danger of flooding?"

Roche smiles. "Indeed there is and there was a very bad flood a century ago in which five people tragically lost their lives. But that was the only spot the landlord would give the tenants for their church, at the time. And as it had been the site of secret Masses during Penal times, you see, it had a special resonance for the people. Different times. Different issues."

"History all around us."

"Indeed. You only have to look across the border to its legacy – a gerrymandered state that's a prison house for Catholics. Origins in a plantation four hundred years ago."

But Frankie is not here for a lecture or to be drawn into a debate about the North. She knows where her sympathies lie, but that's for another day. Her attention turns to an antique oak chess table with fine marquetry inlay squares, by the window. She walks over and glances at the volume of *Great Chess Games* that rests on a stool nearby. "'*Napoleon versus Madame du Rémusat, 1804*'," she reads aloud.

Roche beams. "Are we an aficionado then?"

Frankie examines the state of play on the chessboard. "I wouldn't go that far, but I like to study classic chess games too."

Their eyes lock. That moment of recognition when people discover they have something in common, a connection that tells more in one moment than a hundred introductions. It's like you have a way into their life: show me what you love and I will tell you who you are.

Father Roche smiles, revealing even white teeth. "Well, this game was certainly interesting for its tactics."

Frankie can't help herself. She's drawn in, seduced. Roche gestures for her to sit. He sits on an armchair opposite. *Napoleon versus Madame de Rémusat.*

"You will, of course, have to take off all your clothes first," says Roche, deadpan.

Frankie looks at him in consternation.

Roche's eyes are twinkling, pleased at the effect his words have had on her. "You did know the good Madame used to play naked? Or at least the records of the time – the paintings – indicate as much."

To her annoyance, Frankie finds herself flushing. She can't help but imagine the scene, now the idea has been planted. She smiles uneasily, rises and looks out the large bay window for a change of scenery and takes in the broad expanse of beach and sea.

Roche comes up behind her.

"A magnificent place, isn't it?" He points. "What a view – Magheraclogher strand, Gola Island in the near distance, and further north – Tory."

Frankie is uncomfortably aware of his presence in her space.

When she turns he gestures, palm upwards, indicating that she should sit again.

She feels like a youngster in his presence. How do particular men achieve this? Or is it that this man's office compels ordinary mortals to bow down to him? She remembers the way Brannigan grovelled at the station. As she sits, his eyes fix on a small red beetle that is crawling across his desk. He teases it onto a sheet of paper and pops it into a tumbler of water on the sideboard. He sees her looking and holds her gaze, daring her to comment.

The moment passes.

"Would you like some tea?" he asks her, charming again. "Black? Herbal? Aoife – my housekeeper – stocks a mean peppermint tea?"

"Yes, thanks," says Frankie, "I'll have the peppermint."

Roche rings a little bell on the coffee table by his armchair. Almost immediately, a young woman opens the door, as though she had been waiting outside all along, listening, on the ready. She is a pretty, in her late teens, shy but with expressive dark eyes, almost black.

"Aoife, could we have tea and biscuits, please ... mint tea for the detective and green for me. There's a good girl."

Aoife bobs and bounces out as quickly as she came in.

Roche nods in the direction of the door. "Aoife hails from Tory Island. Have you ever been to Tory?"

Frankie shakes her head.

"Wonderful island. Never lost the old traditions." He settles back comfortably into his armchair, legs spread out, enjoying the moment. "Famous too for its poitín."

Frankie raises an eyebrow, bemused.

"Y'know, it was the main source of income – in some cases, the only source – in times gone past and, being an island community, it was very hard for the authorities to stop the distilling. And, in a way, could you blame the beleaguered people?"

Frankie shrugs. She knows the history. She knows the law. She has a job to do.

"Ever tasted poitín?" Roche grins.

Frankie stiffens. Good God! Is it her imagination or is he inclining his head towards that sideboard? Does he have a stash of the illegal brew in his possession? Is he being suggestive?

She lets the moment pass. "You obviously know this area and its surrounds and the people very well."

"This place has changed so much. When I used to visit here as a child in the sixties with my parents it was one long street, hostage to poverty and emigration. I knew every rock, every house, every shop. Everyone."

"Isn't there emigration now?"

"Well, yes, of course some of the youth are emigrating. But it's different from before. Now you have free education, and excellent training schemes for young people when they leave school, for those who don't get into university, or who don't want to go."

Aoife comes in with a tray. She places it on the coffee table beside Roche. On it is a fine porcelain teapot patterned with pink and blue flowers, cups and saucers that match. A plate of Mikado and Marietta biscuits. "Anything else, Father?"

"Thanks, Aoife, nothing else," Father Roche smiles at her and she leaves.

He opens two teabags – one mint, the other green – and drops them into the bone china cups. He pours the boiling water from the china teapot into the cups and hands one to Frankie. She breathes in the aroma of mint from the delicate wisp of steam that spirals upwards, like incense.

"Thank you." Frankie places the cup on its saucer on the occasional table beside her, to let the drink cool. She gets to the point of the visit.

"I'm really here to talk about Sarah Joyce."

"Oh dear. Poor Sarah." Roche holds out the plate of biscuits, but Frankie shakes her head. "What a sorry business that is. Can't believe the poor girl is in so much trouble." He takes one of the marshmallow biscuits and bites into its soft centre. "I'd better tell you all I know, I suppose."

Frankie registers *The Sexual Life of Savages* that's visible on the shelf behind Roche. Clearly, he reads widely. She pulls herself back to the present. "Yes, that would be useful."

"Such a sad business." He looks out the window for a moment and shakes his head. "She was always a bit wild ..." He lifts a teaspoon and slowly, meditatively, stirs his green tea. "But having said that ... she wouldn't harm a fly."

Frankie glances at the dead bug in the glass. "You would have known the family for a while?"

"Indeed I did. A very dysfunctional family, if I may say so. Poor Mags had her hands full rearing Sarah on her own ..." He looks at Frankie. "You know the story?"

"I've heard bits. I'm trying to join the dots."

Aoife knocks, pops her head around the door. "Everything all right, Father?"

Roche raises his hand as if in blessing and his servant smiles and leaves. He leans back in his chair.

"Mags came from a large family, most of whom emigrated. Well, there simply was no work here in the fifties. Things changed somewhat in the sixties but nevertheless emigration continued." He glances out the window at the wreck on the strand as if looking for clues. "When Mags' daughter Hannah became pregnant, the father left the country."

"Do you know who the father was?"

"The less said about that fella, the better."

"So even though Sarah refers to Mags as her mother, in reality Mags is Sarah's grandmother."

"Mags is approaching her eightieth this year as far as I know. It's not hard to do the maths."

"Indeed."

"Hannah, poor soul, never recovered. I mean in those days it was a terrible disgrace to have a child outside of wedlock. She became very depressed."

"Post-partum blues?"

Roche shrugs. "Whatever it was, she's suffered from it ever since. Doesn't even leave the house for Mass." He lifts one of the Marietta biscuits, smooth as a communion wafer, and brings it to his lips. "I occasionally go over and administer the sacraments. Poor unfortunate woman. You'd have to have compassion."

He bites into the Marietta, and looks out the bay window, as if lost in reflection.

Frankie follows his gaze to the rotting ship's skeleton on the beach. So Roche had inside knowledge of this family? Intimate knowledge. Of dark secrets or dark deeds. She turns to the curate. "Is that how you met Sarah?"

Roche carefully brushes biscuit crumbs off his black waistcoat, smooths the sateen fabric and tugs at the twin triangular points of the hem to adjust. "Yes, she used to make me a cup of tea after I'd been with Hannah … you know, of course, she was going out with young MacAllister from Bloody Foreland? Well, it's common knowledge. Although to be honest, I don't know the status of their relationship since they broke up. But I wouldn't be surprised …" He falls silent.

"You wouldn't be surprised?" Frankie presses.

But Roche pulls in his lips, deciding against.

"Is there any other information you can give us? Anything at all that might throw some light on the case?"

Roche sighs. "The confessional, as you know, is sacrosanct."

The phone rings. They can hear Aoife answering it.

Roche stands. "I'm sorry I can't help you more."

The interview is over.

They shake hands again. "Thanks for the tea," Frankie says as she leaves. "If you hear anything ..."

"Of course. Of course."

As she drives back to the barracks, Frankie mulls over her conversation with Brendan Roche. He's been in the Joyce household, by his own admission, many many times. He's a bright man. Surely he would have seen something? Plus he seemed to be hinting at something regarding Mike MacAllister. Does he know more than he's letting on?

CHAPTER 20

Mary Rose Ferry takes a sleeping tablet every night at midnight, wakes up six hours later – regular as clockwork, rises, has breakfast, dresses and walks the short distance to the cathedral for Mass at eight. She likes to arrive a half hour early to light a candle for poor Éamon who passed away thirty years ago. He was a good man, no matter what anyone says. What of it if he liked a drink now and then? He never lifted a hand to her.

At seventy-seven Mary Rose prides herself in her ability to walk up the hill to Letterkenny cathedral. Thanks be to Almighty God, she has great joints. Or so her GP told her at her last full medical. "You'll never get arthritis," he said, marvelling at her flexibility, which made her feel wonderful. Whenever she feels a little down in the dumps she thinks of the doctor's words: "You have great joints, Mary Rose," and she smiles to herself. *Sure, the Lord knows, I suppose you take what you get.*

Mary dips her fingers into the stone water font, into the pure sacred water, and blesses herself. She steps into an interior, always so dark even when it's a day of bright sunshine outside. There's plenty of dark in the world, but here it's the true dark. That's not a bad thing in Mary Rose's books. She likes the dark, it helps her to think, and she values time alone with her thoughts. She's of an age where the past is more real to her than the present. She has a storehouse of lifetime stories, dramas, heartaches, betrayals and grief behind her. At any time, she can resurrect a memory and experience the feelings all over again. It's not that she ignores the present, more that she can wander from past to present and back again in her mind with ease. The practice induces melancholy at times, but then she prays and that always helps.

The church is empty. Later it will fill for the morning Mass, the organist will raise her thoughts to heaven with wonderful music written by some medieval monk or other, tall candles will be lit. But for now the dark and silence. She genuflects as she crosses to the left side of the church in the direction of her favourite pew. She kneels, buries her face in her hands and prays. Ten Our Father's, ten Hail Mary's, one Glory Be. She gets up to light one of the penny candles. There's something soothing about ritual: first the prayers, then the penny candle and after that, Mass – that's her routine, her life. She likes the orderliness of it, the predictability.

When she first notices the suitcase in front of the altar, she's puzzled. *What in God's name!* She stares at the battered brown case, fashioned from tough cardboard, frayed and worn at the corners.

Suitcases have a resonance for Mary Rose . She packed many a one traipsing over and back to Scotland. She might have married young if she had not had to go to Glasgow to earn money to send back to her poor mother, widowed and much in need of the wherewithal to feed and clothe nine young children. But that's the way it was back then, you did what you had to do. After her dear mother passed away, Mary Rose hooked up with Éamon and they got married – too late, unfortunately, to have children.

Cautiously, Mary Rose rises. She looks to her right and left, then walks slowly up the aisle. Her heart is fluttering, like there's a small bird trapped inside, struggling to get out. Involuntarily, she places her hand over her chest. She has a sense of impending doom and she moves closer to get a better look at the suitcase.

The case is open. Mary Rose peers in.

The infant's hand pokes out from the blanket, five miniature digits raised as if in greeting. Mary Rose gasps. She reaches out to touch, to see if the child is alive. The tiny fingers are stiff and cold as marble. Mary Rose shrieks – a loud thin gut-wrenching cry of horror – as the contents of her stomach rise to her throat. She gags, puts her hand over her mouth, turns and rushes down the aisle and out of the church, the sound of her low-heeled court shoes *clop-clop-clopping,* echoing eerily through the chambers of the empty cathedral.

* * *

Brannigan places his pipe in the side of his mouth, emitting little plumes of smoke from the other side as he sucks greedily on the stem. McGinley stands to attention by the door.

Father Roche, in black soutane and dog collar, positions himself in front of the Sacred Heart, clasped hands behind his back, in the stance of one who understands the importance of appearances, of occasion, of power. He pulls back his shoulders and thrusts out his chest to deliver his sentence.

"Regrettably, we can't give either baby a Christian burial."

McGinley crosses himself. "Oh, the Lord save us and bless us!"

Frankie pauses in her search for a document in the filing cabinet, and turns, eyebrows raised. "Why not?"

"Against Canon Law, unfortunately. We have to assume neither were baptised before death ..." he sighs – "so, sadly, they are not properly absolved of original sin."

"Limbo it is so for the little beggars, I suppose," grunts Brannigan out of the side of his mouth.

Frankie knows her catechism, she should do – she spent fourteen years learning it. Heaven is for the good souls, purgatory for those awaiting entry, hell for the damned. And then there's limbo, an airless place for the lost, forgotten or unwanted, with no prospect ever of progress or improvement. Of course, she knows it could be argued that Limbo was invented as a mercy, as previous ages had to believe unbaptised babies went to hell. Nevertheless, she feels a sudden aversion to Father Brendan Roche and what he stands for. Where before she had felt drawn by his charm, his charisma, his powerful presence, now she is overwhelmed by a sense of the cold-hearted misanthropy that underpins his power.

She retreats to the prefab. "Pat Mullarkey is right," she announces to no one in particular.

Moran presses return on the typewriter, pulls out the sheet of paper from between the rollers, signs it, and sticks it in an envelope. He leans back. "At last! Done! Who?"

"Pat Mullarkey. The journalist. She says women are considered murderers if they have an abortion because the foetus is a person in the eyes of the Church, *but* ..." she raises a finger, "it is not a person when it is born unless it's been baptised ..." Frankie sits and leans back in her chair, arms folded. "How many angels can dance on the head of a pin?"

Moran looks up, bemused. "Are we a feminist now or what? And, anyway, I thought you were an atheist? Or has there been a conversion on the road to – to Donegal? No?"

Frankie makes a face at him.

"Anyway, since you think it is all mumbo jumbo, why are you bothered? What has all that got to do with us or the case?"

Frankie opens a file and glances at the forensics report they received the day before. The garden baby's death: no foul play involved.

Moran picks up a biro and taps it on the desk as he looks out onto the harbour. *De-dum de-dum de-dum.*

Frankie looks up – *what?*

Moran tosses the biro onto the desk. "Okay, I've changed my mind. My theory now is: Sarah *did* kill the Strand baby."

Frankie studies her thumb, discovers a rag nail, nudges it. This is going to be painful.

"Sarah's lover was two-timing her," Moran says. "The Strand baby was his by another woman." He lifts up the biro again and taps out his point. *De-dum de-dum de-dum.* The biro takes on a life of its own. "Having just delivered – and watched die – her own child by this man, Sarah sneaks into the maternity ward, steals her rival's baby in a jealous rage and kills it."

Frankie snorts. Ridiculous. "It doesn't seem plausible." She tugs at the rag nail, winces, decides to leave it alone. "I mean, for starters, how could she even get into the maternity ward without being noticed or stopped?"

"Well ... hospital maternity wards are notoriously busy places." Moran is determined to give his theory a good airing. "Nurses are overworked, on strike most of the time for God's sake."

"They're on strike now," retorts Frankie. "Not most of the time." She glances sideways at her thumb, red and throbbing on one side, urging her to try again and get rid of the villain. "But go on."

"Where before they had a patient to a bed per day, now they have two patients. That means they are preoccupied with all the paperwork, cleaning the beds and so on and so forth. They haven't the time to be noticing strange happenings. All it takes is for a woman to act coolly, keep her head and find her moment." Moran leans back in his swivel chair, hands clasped behind his head, satisfied with his theory. "And don't forget lots of women come to visit in maternity wards, so a lone woman walking into the place would not seem out of place. She could have been a sister coming to have a peek at the child."

"But ..." Frankie looks for holes in the argument – there have to be holes, it's so outlandish. "But ... okay, so let's suppose she manages to make it to the nursery without raising any eyebrows or causing alarm, how on earth could she have spirited the baby away without detection? I mean you can't put a baby into your top pocket."

"No. Not into your pocket – but remember we're talking about an infant that probably weighs about eight pounds in weight ... think eight pounds of potatoes – it would easily fit into the large handbags most women carry around with them these days – some of those things are as big as a case."

"But you're missing the obvious: any poor unfortunate

mother would lift the roof if her baby went missing. It would be the talk of the town, not to mention the media, for weeks after. So that can be ruled out."

O'Toole rushes in. "Another baby found – in Letterkenny cathedral."

Both detectives stare at him.

"Dead. With a note attached to it that says: *This belongs to you.*"

Moran scratches his head.

"Maybe Sarah had three babies, sir."

Moran glowers at the intern.

* * *

"We are appealing to the mother to come forward." The Superintendent pulls himself up to his full height, sucks in his stomach, conscious he's on TV. "This is an emergency, a tragic case of a mother, possibly a young unmarried woman, panicking after a birth. We want to assure the mother that she will receive all the necessary help."

Doctor Long steps forward to the microphone. "In a case like this," the doctor from Letterkenny General, says, "medical help is needed. The woman clearly gave birth in traumatic circumstances. So not only does she require physical care at this time, but she also needs psychological assistance, which will be available to her in the strictest confidence."

Presenter Seán O'Rourke details the media interest there is in this story: three babies found dead one after the other. Unprecedented. The huge international attentiveness to the case shows no sign of abating – the number of television crews and press reporters arriving in northwest Donegal continues to grow. A cold weather front is blowing in from the Atlantic, he warns.

* * *

"The pathologist confirms the Church baby's death is a tragic case of suffocation due to clumsy birthing," Moran says. "There's no evidence of foul play. Although it seems parishioners are wondering who would leave a note attached to the infant's shawl that says: *This belongs to you*."

"And why leave the baby in the church?" Frankie wonders.

"Brannigan's take on it is this is a sad case of a poor unfortunate woman offering her dead baby up to God. In any case, the girl involved hasn't committed a crime. We should interview her all the same. I'll do it. Even if it's not a criminal case, there's something suspicious about the whole thing." Moran pulls on his coat. At the door, he turns. "By the way, McGinley tells me a boat has been seen coming and going from Umfin to Port Arthur. We need to check that out. The Biddies are not written off yet." He nods at the intern.

"Done!" says O'Toole.

* * *

It takes O'Toole less than a couple of hours to establish that the furtive coming and going in the night had nothing to do with the Children of Bríd. Another dead end.

When Frankie arrived in Bunbeg, the Biddies were suspect number one. Within a day Sarah turned up and there were two dead babies and two suspects. Then in a puff of smoke there were none. Now a third baby is found. And still no leads, no suspects.

CHAPTER 21

Moran and Frankie arrive together at the barracks in Bunbeg. As they wend their way around to the office via the side gate, Moran is seized by a paroxysm of sneezing. Frankie points towards the wild ferns clustered in a sullen clump in the corner of the yard. "Stay away from those things – they're lethal for allergies."

Moran sneezes again, opens the prefab hurriedly to get away from the offending plants. Then, remembering something, he turns towards Frankie and holds an index finger up for attention. "By the way," – *sneeze* – "Happy Birthday!"

"Thanks."

"So what great age is we celebrating today?"

Frankie makes a face. "Thirty-five."

"Ah ... I remember thirty-five," he says, mocking her. "It's

Saturday. Let's take tonight off."

Frankie frowns. "We're getting nowhere in the case – I'd feel almost guilty ..."

"There's nothing happening on Saturday night. We're due a night off. All work and no play and so on ... I'll book us a table for somewhere grand tonight. We can discuss the case, if you like. What about the Beach Hotel?"

Frankie smiles. "The Beach Hotel would be splendid."

Moran nudges her suggestively, but she moves away. Moran slumps his shoulders, turns his lips down and assumes a clownish faux-dejected look. Frankie can't help smiling. He's quite the comedian. She likes that about him.

"Anyway," he says, snapping back to action, "enough of this nonsense – *chop-chop!*"

They collect folders from the prefab, return to the barracks, and join Brannigan in the back office. Through the glass window partition they can see the tall thin youth from Bloody Foreland in argument with McGinley.

Brannigan nods in their direction. "We got him. MacAllister."

Frankie frowns. "But Mike MacAllister has an alibi for the eighth of May. Until we come up with evidence, he's off the hook."

Brannigan's face lights up as he pulls out his tobacco pouch. "*Ah ha!* That's where you are wrong. This boyo is up to his eyeballs in trouble." With care he lifts out shreds of gold-brown nicotine and stuffs them into his pipe. "Maybe not in the murder case, but deep trouble nonetheless."

Moran leans against the desk and reaches into his pocket.

Frankie lifts her palms upwards in question.

"Me bould Michael John Daniel MacAllister has been caught red-handed." Brannigan pats the tobacco, strikes a safety match and lights up. "Growing herbs."

Moran, sticking a cigarette between his lips, leans across for the sergeant to add flame to his cigarette: a communion of smokers.

Frankie remembers the pungent smell in MacAllister's house.

Brannigan shakes the match to quench the flame, puffs a few short staccato pulls in succession, in the now familiar ceremony of getting the pipe going. "And not of the medicinal type, I should hasten to add." He exhales sickly sweet-smelling plumes into the atmosphere. "If you get my drift." Pipe dangling from the side of his mouth, he picks up his car keys and puts on his sergeant's hat. "So you see," Brannigan removes the pipe from his mouth momentarily, pulls himself up to his full height, straightens his jacket and pulls in his enormous gut, "we've got him by the short and curlies." He swaggers to the door and turns. "He gives us information about where the IRA plant bombs – we keep him out of the slammer." He smirks. "There could be a promotion in it yet." He leaves.

"Roseanne told me she thought MacAllister was no longer in the organisation," Frankie says.

"If he is and they find out, they'll knee-cap that young Turk," Moran says.

"Who will?" O'Toole asks.

"The Ra, O'Toole. The bloody IRA."

Frankie shrugs. "You wouldn't think he had it in him."

Moran stubs his cigarette out in the sink. "So that's what Brannigan is up to – looking for the big 'find', so he'll get promoted and retire with a fat pension pot."

Back at the hotel, Frankie checks at reception once again to see if there is a message for her. It's four o'clock. Rory has never missed a birthday before. The sky has suddenly darkened. Too wet now to go for a walk. Too cold. She looks out of the window. Nothing.

Frankie runs a hot bath, puts some bubble-bath cubes and several drops of lavender into the water. She strips, eases into the warm welcoming suds and breathes in the soothing aroma. Try as she will, she cannot shake of a feeling of unease.

The case is going nowhere – and neither is she. She'd thought the murder case would be solved quickly, hadn't anticipated the many roadblocks the investigation would throw up.

She's a year older and has found the first grey hair in her head. Thirty-five and childless. What is she doing with her life? Her twenties have melted away and now here she is approaching middle age, the bloom of youth gone, with nothing to show. She shakes herself out of her existential trance. Whenever she lets her mind drift to the bigger picture, the trajectory of her life, she feels overwhelmed. In the here and now she's alive, happy even, fully engaged with solving this crime despite the obstacles, the challenge. Because of the challenge, maybe. And isn't that all we've got in life? The here and now? Why can't she be happy with that? Is it the human condition to operate at two levels – a yearning to have everything in the big picture go according to a plan in our heads while we live our lives minute by minute? But we will only see the big picture in time, at the end of our lives perhaps, when the pattern – as it were – fully emerges on the carpet.

She steps out of the water and wraps a bath sheet around her. She likes the feel of fluffy terry cotton on her skin. Back in the bedroom she allows the towel to slip to the floor and surveys herself in the full-length mirror. She sees a body that pleases her, one that's lean and well-toned: a steady routine of jogging and exercise for strength and flexibility shows. She's never minded having small breasts. All a man needs is a handful, Rory said once. She was slim, and he liked that: *"My very own Modigliani."* He even went to the trouble of showing her the artist's *Reclining Nude* to prove his point. A very elongated model reclines on a deep-red throw. Her eyes are closed. She has one arm up behind her head, the other tucked under her chin. Small firm breasts point upwards. Her flawless skin glows, its bloom and peach tones startling bright against the deep-red tones of the textured cloth. The left hip is raised and twists so that the lower body faces the viewer. A neat triangle of dark-blonde pubic hair forms a V at the top of closed thighs.

"That hip looks dislocated," Frankie had said.

"Ah, maybe it is, but look at the harmony," Rory said. "The model was Modigliani's lover. It's a painting about intimacy, about being in love."

Dislocated hip notwithstanding, Frankie did like the image, its radiance, its sensuous colour, felt tenderness towards Rory for making the comparison.

She pads over in bare feet and examines her wardrobe. She hadn't expected this investigation to take so long, so she doesn't have much of a selection to choose from. She puts on a pair of black jeans, tries on a black low-neck top with it and looks at herself in the mirror. No, that won't do. Off it comes. Next up a midnight-blue top. Still not right. Her final choice is a fitted red knit top that accentuates her shape. She opens the top buttons to show off a bit of cleavage. *Yes!* She puts on the chain Rory gave her for her thirty-fourth birthday: a silver pendant of an ancient Celtic icon. She opens one more button, wiggles her shoulders. The pendant falls between her breasts. That's better. She twirls, takes off the band tying her hair back and shakes it loose. She grabs her keys and jacket. She's late.

Moran is waiting in the lobby. His eyes light up when he sees her. She observes him as he looks her over from head to foot. He's wearing a dark-blue linen jacket over a blue check shirt and light-coloured trousers. Suede shoes. To her eyes he looks spruce and attractively turned out. *Very attractive, indeed. What am I like*, she scolds herself. *This is not a date.*

Moran smiles, cheeks dimpling.

Oh lord! Those dimples!

The Beach Hotel on her birthday. What the hell! A glass of wine and the world will glow. They drive down the long narrow strand-road to the beach, a mile from the main road. The evening is balmy and warm. Moran turns on the radio and switches the dial to 2FM and *Top of the Pops*.

"*Next up, 'Like A Prayer', Madonna's iconic hit*," the DJ intones, "*into its fourth week in the top twenty*."

"I like the hussy," says Moran, and hums along.

Frankie is preoccupied, finding it hard to shake off the hurt that Rory hasn't made any effort to contact her. Or sent a card, at least. Where is he now? Is it over between them? He could have rung or left a message. Put him out of your head, Kate Francis, she tells herself – it's your birthday, tonight you're going to enjoy yourself. With an effort she pulls herself back to the present, picks up on lyrics and sings along with Moran and Madonna. She likes the hussy too.

The dark clouds have vanished. The sea slithers over the sand, blindly obeying the pull of the full moon. A thin film of water glistens as it forms a slick over the dark gold grains on its forward glide to the hotel. Just shy of the building, it will stop and begin the long slide back to the channel. The mesmerising draw of the tide. Frankie can almost feel its power.

A waiter escorts them to the table Moran reserved, by the window, overlooking the beach, a bottle of Rioja already ordered and sitting on the table at room temperature.

The waiter, linen towel over arm, lifts the Rioja and pours a small amount into Moran's glass. Moran waves his hand for him to get on with it, fill it up, no need for tasting. The waiter pours and leaves.

Moran raises his glass in a toast. "So ... thirty-six?"

"Thirty-five," Frankie corrects, clinks his glass and sips.

"*Oops!* Thirty-five. Sorry." He takes a slurp. "Here's to ..." – pauses – "life."

The dining room starts to fill up. The new waiter is slow taking orders. After a couple of glasses of wine, Frankie feels lightheaded. Wine always makes her giddy, especially on an empty stomach. She becomes talkative.

"Do you believe in God?"

"God? Oh! We're getting into deep territory." Moran tips out a cigarette, places it at the corner of his mouth, lights up. "What's brought this on?"

Frankie looks out the window at the boat, lying forlorn and abandoned on the damp sand, pondering the folly of mankind with all its worries and pointless endeavours. Soon you will all be dead too, it seems to say. So just live for the day: you only have one day.

"Visiting that church down in the hollow the other day, I

229

suppose. Father Roche. Not that we talked religion. In fact, you would forget at times that he's a man of the cloth."

"A man of the cloth." Moran squints at her through the smoke. "Funny expression that. What does it mean anyway?"

The waiter comes and takes their orders, offers some light banter and leaves. Despite the new waiter's slowness, Frankie is glad Lucy is off duty tonight. It's her birthday, she doesn't want competition.

"My question about believing in God ... I'm just thinking of that baby on Port Arthur Strand."

"And that reminds you of God because ...?"

Frankie sighs. "Just ..." She pauses, trying to think it through. "It's just ... how could a God allow a defenceless baby to be beaten to death?"

"Well, sorry, but tonight I am on my night off from wondering about God."

The food arrives. Moran eyes his chicken supreme and cauliflower in white sauce. He sticks a fork into the vegetable, looks at Frankie with twinkling eyes. "*Ah!* There *is* a God!"

The evening wheels along in a pleasant haze of agreeable food, alcohol and banter. They become oblivious to the other diners, engrossed as they are in their own bubble. One topic follows another seamlessly. Dessert follows. Then coffee.

Darkness slowly closes in.

Moran pours wine into Frankie's glass. He leans in towards

her. "You know, you have exceptionally high cheekbones, Kate Francis."

The room is beginning to spin ever so slightly. Diners rising to leave appear to weave through space rather than walk in straight lines.

"Oh stop. You'll give me a big head," she says, aware she's blushing.

Moran gazes at her. "You must know you're beautiful?"

Frankie finds herself losing the battle against the feelings overwhelming her. Anto Moran may be grumpy at times but still ... he's a very attractive man. He did tell her his marriage is over, that day they drove back from Galway, that it's been over for a long time, but they never got around to the mechanics of breaking up. Oh, what am I thinking of? Don't they all say that!

Moran lifts her hand and kisses it. She makes no effort to resist the gesture. She feels the warmth of his moist lips on her skin as a sensual pleasure.

"Shall we leave?" Moran gestures for the bill. "I'll call a taxi. I can collect the car tomorrow."

She nods happily. The next day she'll wonder how she managed to get from the dining room to the taxi for she'll have no recollection of it at all. What she *will* remember is that back at the hotel, Moran walks her to her room, both of them tipsy and talking animatedly. Frankie's in full flight about chess, what draws her to it, the challenge of it. She's on an alcohol high, thrilled with Moran's attention, the frisson between them. Uninhibited, she explains to him why it is the supreme game, why she's become addicted to it.

At her bedroom door, they turn towards each other. Moran tilts in and whispers, "Do you have a chess set in your room?"

Frankie laughs. He knows damn well she has a chess set in her room because she's already told him she has. She knows where this is going, that she should stop the flow, but what the hell, she thinks, let it rip.

As she fumbles to get the key into the lock, Moran rests his hand on her shoulder, slides it slowly down to the small of her back.

"Let's have a look at this famous chess set of yours, then."

He follows her into the room and pushes the door closed. Frankie kicks off her shoes, and drops onto the carpet in front of the chess set on the locker. She re-arranges the pieces on the board, white facing black. *Game set.*

Moran saunters over and plops into the armchair nearby, opens a pack of cigarettes. He nudges one out a little and extends the pack to Frankie. "Want one?"

Frankie, a golden strand of hair falling down over her cheek, kneels, and sits on her heels. Unable to resist, she takes the proffered cigarette and places it awkwardly between her lips. Moran flicks his lighter on. The flame leaps forward, orange and hot. Their eyes meet as she steadies Moran's hand to bring the fire to her cigarette. She breathes in the sweet smell of kerosene blended with toasted tobacco, leans back and draws deeply. She coughs and splutters, eyes tearing momentarily. Moran pats her back and she regains composure. She quivers at the brief touch of his warm hand on her back again.

Moran sits on the floor beside her. He nods at the chessboard. "So, teach me."

"You're serious? You want to learn how to play chess?" She tries hard to articulate without slurring.

Moran nods disarmingly. Frankie smiles, aware she's feeling very woozy. Oh, I know what you're at, you sly old fox. You've no more interest in chess than the Man in the Moon. But sure, what the hell. Let's play. She hands Moran her cigarette and picks up a pawn.

"This is the little guy. Very important as a team player but not much power on its own."

"That'd be O'Toole."

They laugh at the mention of the intern. Moran stubs out the cigarettes. He selects one of the royals, like he already knows what's important. "Tell me about this one."

Frankie takes a deep breath. "That's the queen. Now she has the power. She can move anywhere she damn well likes."

"That'd be you, so," Moran says, looking into her eyes. "Women have all the power. Men are putty in their hands."

His eyes are green, Frankie notices. How did she not spot that before? *Green with brown flecks – dancing eyes, full of fun.*

Frankie examines the chess piece to distract herself. But she can't help it. She turns to Moran to find him moving in towards her. They hover for a moment, mouth almost touching mouth. It's as if everything slows down, as if time itself has stopped, as they breathe into each other. They move closer almost in slow exquisite motion, until finally they connect in a kiss. *The smell and taste of him!* Frankie drops the queen and puts her arms around him. She pulls him in.

The queen rolls onto the carpet, face to the wall.

CHAPTER 22

Roseanne gives Sarah a hug. "How are you holding up, hon?"

The room is hot and stuffy. Nevertheless, Sarah shivers and pulls her dressing gown tightly around her, two fists holding the cowl up under her chin.

"Are the papers still writing about me?"

Roseanne sighs and sits. "You did nothing wrong, Sarah. You've got to remember that."

Sarah sticks her thumb into her mouth and chews her nail. "Why am I still in this place if they've nothing against me?"

Roseanne appraises Sarah, hair scraped back from her face and tied with an elastic band. A beautiful young woman, with a mass of flame-coloured hair now bunched behind her head in a pony-tail. She sees anxiety and fear in her eyes. How small and waif-like she looks. How vulnerable.

"You'll be out of here soon."

"Y'know, sometimes I think I should have taken the boat to England for an abortion while there was still time. Just gone and done it."

Roseanne reaches out and puts her hand on Sarah's. "Put all that right out of your mind, Sarah. Try and be patient. They'll have to let you go soon."

A nurse looks in. "Are you receiving Holy Communion?"

Sarah glares at the nurse. "No, I'm not receiving. I've told you before, but you keep asking me. *How many times do I have to tell you I'm not receiving?*"

The nurse raises her hands in the air defensively and backs out of the room.

"Jesus!" exclaims Roseanne. "Don't shoot the messenger, *a stór.*"

Sarah shoulders slump, a vein in her right temple pulsates. She sighs. "It's my nerves. They're shot to pieces. You've no idea, Roseanne, it's all enough to make you sick."

"You are sick," says Roseanne.

"Well, sicker then."

* * *

Frankie swings in towards the pier and parks. She sees her boss further up on the grassy embankment, leaning against his car, smoking. She regrets now having arranged this meeting when they were at the meal last night, before they ended up in bed.

When he sees her, Moran tosses his cigarette, and comes towards her, smiling, a sheepish look on his face.

"Sorry I had to leave early this morning."

Frankie squirms, waves her hand dismissing the subject. She feels a flush rising from her neck right up to her face, feels uncomfortably hot despite a breeze wheeling in from the Atlantic. The events of last night keep plunging into her mind. Just when she thinks she's tamped them down – *bang!* There they are again. Oh please, please, let's not go there, last night was a mistake, it will never happen again. Ever.

A high blanket of cirrus cloud has begun to disintegrate, like pieces from a jigsaw puzzle and sun breaks through the gaps, imposing patches of silver onto the grey green of the sea.

As they walk down the sandy path that leads onto the beach – there is a proper path, she discovered, that doesn't involve treading over dangerously slippery rocks – and towards the fateful dune, Frankie is acutely aware of Moran's closeness. Almost perversely, she keeps stumbling on the uneven ground, bumping into him. At one point, as she flings her hand out to steady herself, Moran holds it and draws her in. She smiles at him momentarily – caught off-guard, confused – before moving away. *What are you encouraging him for?* she scolds herself. Rory used always say to her: "*Nature hates a vacuum.*" And Frankie would always reply: "*Is that the only reason we're together – because we can't bear to be alone?*"

With an effort, she switches her mind back to work, to the job on hand.

The detectives measure the distance from the dunes to the pier, carefully scanning the area.

"I've already scoured the place twice," says Frankie. "Not a trace of anything,"

"Still, it bears repeating: every contact leaves a trace. They take something with them, leave something behind."

"Rule 101, I know. But we've not found any traces so far."

"Motive, we must focus on motive," says Moran, digging his hands deep in his pockets. "This is your territory, Detective Francis. I think, given the severity of the wound, we can rule out that it was some kind of horrible accident, so the question is why someone would kill a new-born child?"

Frankie zips up her jacket against the light cool breeze rolling in. "It could have been post-partum blues. Or a mother might kill her child out of fear of being shunned by her community."

White horses ride the deep-blue waves and they hear the *whish-whish* as the water advances and retreats, throwing a thin skin of water forward, as if an invisible might has upended a bucket of suds and flung them horizontally onto the strand in a bid to cleanse the place of the memory of the crime. The sea here is different from the other beach, Magheraclogher, Frankie notices. There, the sea retreats to a narrow ribbon between mainland and promontory – here it's straight out to America.

Moran opens a pack of cigarettes, sticks one in his mouth and pats his jacket pockets to locate his lighter. "A family might kill the child out of shame."

"A lover might kill the child because he fears he'll be disgraced if he is a married man."

Moran stops and bends his head towards his chest, as he cups both hands and flicks the lighter into action; it takes several attempts before he can get a flame that lasts long enough to take hold.

Frankie moves to his other side. "We still don't know who the mother is. But if it is Sarah, then her motive might have been fear."

"I thought we'd already established that Sarah is not the mother of the Strand baby."

"I'm just running through scenarios that might pertain if Sarah did have two babies."

"What? Are we going back over that again? I thought your conclusion from the nods and winks from her ladyship – Hannah – well, nods, anyway – was that Sarah did not have two babies, that Mags was either doting or playing us for fools when she said she had."

"Yes, I know. I'm just going over possibilities. And then, of course, there's Hannah herself."

Moran frowns. "We've already interviewed Hannah."

"But think about it – she tried to kill her own illegitimate child – now her daughter has a child out of wedlock – that would still be a disgrace in Donegal even if it isn't in Dublin any longer. Is it unthinkable that she might want to help her daughter?"

"You're suggesting we should bring her in again?" After several tries, Moran manages a smoke ring. "Okay, we'll bring her in again."

They retrace their steps back up the sandy path onto the pier and down to its end. They stand at the edge, looking out to sea and breathing in the briny air, as the green waves crash against the granite wall, whooshing a fine spray onto their faces. Mesmerised, they watch the seaweed bob and tumble in the tide, over the rocks, a swirl of water and weed and foam against and around the granite and quartzite rocks.

Moran steps up behind Frankie and envelops her in his two broad arms, rests his chin on her shoulder. "Next stop, America."

He smells of tobacco. It's him. For a moment she allows the feeling to linger and sinks into the embrace, momentarily luxuriating in it.

A shout from the embankment shatters the moment. "*Frankie!*"

She jumps, startled, frees herself from Moran's embrace.

Again, the sharp call, "*Frankie!*"

A familiar voice.

Both detectives turn to face the embankment where the cars are parked. A feeling of dread overwhelms Frankie. Oh no. Surely it can't be ...?

A man is walking hurriedly towards them down the length of the pier. It's not who she wants to see at this precise moment, caught as she is in a compromising position. What on earth is *he* doing here?

Frankie pulls further away from Moran. "Rory."

A fit and tanned Rory marches all the way to where they stand at the pier's end.

Rory glares at Frankie, then at Moran, and back at Frankie. "What's going on?"

She stands transfixed, frozen, as panic sets in, and finds herself stammering. "Rory, I thought you were in Barcelona."

Rory raises his hands in the air, palms up. "Oh, yes, very convenient," he says, his face beetroot-red. "So this is what's been going on. Oh, my God, Frankie ..." He shakes his head, choking with emotion. "You could have just told me." He stares at her, eyes welling up, then turns abruptly and hurries back up the pier.

Frankie runs after him. "*Rory, wait!*" Her heart is thumping. "*It's not what it seems!*" It sounds so feeble, she knows, but she has to fix this.

Rory is already at his car. He hops into the old Toyota and is gone, wheels screeching, raising a cloud of sand and dust, a broken exhaust puffing out a miserable plume in its wake.

Out of breath, Frankie stops running and looks after the retreating banger. How can this have happened? Moran joins Frankie and both stand looking after the car – now a dot in the distance – as it shoots up the narrow sandy road.

Moran puts his hand on Frankie's shoulder. "Sorry ..."

She shrugs him off. "Don't."

Moran backs off.

She marches off to her own car. *What on earth is Rory doing here? Didn't he go to Barcelona after all? How did he know to find her on the pier?* She drives back to the hotel.

CHAPTER 23

Mags twists her abalone rosary beads around her gnarled fingers. She has refused to take off her coat and hat, despite the heat in the room. She hates hospitals, never liked them, can't wait to get out of the place. Sarah sits opposite, her cheeks burning, heart palpitating – she's determined to raise the matter that's burning a hole in her brain.

"Ma ..."

Outside in the corridor, the business of hospital carries on: nurses calling out, bells ringing, people being hurried to theatre. A tea lady trundles along with her trolley, knocks on the door and pokes her head around. "Tea?"

"No, thanks," says Sarah. "Sorry, Ma ... would you like some tea?"

Mags shakes her head.

The door closes.

"Ma ..."

Mags looks at her daughter. "What it is, hen?"

Sarah is clearly struggling and ill at ease. Finally she blurts out in a rush, in the manner of one who fears they won't have the courage to say what they need to say if they don't say it fast.

"Ma, I know Hannah is my mother."

Mags takes in a deep breath, closes her eyes, lifts the crucifix at the end of the rosary beads, kisses it, blesses herself. She remains completely still for several moments, with only her lips moving as if in prayer. Sarah waits.

Finally Mags opens her eyes, wraps the beads around her fingers, kisses the crucifix once more and sighs. "Yes, *a stór*, I thought you knew. Sure it wasn't that I was trying to hide it from you, it was just ... ah sure, I don't know. I'm only an old countrywoman getting on in years."

Sarah chews her thumbnail. She looks up at Mags under long lashes. The moment hangs awkwardly, neither of them used to conversations like this, neither of them sure how to proceed. But the conversation has begun and must continue.

"You've been a good mother to me, but I'm not a child any more. I need to know the truth about who I am."

Mags works her beads, nods.

Sarah frowns, trying to summon the courage to say what she

has to say. There's no going back now. She straightens up, the better to stiffen her resolve, clears her throat.

"Ma, there's something else ..."

Mags looks up, alarmed, wondering what's next.

"I want to know who my father is too."

Mags freezes. She stares at Sarah. Sarah can see the whites of her eyes. She's reminded of the horse in the meadow at home who always shows the whites of his eyes when frightened.

Mags looks down, stares at her feet. Slowly, she struggles to get up, stands and arches her stiff back. "The smell of hospitals does me nerves in."

* * *

Roseanne leads Frankie into the kitchen. "Sit down, sit down. I just have to stir this once and I'll be right with you." She has her thick hair tied back and is wearing a striped apron. She moves a large stainless-steel pan off the electric ring, tips its contents into a colander over the sink and allows the water to drain off. She shakes the remaining moisture off before placing the utensil on the draining board. Using a fork, she scoops up a portion of slimy green vegetable – in appearance not unlike spinach – and dollops it onto a plate.

Frankie pulls back and makes a face. "What on earth is that?"

Roseanne chuckles, amused at her friend's reaction. "This, my dear, is sloac, a seaweed purge straight out of the sea, a thousand times more effective in removing toxins from the system than any pharmaceutical concoction. Good for the soul."

"I could do with my soul being purged right now." Frankie wrinkles her nose. *But God almighty! What a smell!*

"I thought you didn't believe in souls ..." Roseanne holds up a forkful of the green seaweed. "Anyway, if you eat this you'll live to be a hundred."

Frankie takes a deep breath. "I think I'll take my chances."

Roseanne sits. She smiles as she twirls the sloac onto her fork, pushing down on a spoon the better to make it hold. "Anything else I can offer?"

"No, I'm only here for a flying visit. I needed to talk to someone."

"Shoot. You say you saw Rory on Port Arthur, when he was supposed to be in Barcelona ..." Roseanne tucks into the dish of seaweed.

Frankie looks out the window and addresses the fuchsia in the lawn, in an effort to avoid looking at Roseanne eating. "I just can't figure out why Rory is here? He told me he was booked for Barcelona so why is he in Donegal? And how on earth did he know to find me at the strand?"

The purple florets nod silently in the light salt breeze from the Atlantic as if in sympathy with her predicament.

Roseanne lifts a jug of water and pours some into two glasses, one of which she hands to Frankie. "What do you think is going on?"

Frankie takes a sip of water. "I don't know what to think."

Roseanne tears off a piece of bread roll, wipes her plate with it in order to soak up all the seafood juices, bites into it. "And of course, the other thing is," she says, mouth full, "the question must be asked – what is *really* going on here?"

"What do you mean?" asks Frankie.

Roseanne lowers her head and taps her nose. "I mean between you and the lovely Anthony Moran?"

To her annoyance, Frankie finds herself blushing. "There's nothing going on. I have no interest in a married man."

Roseanne nods and smiles. "And if he wasn't married?"

Frankie glances sideways at her friend. When is she going to finish that stuff so I can look at her without my stomach upending? She gets up, walks to the window and stares at the fuchsia, still nodding. She doesn't answer.

Roseanne doesn't need an answer. She finishes her dish, takes the plate over to the sink and rinses it. She takes off her apron, opens the washing machine under the sink and throws it in "Well, for a start you need to confront Rory about all this. There's no point in second-guessing what he's up to. There could be a number of reasons why the Barcelona trip is off and he's in Donegal instead. You're the detective – you'll figure it out. I mean, his mother lives in Dungloe, right? Couldn't he have simply changed his mind about the Spanish trip and decided to come home for a visit instead? Look you up while he was here. And then finds you in flagrante, as they say."

"Hardly in flagrante."

"As good as. Anyway, best thing, I would say, would be to have it all out in the open." Roseanne fills the kettle. "But also, if you don't mind me saying so, it seems to me you are conflicted. It's not clear – to me at any rate – where your affections lie."

"With Rory, of course! I want us to get back together," says Frankie.

"But would you also like to keep things open with Moran in the hope that he will leave his wife?"

Frankie shakes her head. *No! No!* She's beginning to find this discussion unsettling.

"Or is it that you have marked Rory out as the poor schmuck you'll marry in order to have a baby in the distant future?"

Frankie winces. "Jesus! No! I love Rory."

Roseanne raises an eyebrow. "*The lady doth protest too much, methinks.*"

"Okay ... I can't deny I find Moran very attractive. He's fun to be with. He makes me laugh. Isn't it possible to love people in different ways?"

"*Whoa!* You're beginning to sound like that lot out in Umfin. Are you saying you want them both? The one for making a baby, the other for fun?"

Frankie shakes her head. "No, of course not. There's no

question of anything with Moran. That was a mistake. I want to be with Rory. He's kind, considerate, we're compatible ..."

"And fun?"

"Stop. What I want to know is how do I explain what he saw on the pier, that's all."

Roseanne folds her arms and leans against the countertop as she waits for the water to boil. "Want a bit of advice from Agony Aunt Roseanne Doherty? Sort out where your affections truly lie, and as soon as possible. Once you are clear in your own mind, there'll be no need for explanations."

Frankie's mind is a blank.

Roseanne takes two earthenware mugs off the shelf and puts them on the table. "Changing the subject ... I talked to Sarah Joyce yesterday."

Frankie snaps back to attention. "Oh?"

"She said she's wondering now if she should have gone for an abortion after all." She opens the fridge and takes out a carton of milk.

Frankie sits on the windowsill.

"I 'took the boat' once, y'know?"

Toby saunters into the kitchen, marches to the middle of the room and looks up at the detective interrogatively, as if to let her know she won't get away with it.

Roseanne, milk carton in hand, stares at Frankie. "For an abortion? I didn't know."

"That night at the graduation party." Frankie sighs. "That stupid party."

The tabby sniffs the air, screws up its nose, decides he doesn't like the smell in the room, and drifts away into the living room, his tail a curled up into a question mark.

"My God. You went to England!"

"No options here."

"There was CARE," says Roseanne.

"Like I'd go to CARE."

"*Wow*. You've got me there."

Secrets. Damn secrets.

CHAPTER 24

Aoife arrives at the barracks just as Frankie is about to lock up. "Oh, I'm glad I caught you. I was afraid no one would be here." She's been peddling hard and is out of breath. She places her hand on her chest as if to calm her beating heart. "It's Father Roche – he's gone missing." Aoife reels off a litany of detail, mostly to do with people ringing to ask where he is.

Frankie leads the young woman into the main office. She pulls out a chair for her, puts a reassuring hand on her shoulder. "Would you like a glass of water, Aoife?"

"No, thanks. I'm okay."

Frankie sits on the end of the table beside her. "What makes you think Father Roche is missing?"

Aoife frowns. "I haven't seen him since Monday last. He had

a load of appointments lined up for this week. And today he was down for a baptism and a funeral. All these people are ringing me and I don't know what to say. They expect me to know what to do. But I don't know what to do. I have no idea where he is. He just seems to have vanished."

Vanished? Seems like an extreme conclusion to come to. "But couldn't he just be away? I don't know – at a conference maybe? Visiting his mother?"

Aoife shakes her head. "His mother lives in Cork."

"But he could be away somewhere on Church business?"

"I don't think so. He would have told me. He always let me know where he was going, if he was to be gone for long, just in case anyone was looking for him. And there's nothing in here to let me know where he is now."

Frankie glances at the black-leather-bound book Aoife is clutching. "Is that Father Roche's appointments diary? Could I have a look?"

Aoife hands the book to Frankie. She flicks through recent entries. Aoife's right. No clues. Nothing.

Frankie hands back the diary. "You're a very loyal worker, Aoife. Have you been long in Father Roche's employment?"

"Since he came to Gweedore three years ago. He's been so good to me. Got me a place in the college recently."

"Before Bunbeg, he was stationed in Letterkenny, as I understand it?"

"That's right, yes. He was always up and down to Letterkenny."

"I'll make some enquiries, Aoife. Meantime, if you hear anything new, please get in touch with me. And try not to worry."

Aoife takes a deep breath and smiles as she leaves, as if grateful she no longer has to bear the burden of responsibility of the priest's disappearance. That's now firmly on Frankie's shoulders.

* * *

Dark charcoal-grey clouds form a thick mantle over the Poison Glen that seems to chime with Frankie's thoughts, as she drives to Letterkenny. With the low visibility, the whole landscape seems to have vanished, disappeared. It's entirely possible Father Roche is just away: his mother is ill, he's sleeping off a hangover, or got a boat out to one of the islands and got stranded, or something. Still the doubt. She must find out if Father Roche's disappearance is in any way connected with that baby found in the church. It must be, otherwise it's a coincidence. Frankie doesn't believe in coincidences.

Nothing makes sense. Is there a spell on this place, she wonders, a jinx? Or something worse?

She find St Eunan's easily enough, its steeple a lightning rod to God. *We are the power and the glory. Come all ye faithful, raise your eyes to heaven.*

Judging by the number of cars in the church carpark, Mass is being celebrated.

She parks near the Celtic cross, and makes her way into the sombre gloom of the Victorian neo-gothic building. The church is half-full, people in small groups here and there in the pews. A knot of old men hover at the back, standing, presumably the better to take off once Mass is over. The congregation face the altar and the celebrant. Brilliantly coloured stained-glass windows illuminate the sanctuary, depicting thirteen scenes from the life of Christ, and form a backdrop to the service. Cut pieces of glass slab in diamond shape create each of the windows, each window unique. Frankie momentarily marvels at the artistry of Harry Clarke, Ireland's internationally famous stained-glass artist. At another time, she would pause to appreciate it fully.

But today, her focus must be the murder. She slips into the back seat, as quietly and unobtrusively as she can. She kneels on the cushioned hassock and breathes in the sweet intoxicating aroma of incense. As a child she always loved the smell of incense, its promise of pleasure, exoticism, magic.

She leans sideways to tuck her bag under the pew. In the effort to execute this as quietly as possible, her car keys slip out of her hand and fall with a noisy clatter onto the tiled floor. A couple of teenage girls, eager for distraction, whip heads around to gawk and giggle. They are smartly nudged back to attention. Someone coughs loudly. A mother hurriedly rushes out with her wailing child, the noise amplified by the splendid acoustics of the cathedral.

Go forth, the Mass is ended ... The old familiar refrain plunges Frankie back in time to all the church rituals she remembers as a child growing up: First Communion, Confirmation. Novenas at Advent and during Lent. Despite herself, she cannot deny the comfort of it all, understands the draw it has for man. At some deep level she misses the sense of community it offers, the belonging. But she also feels resentful at how the Church has commandeered all the major events in people's lives.

The curate crosses himself, genuflects and bows low in front of the tabernacle. Then, holding the chalice high in both hands, he ceremoniously leaves the altar, embroidered white vestment billowing out behind him, altar boys in their white vests and red skirts scurrying in his trail like so many little worker bees. The Mass is over.

The congregation heave as one and rise to a standing position, before streaming out into the light, Frankie swept along with them. She blinks in the raw sunshine after the dark of the church interior. Gradually, her eyes adjust to the world of men and women: transitions from the metaphysical world to the physical.

Parishioners stand around in groups, chatting, feeling good, duty done for another week. In a cluster outside the great oak church door, men smoke, heads together as they exchange the latest racing tips or football scores, enjoying that wonderful feeling of the reward that follows sacrifice or endurance. A little further away a group of teenage boys shove one another about like young colts. Teenage girls – huddling nearby the better to observe the boys – scream sporadically, each scream prompting more extreme display of testosterone-fuelled horseplay. Three women close by look at them in remonstration: two in their thirties, parents perhaps, the other about sixty, grandmother possibly.

Frankie approaches the group of women and identifies herself. "I'm enquiring about Father Brendan Roche? He was curate here for a few years. Do any of you remember him from his time here?"

One of the thirty-somethings turns away at the mention of Roche, tutting and shaking her head in apparent disapproval.

The old woman steps forward towards Frankie and grips her in an elbow-clinch. "Father Roche, is it? I'm telling you, there was a good man if ever there was one, and bad cess to the begrudgers. There'll always be begrudgers. He brought life to this parish when he was here, so he did. Introducing lively music to the choirs, modernising, like, with guitars." She releases Frankie, straightens her scarf, tightening the knot more firmly under her chin. "My young grandson learnt the guitar through the Father. A good man, he was."

More shrieking hilarity charged with sexuality emanates from the teenagers, as the girls egg the young fellas on to more outrageous boisterousness and showmanship. Dirty looks emanate from the adults, to no avail.

One of the younger women challenges the older woman. "Good man indeed! What are you talking about, Granny? What about Madeleine Byrne? The rumours? No smoke without fire!"

"Yes, a disgrace he was," her companion says, bolstered by support. "That poor girl!"

Granny swings around and glares at her. "Ah, Treasa, will you wash your mouth out! It's a tragedy you'd want to go joining the nay-sayers! How you live with yourself, bad-mouthing a holy man of the cloth, beats me. He did mighty work for this parish, indeed and he did, so he did!"

Treasa shrugs, unwilling to face the alpha-female matriarch down.

"And poor girl, my eye! I've heard stories about that hussy!" Granny continues, making good her gain in the debate, as she nudges uncomfortably close to Frankie, the better to impart a confidence. "That one was no angel, let me tell you. There are things happened would put the hair standing on your head."

Having delivered her killer blow, the old woman turns back towards the church.

"*Stories?*" calls Treasa. "*What are you on about?*"

But Granny is gone, swallowed up in the gothic dark. Treasa and the other young woman look at Frankie apologetically, heads together in close conference.

Frankie addresses them directly. "This Madeleine Byrne – who is she?"

The woman called Treasa speaks. "A poor young one who got led astray is who she is."

"She was Father Roche's housekeeper," her companion explains, "when he was serving here in Letterkenny. It was nothing short of a scandal. Everyone knew they were at it."

"*At it?*" asks Frankie.

"You know yourself, and as usual it's always the woman who gets the blame."

"They were having an affair?"

"Oh, yes," says Treasa. "People look up to priests but, in the end of the day, it's the woman who's always the slut. They just move the priests around and the woman is left shamed."

"You're saying Father Roche was moved to Gweedore because a scandal was being created?"

"Everyone knew about the affair."

"Where is Madeleine Byrne now? Is she still around?"

"No idea," says Treasa. "She doesn't come to Mass any more – not to the cathedral anyway – so we never see her. We didn't really know her anyway, but you'd hear the stories, and you'd just feel sorry for her. She was only a teenager in the end of the day."

A young girl comes running over crying, complaining she is not being included in a game. Treasa comforts the child, looks at Frankie apologetically and both women take their leave.

But Frankie has heard enough. There's much more to Roche than meets the eye, just as she suspected. She needs to find out about him: where he started his career, what has been his trajectory within the Church, why he ended up in Donegal.

A brief conversation with the celebrant serving Mass yields nothing of interest – he's a visiting priest and not from the locality.

Frankie calls O'Toole.

* * *

Moran lights a cigarette. "Just got word back from forensics. The garden baby's death was due to clumsy birthing."

"As we thought," says Frankie.

"Any news, you?"

"Indeed I have. On Sunday, Aoife, Roche's housekeeper, visited me in a state of distress. She was concerned that Roche had disappeared. Acting on a hunch I paid a visit to Letterkenny, attended the Mass, met a few people afterwards, and found out that there are stories aplenty about the man, not all favourable." says Frankie. "You may be surprised to hear it, or you may not, but it seems our flamboyant Roche has a past."

"Not surprised. If someone looks too good to be true, they usually are," says Moran.

"Originally from Cork. Second oldest in a farming family.

Singled out at an early age to be the one to go into the Church."

"Indeed. Every good family had to have at least one in the family take the vows. Continue, madam ..."

"Ordained in nineteen-sixty. For a while worked in a working-class parish in north-city Dublin. But his superiors felt he was getting too friendly with some of the young teachers there so he was sent to a quiet parish in Wexford."

"You've been digging ..."

"O'Toole has."

"And don't tell me – Roche got friendly with the young teachers in the sunny south-east?"

"Worse. He was caught in flagrante in the sacristy."

"In flagrante, is it? With a boy? A girl?" Moran smirks. "A goat?"

"Will you stop!" says Frankie. But she can't help smiling. "With the daughter of one of the sacristans."

"Okay ..."

"And guess what?"

"Tell me."

"Can you believe it? They just moved the problem."

"I see, said the blind man," says Moran.

"Wait, there's more. It seems Roche had an affair with a young woman while he was in Letterkenny. A Madeleine Byrne."

"The plot thickens. Great work, Detective Francis," says Moran. "And did said young one get pregnant?"

"I don't know whether she did or not. All that the women at the church told me was that he was moved as soon as the affair began to create a scandal."

"Where is Madeleine now?"

Frankie shrugs and shakes her head.

Moran pulls on his jacket and lifts his car keys from the desk. "Unfortunately, I have to go back to Dublin for a couple of days, another brief I have to look into. But that's a great breakthrough regarding Roche. Well done. Needs to be followed up. I take it you're chasing up this Madeleine Byrne for interview?"

Frankie shakes her head. "I've made several enquiries, but so far nothing. Can't find her to interview. Despite the breakthrough, sometimes it seems you get so far and then you reach a dead end."

Moran walks over and with index and middle fingers on Frankie's chin turns her around to face him, looks her straight in the eye. "You know how the mouse ate the elephant?"

Frankie feels a shiver run down her spine at the touch, as she's reminded of that night a week ago. She tries to focus. Mouse? Elephant? She hates riddles. "How did the mouse eat the elephant?"

Moran smiles. "Bit by bit."

CHAPTER 25

Jon McCarthy loves walking his dog on the strand at this time in the morning. Not a soul around. The sky is deep blue, pink and yellow at the edge where the sun is coming up. It will be another scorcher of a day. He can see Gola in the distance. Just about. The grass is scratchy under his bare feet. He'll go a little bit further before he starts his exercise. The waves hiss softly over the pebbles at the shore's edge, the tide coming in.

Later, the place will be thronged. The woman from the hotel will come down here with her two children, first thing. She arrived at the hotel the same morning he did. Always tearing around with the kids: the anxiety of the separated – now single – mother, who overcompensates. Then there are the elderly sisters, also from the hotel, here for a fortnight on a budget holiday. They will come to the strand around ten o'clock, with flasks of tea and sandwiches. They'll spend the day here. Make it stretch, a cheap day, little expense. Two young American campers, on a tour around Ireland will come for a vigorous dip and a jog, then skive off, laughing and talking, energised. The vigour of youth. Some locals with visiting relatives. Always pairs. Or groups. No loners like him. Life is so much harder for singles. These beaches in Gweedore never suffer the busyness that you'd get in the Costa del Sol. Which is a good thing, of course, except that can make it more difficult for him. Makes him more obvious. A lone man with a dog.

The other evening, he hadn't really been doing anything, just sitting alone with Rua and reading his book of poetry. *I must lie down where all the ladders start ...* His favourite poet, Yeats ... *In the foul rag and bone-shop of the heart*. It was late. The beach was empty. He heard children's voices, looked around and saw the mother approach with her two children. "Can we go in now?" he heard the little girl shout, already on her way, rushing headlong to the water. He was sitting between the trio and the water. The mother spotted him. "No, no!" she cried in alarm. She yanked the child back and hurried both children away up to the pier. A lone old man sitting on a beach. With a dog. Doing nothing. Weird.

This morning he can be as weird as he likes. He takes the lead off Rua, who scampers off like a clown over the dunes and down to the hard damp sand, where she runs easily along the shore. He pushes his glasses up onto his forehead. Places the black patch, hanging around his neck, over his left eye. Every morning the same routine. Exercising the right eye to see with central fixation.

He breathes in the salty air. Seagulls screech overhead. The smell of seaweed. He loves Port Arthur Strand. Of all three beaches in Gweedore, this one is his favourite. Magheraclogher is the more popular and probably the best for swimming. Then there's Gallen with its enormous waves. But Port Arthur has something special. Good for swimming and beachcombing and then the sand dunes.

The sun is up. He sloppily traces an imaginary shape around Errigal, majestic in the near distance. Through his amblyopic right eye, all he sees is a blur, but he visualises the mountain from memory. The number of times he climbed Errigal as a youth! From the top you can see for miles around: Tory Island to the west, Lough Swilly and Foyle to the north, the Blue Stacks to the south. God, this part of Donegal is heaven. Or would be. If it weren't for people. *Arrah,* when did he become such a curmudgeon?

He holds his wrist close to his face to peer at his watch. Still only six thirty. Plenty of time yet before anyone appears. People make him anxious now. He'd come here hoping for some respite, but you take yourself wherever you go. Not that he wants to get away from himself. He's happy in his own skin. If only people would leave him alone.

The wet sand is firm beneath his feet. As he strolls along, whistling, Rua comes bounding back to him, tongue hanging, pink and quivering. He veers towards the path via the sand dunes. Bluebells nod their heads in the early morning sun, a sea of dancing blue. The coarse vetch clings to the hair on his legs, but it doesn't bother him. He loves the solitude, the conviction he is finally at peace with mankind and the world.

He stumbles. Falls into the white sand. He curses and struggles to his knees. He feels something just under the surface. What is that? He scoops away the sand.

A hand shoots up. His knees collapse. The man is dead.

CHAPTER 26

The orderly in a white coat leads Frankie and O'Toole up the corridor and opens the door into the narrow hospital morgue. They step inside. Nothing in the room except a single bed on which lies a bulky form covered with a white sheet. O'Toole turns deathly pale, threatening to faint. He leans against the door jamb. The attendant puts his hand on his shoulder. Frankie walks over slowly, stands for a moment beside the bed, then gripping the corner of the cotton sheet slides it back a little to reveal the identity of the dead body: it is undoubtedly that of Father Brendan Alphonsus Roche. She feels suddenly queasy, her stomach churning over. Stay calm, she commands herself.

Strange to see the curate lying there – once such a force of life, now so powerless. Inert. An ordinary mortal after all: no pomp or ceremony to enhance his status now.

Frankie studies the corpse. She observes the waxen pallor, the swollen cheeks, puffed up. From what? Immersion? Or the natural process of decay? Pockmarked too, as though it had been pecked at by seagulls. Do gulls do that? The undertakers will, of course, later dress the remains after the investigation, make it presentable for viewing if that's what the family wish. She knows the score, knows how skilled these people are, how they can transform even the most broken body back into a shape that makes it easier for the relatives. They look on it as a form of art, which indeed it is. But all that will come later. For now the investigation. She will have to find out where the body was found, examine the area.

Frankie moves closer and narrows her eyes as she peers at the forehead. Among many marks that most likely are from birds pecking at the flesh, she notices a strange round indentation on the skull, at the hairline. She stares at it for several moments. She beckons O'Toole, who shuffles forward cautiously, unsure of himself, not entirely confident he won't gag. He plants himself beside Frankie and reluctantly leans forward to scrutinise the remains, at the area she points to. They both stare at the mark. O'Toole looks back at her with eyes large as saucers. A moment of recognition. Can there be any doubt about what they're looking at?

* * *

Frankie faces a grumpy Brannigan and attempts to analyse the tension between them. The death of the priest, Father Brendan Roche, is another murder, she's sure of it. Both she and O'Toole concur on the mark they saw on the dead priest's forehead: it could have been from the blow of a small hammer.

The sergeant riffles through documents, preoccupied. He rummages in his drawer, and without looking up, mutters, "Poor devil. You'd think he'd have been aware of the currents."

Frankie frowns. *What is he talking about?* "Currents? He was found near the dunes. The tides don't come up that far. Who found him?"

Brannigan leans back on his chair until his head is almost touching the cabinet behind him, chewing. "A regular visitor at the Seaview hotel." *Munch.* "Out walking his dog." *Munch.*

"And the pathologist has examined the remains?"

"He has indeed."

"Why is this not being considered a murder case?"

Brannigan screws up his face, waits for the spasm to pass before answering. "The pathologist ..." *munch* "... says the condition of the body allows for no firm conclusion. The poor man drowned. It was an accident." He leans back a little more. His chair wobbles, almost toppling over. He steadies himself, cursing.

Frankie can feel the muscles on her jaw tightening. With an effort she keeps her voice calm. "I want to query that result. I've just been to the morgue. There's something more than suspicious about this death."

Brannigan narrows his eyes. "We have the expert view that the condition of the body allows for no firm conclusion. It was immersed in water for a time, as I've told you. Clearly a case of accidental drowning."

Frankie stares at Brannigan. Maybe its blood type – its DNA even – changed while it was immersed. Maybe it's not Roche at all! Why is he being so belligerent? "He drowned and yet he was found near the dunes? This surely needs investigation. Also, I clearly saw a suspicious mark on the priest's forehead."

"Are you questioning the findings of the state pathologist on this?"

"I think we should consider it a murder."

Brannigan's face reddens. "This death is *not* a murder. The pathologist found water in his lungs which indicated that he drowned. There were many marks on the body but due to the condition of the body, there was no way to ascertain whether this was foul play or otherwise. Therefore the pathologist's verdict is an accidental death. As if the people of Donegal would murder a priest! There will be no investigation into the death of Father Roche. *None.* We have one murder on our hands – the Strand baby. And that's it."

Brannigan writes something in the ledger open in front of him, closes it, stands and pulls on his jacket. He has work to do, a plan to realise.

"So if you'll excuse me now, Detective Francis ..."

What's going on here, Frankie wonders? Here they have a new development in the case – a blatant link – and she's being blocked by Brannigan. Why on earth would he want to block something like this? And where is Moran? He was supposed to be back by now.

CHAPTER 27

Moran has a terrible thirst on him after the long journey from Dublin. He stops off at Sweeney's in Lifford, for a pint. The county capital, though not the largest town – that would be Letterkenny, Brannigan had told him – a haven for Shinners. He'll soak in the atmosphere, and you never know, you might hear something, someone might talk. There's been a lot of activity around here. While he's in the area he might as well check it out. You hear a lot in pubs, tongues loosen. He finds himself a tall stool at the bar and orders a pint of stout and a chaser.

The barman pulls the pint carefully until it's halfway to the top, waits for it to settle. "You don't rush the black stuff," he says.

Moran surveys the place. The light is low and the smoke lends a bluish hue to the place and a distinctive smell. On the back wall hangs a large green, white and orange flag. Framed photos and posters cover the other walls. Hurlers and football players: groups of men kneeling and holding aloft a cup to signify many glorious wins, a couple of publicity notices for Wolfe Tones gigs, the 1916 proclamation, and the centrepiece: a poster from Bobby Sands' election campaign – now slightly yellow and ragged at the edges. You'd be left in no doubt that this is a Republican watering hole.

The bar fills up slowly, stools are commandeered and positions held. Apart from two couples who occupy a table just inside the door, mostly the clientele is male.

Moran is halfway through his pint when four men in their early twenties fall in through the door, sozzled, arguing and pucking each other like young goats. Distinctive Derry accents. Trouble, thinks Moran. He turns sideways to survey the newcomers. One of the group, well over six foot, throws a punch at his companion, a thin streel of a lad. A long drink of water, as the fella might say. Or a short drink, in this case. The walls quake as the two flail and kick and punch. The little fellow is bleeding heavily from the nose.

Moran steps down off his stool, takes a step or two towards where the two are fighting and says, "I'd advise you to stop now."

The big man straightens up to his full size, a head and more above the detective.

"Or else what?"

Moran squares up. He is about to pull out his Garda badge

when the giant swings an enormous fist at him. Moran dodges and gives him one in the solar plexus. One of the other men from the group catches him offside with a punch and he falls. Moran grabs the giant's ankle. Out of the corner of his eye, he sees one of the cronies lift a hurley off the back wall, prized trophy from some long-ago match. *Oh Christ, I'm done for*, he thinks.

Moran watches in slow motion as the man brings the stick down hard, on his leg, just below the knee. A loud crack.

"*Jaysus, me fuckin' leg!*" Moran groans, rolls onto his back and holds his knee. What happens next, he will only hazily remember afterwards.

"*Frig's sake, fellas, that one's from the squad!*"

A flurry as several of the patrons escape in a hurry.

"*Is that 999?*" someone shouts into the phone. "*There's a man in a bad way!*"

The next thing he knows, he's in the ambulance with a medic putting a splint on his leg.

And so Anthony Moran spends his first night in Kilmacrennan Hospital, the first of many as it transpires.

* * *

Rory strokes Frankie's hair. He winds a long strand around his hand, brings it up to his face and breathes in its smell. She smiles, kisses him on the shoulder and snuggles contentedly into the crook of his arm. She's taken a day off to mend things with him. The truth is she needed a break anyway, to get some perspective on the double murder case. Sunlight penetrates the pale yellow curtains of their hotel bedroom, drenching the room in a golden hue. Frankie feels very relaxed.

Rory kisses her head and says, "God doesn't close a door but he opens a window."

"I don't believe in God."

"Look at the upside, we're back together."

Frankie nudges him affectionately, snuggling closer. "Are you arguing with yourself?" She traces a circle on his bare chest with her fingernail. "I'm glad you came to Dungloe to make your peace with your mother. Glad you came to surprise me. For surprise me you certainly did!"

They've already had *that* conversation – about what happened, why Rory came to Gweedore, how he'd first called to the barracks, then taken a chance she might be at Port Arthur – which she was – his fear that there was something going on between herself and her boss.

The phone rings. Frankie glances at it, shakes her head, then turns away.

Rory raises himself on one elbow. "It's okay."

Frankie gazes at him to assess if he means this. "You sure?"

Rory reaches over, lifts the receiver and hands it to her. He ruffles her hair. "Go on."

Frankie takes the phone and sits up. Brannigan. She closes her eyes, takes a deep breath and counts to five. "Yes?"

The sergeant growls at the other end of the line. She's to come to the barracks asap.

She puts down the phone, glances at the radio alarm – eight thirty – then at Rory.

"I heard," he says wryly. "Go on. I'm eager to see the end of this sorry business now too." He runs his fingers down her back, articulating each vertebra as far as the coccyx. "As you know, I was planning to go back to Dublin this afternoon anyway – I can't take any more time off work. Give me a ring later and let me know what's happening."

She kisses him on the mouth, has a quick shower and dresses. Moran was due back yesterday. What does Brannigan want that Moran can't deal with?

* * *

She hops in her car, motors north to Bunbeg, and down the harbour road to the barracks. Typically, there are no car parking spaces. She drives to the end of the jetty, and parks behind a fisherman's truck. The two old men watch her as she hurries back up to the station.

O'Toole is standing to attention in the front lobby, the air thick with mystery. "Oh, am I glad to see you!" He inclines his head in the direction of Brannigan's office. "They're waiting for you."

She knocks and enters, O'Toole at her heel. Brannigan is behind his desk, flanked by McGinley. No sign of Moran. "Is something up?"

Brannigan riffles through papers on his desk. "There is indeed something up, as you put it, something very much up." He abandons his search for whatever he was looking for, feels about in his pocket instead and pulls out a fresh packet of antacids. He fumbles with the foil to open it, removes one and pops it into his mouth. Like a coin into a fountain.

Make a wish now, sir – the way you're going, there may not be too many more.

"Where's Moran? Isn't he back yet?"

Brannigan looks down at his folder without answering, pokes absentmindedly at his tooth with a match.

Frankie registers he's ignoring her question, as she's meant to.

"Haven't you heard?" says McGinley.

Heard what?

"He's beyond in the Community Hospital in Kilmacrennan."

"What's wrong with him?"

"Shenanigans up in a pub in Lifford. Seems he found himself on the wrong side of the Shinners." McGinley makes a clicking sound with his tongue. "Leg caput."

"*What!*" Involuntarily Frankie puts her hand up to her mouth in alarm. "They kneecapped him?"

"No. Got himself into a fight and came out the losing end with a broken leg. We don't have the details yet."

"We're looking into it," says Brannigan. "Never fear. We're looking into it." He chuckles smugly. "Grist to the mill, you might say. We're down personnel and I want to wrap up the Strand baby murder case. I've been on to head office about it. Far as I'm concerned, Sarah Joyce is number one suspect, I've thought so from the beginning. Unfortunately, we have insufficient evidence in that regard and we're going to have to let her go."

Does Brannigan think he's in charge now, that Moran is out of action? "Sarah Joyce was in hospital when the priest was found dead."

"Do I have to repeat myself – the priest's death is *not* a murder. And just because we can't keep Sarah Joyce in custody any longer doesn't mean I don't think she's guilty of the Strand baby murder."

"I don't believe Sarah Joyce is in any way connected with the Strand baby," says Frankie.

Brannigan ignores her remark. "Failing that, you have the Biddies."

Surely Head Office haven't put Brannigan in charge!

Frankie shakes her head. The Biddies are not on the agenda. Neither is Sarah Joyce. She needs to start over again, try new avenues of investigation. She's looking for the murderer of both the Strand baby and the priest, who she is convinced was also murdered. And most likely by the same person.

"Madeleine Byrne might know something useful," she says. "I'm trying to find out where she lives."

Brannigan frowns. "Who in God's name is Madeleine Byrne?"

"She had an affair with Father Roche in Letterkenny for three years. Before he came to Bunbeg." As if he doesn't know. The guards know everything that goes on about the place. They would certainly have got word about the curate's philandering. *Could that be why he's so reluctant to broaden the case? Is he protecting the curate from scandal and by extension the Church?*

"While Detective Moran is out of action, head office have appointed me in overall charge."

Oh lord! What a backward step!

"There is no investigation into the death of Father Roche. Your job, Detective Francis, is to nail Sarah Joyce for the Strand baby murder. O'Toole will work with you as before. You have a week to ten days."

O'Toole smiles broadly at Frankie: the cat that got the cream.

Frankie and O'Toole retire to their office out the back. She'll have to touch base with Moran. But a broken leg doesn't heal in a week or two; it takes weeks or even months in plaster or with a walking stick. How much work will he be able to do on the case? The appalling thought strikes Frankie: she could be on her own now. O'Toole shuffles his feet. Frankie looks up slowly at her side-kick, sighs and moves her stuff over to Moran's desk by the window where she sits and looks out for a moment. The river glitters under the raw sunshine, fishermen are pulling in lobster pots, a heron stands to attention on a rock, perfectly balanced on one leg, conserving heat, its long yellow harpoon-like bill pointed downwards, always on the ready for an unsuspecting frog, fish or small mammal to pass by. The great wheel turns. O'Toole settles himself into the seat Frankie has vacated, leans back in the chair, thumbs under his belt, and gazes happily at her.

CHAPTER 28

Sarah is sitting by the window reading when Frankie walks in. She starts initially, her instinct to be on guard, but after a moment she makes eye-contact, and relaxes.

"Sarah, as you know by now, you have been cleared of all charges and are free to go when your health permits. Okay, if I ...?" Frankie sits on a chair beside her. "You've heard about the baby found in the church in Letterkenny."

Sarah harrumphs. "With a note attached: *This belongs to you.* I heard."

"And you've heard about Father Roche's death?"

Sarah gazes out the window but says nothing.

Frankie sees the woman in front of her as if for the first time: the flame-red hair falling loose around her shoulders, the face with its creamy complexion free of make-up, the large green eyes translucent. The woman is beautiful. There's a brightness about her that she hasn't noticed before. A determination. And something else that Frankie can't quite put her finger on. Autonomy perhaps?

"Father Roche was the father of your child, Sarah, wasn't he?"

Unprepared for the question, Sarah turns to face Frankie, eyes wide. She wells up, wipes tears away with the corner of her cardigan.

This woman has been through so much, and innocent all along. But Frankie still has a job to do, needs to follow up on a new line of enquiry. She waits a moment.

"You knew about Madeleine Byrne?"

Sarah's eyes flash at the mention of Madeleine.

A loud clash from the corridor, like something metal falling – a bowl or tray of instruments – captures their attention momentarily. They listen to the mini-commotion outside their door. It passes.

Frankie probes deeper. "Would you be willing to tell me how you met Father Roche? And what you know about him and Madeleine? Anything. It's very important. Take your time."

Sarah breathing becomes shallower, as if this conversation is about to bring her to a place she'd rather forget, regurgitate painful memories. She closes her eyes for a moment, then takes in a deep breath and sighs resignedly. She has the demeanour of one who wants to help, and has decided to surrender to the inevitable, to let go.

"Father Roche – Brendan – and I met at a teacher seminar weekend in Letterkenny. He had suggested the event to me on one of his visits to the house – he used to call regularly to visit Hannah, part of his pastoral social work. It was one of those delegate union seminars. I wasn't a delegate, but you could attend as a non-voting observer. I just wanted to be immersed in the whole teaching life. I paid for the weekend out of my savings. I thought if I got to know as much as I could about teaching and the union it would give me start. But it wasn't a chore. I enjoyed it."

Sarah had felt elated. She knew then she would have a chance of achieving her dream of becoming a teacher. Being there had made her *feel* like a teacher. She is speaking so quietly Frankie has to lean forward to catch everything she is saying.

"The seminar weekend was one of those closed affairs, all the activities – talks, debates, meetings – held in the one venue, the Malin Hotel. Father Roche was there. He often attended these affairs. Really he had his finger in every pie. But at that time I just saw him as someone charismatic."

The first evening there was a social in the bar of the hotel. Everyone was there. People had freshened up after all the debates and talks, and there was a ambience of gaiety in the bar. People are relaxed, dressed up and in good form. Brendan was in civvies. It was the first time Sarah had seen him outside of the house setting.

"I felt a a frisson between us, like electricity. We stayed chatting for ages. Brendan ordered a bottle of Merlot at the bar and two glasses and led the way over to a table at the back of the room."

There she was talking to this handsome older man about books, Piaget, the philosophy of education and it felt like the world was opening up for her. She felt exhilarated. She had wanted to spread her wings, explore the wide world, and now everything seemed possible.

Their conversation segued from education and philosophy to war.

"Prostitution is a common feature in all wars," Roche said, gazing into her eyes. "I suppose that as you face death, life becomes so much more vivid, you want to get the most out of it while you can. It's hedonism, of course. But understandable. And who are we to judge?"

Derry's red-light district was well known, he told her.

Sarah's thinking was becoming a little fuzzy with the wine by this stage. How had the conversation turned to prostitution? She didn't care. The daring of it, talking about the erotic, and with a priest no less!

"I've never been to a red-light district in my life," she said.

"Never?" Roche said. "You're kidding me." As he spoke, he had looked at her steadily, his eyes undressing her.

Then he offered to take her on a trip. He placed his hand lightly on the small of her back and told her it would be educational. Sarah had almost swooned with delight at his touch.

The following week they booked into a hotel in Derry. They never made it to the red-light district. A month later Sarah had to tell Father Brendan Roche, curate of St Bartholomew's Church, that she was pregnant with his child.

Sarah wipes the tears that have started to well up again as she revisits painful memories. "I was terrified. I was pregnant, unmarried and I'd just been accepted onto the teaching course in Mary Immaculate Teaching College in Limerick for the following year. My dreams of becoming a teacher were beginning to drift away. I became desperate. I rang Brendan, thinking that he would help. But he told me he couldn't be the father, that I should contact CARE. He said he'd deny that he touched me and who would believe me, an IRA supporter, known for lies and deception? He accused me of having other lovers. I was horrified." Sarah blows her nose. "It was like he'd become someone else. Once so charming, then suddenly so cold, like Jekyll and Hyde. He'd turned into someone truly horrible. I was in shock."

Frankie nods.

Sarah looks at her watch and starts. "Sorry, they're coming to collect me soon. I have to get ready." She opens her locker and proceeds to take things out and line them up on the bed: washbag, hairbrush, towel and other personal items. She pulls a holdall down from on top of the wardrobe and unzips it.

"How did you find out about Madeleine Byrne?" asks Frankie.

Sarah folds her pyjamas and adds them to the collection on the bed. "She visited me."

The tea-lady comes in with a tray and is about to place it on the table but Sarah shakes her head and the woman leaves again.

Frankie prompts. "Why did Madeleine visit you?"

Sarah sits on the bed. "Madeleine and Brendan had had an affair for three years while he was stationed in Letterkenny. I didn't know any of this, of course, when we got together. Madeleine saw Brendan and me in Letterkenny – this was the day before I found out I was pregnant. She was filled with rage and jealousy. She made enquiries about me, found out where I lived and paid me a visit. She forced her way into the house, past Mags – and that's no easy task – up to my room and accused me of stealing her man. I explained to her that Roche and I had split up, that he'd dumped me, that I was pregnant. That's when Madeleine told me that she was too. That was probably why Roche had been so shocked at my news. He'd just fathered two babies."

Frankie's heart leaps. "Are you sure? You're saying Madeleine Byrne was pregnant at the same time you were?"

"Yes."

"So he was two-timing?"

"Yes ... well, no. Not exactly. But it felt like it." Sarah starts to bundle everything into the bag. She sighs. "After he moved to Bunbeg, they'd had an on-off relationship. He would go up to Letterkenny every now and again to meet up with her. After

Christmas last year, he dumped Madeleine because she was getting too needy. She wanted the relationship to be serious – he couldn't allow it if he was to keep his job. He just wanted occasional enjoyable sex. *The bastard!* Anyway, she contacted him in August. They got together, one thing led to another and they ended up in bed – a one-night stand." She stops her packing, walks over to the window and looks out forlornly. "This happened about a fortnight before he and I got ... y'know ..." she blushes, "intimate."

"So you were both due to give birth around the same time, give or take a week or two," Frankie says, more to herself than to Sarah. She stares at Sarah. "You knew that another woman had a child born at the time you were charged with the murder." She waits for a reaction but Sarah just gazes out the window unseeing, thoughts turned inwards. "Why did you say nothing?"

Sarah turns towards Frankie. "Who would have believed me?"

Indeed – hardly credible. Three dead babies, one murdered; and the father – of at least two of the babies – Father Brendan Roche – now dead. Sarah is innocent. Frankie needs to find Madeleine. She's running out of time.

CHAPTER 29

"Gaelic Ireland was dead and gone forever, you could say, after the Flight of the Earls."

O'Toole has launched into a history lesson, no filter between brain and mouth, as Moran would say. It's not that Frankie's disinterested in history – in fact she's very interested – but there's a time and a place and right now she needs to stay focused. But sometimes it's just easier to let him talk.

"First you had the plantation of Ulster, then the Penal laws, then the Union. And of course the Famine. Not that the people of Gweedore suffered the worst of the Famine. But they did suffer with the end of the ancient system of rundale, when Lord Hill divided up their land into parcels and took the mountains from them." O'Toole is on a roll, delighted to have an audience, someone to listen to him.

The sun breaks through the clouds and the landscape changes dramatically.

"The Derryveagh mountain range," O'Toole announces, sweeping his hand in an arc to take in Errigal, Muckish and the Poison Glen. "Can you believe it, that one man – a Captain John Adair, land speculator – bought up this whole area a hundred years and more ago. And actually," he scratches his head resignedly, "McGinley was right – I checked up on it – it was the agent was murdered on that occasion, not the landlord."

Frankie nods and lets him ramble on.

"What happened was," continues O'Toole, "a quarrel between Captain Adair and his tenants about shooting and fishing rights – which the poor people needed to survive – ended in his Scottish agent being murdered. In retaliation, Adair had the sheriff come in and evict more than 47 families – 244 men, women children – all thrown out on the side of the road, the roofs of their cabins broken in."

They're almost there.

"Adair was part of a new breed of speculating landlord, same as Lord George Hill in Gweedore, Nixon in Bloody Foreland."

Frankie sighs, glad they've finally reached Letterkenny. Enough history for one day.

Without too much difficulty, she finds the Glenkeen Gardens, a small estate on the outskirts of the town. Verbal diarrhoea aside – to borrow another of Moran's expressions – her sidekick is a good navigator, Frankie thinks, she'll give him that. She asks the rookie to wait in the car as she proceeds to walk down the row of houses, glancing at the numbers of each as she passes – twenty-eight, twenty-nine, thirty ... She checks the address in her notebook – number thirty-one – this is it.

At last: Madeleine Byrne's flat. She's found it.

The house has seen better days, she notes, the grass in the front trodden on and burnt both from neglect and the sun: the sad derelict garden of the rented apartments. She lifts the knocker, raps on the blue door with its peeling paint, and waits. After some moments it opens.

Standing in front of her is a petite young woman with blonde hair, mid-twenties.

"I'm looking for Madeleine Byrne. I believe she lives here. Have I found the right person?"

"She's not here."

Frankie flashes her badge. "I'm Detective Kate Francis from the Dublin Murder Squad investigating the murder of the Strand baby in Gweedore. Can you tell me your name, please?"

The young woman's face pales. Frankie never ceases to be amazed at how quickly people appear guilty when confronted by an official. But then, why is she surprised if you reflect for a moment on Ireland's history?

"If you don't mind, I'd like to ask you a few questions."

The blonde holds the door wide to let Frankie in.

Frankie surveys the ground-floor flat. Typical bedsit: carpet threadbare, walls papered and in need of refurbishment, heavy mahogany furniture. *Riddled with woodworm, no doubt*, Frankie thinks, reflecting back to her own student days and the many little mounds of sawdust she regularly found under tables, chairs, presses. Despite its down-at-heel appearance, everything seems neat and tidy.

Frankie sits on the settee. She gets straight to the point. "As part of our investigation, we would like to interview Madeleine Byrne. We're just making enquiries at this stage. You knew she had an affair with Father Roche?"

The young woman nods slowly, unsure about breaking confidences. Of course she knows! Young women tell each other everything, especially about their love lives.

"Can you tell me what you know about their relationship? When it started? Anything."

The young woman seats herself in the armchair opposite. Frankie can sense she's thawing out, becoming more at ease, now she realises she's not the one under the spotlight.

"Madeleine was very bitter about what happened, how it ended." She lifts a mug of coffee from the occasional table, pauses, puts it down. "Coffee? Tea?"

Frankie shakes her head, declining.

The young woman nurses her mug. "She told me the story

many times, like she was obsessed with it. In a way, she was obsessed with *him*. I kept telling her she must move on. But she was stuck, infatuated with the man."

The affair started over six years ago, she tells Frankie, in the winter of January 1983. Madeleine Byrne was nineteen when she went for help to Brendan Roche, when she confided in him about her abusive childhood, her depression, her suicidal tendencies. He offered her a sympathetic ear, took her for drives out to Malin Head, to the shores of Lough Swilly, to Gweedore. They talked and before long they are embroiled in an affair. Roche set her up as his housekeeper, encouraged her to go back to school, to take evening classes. She studied arts and crafts at the tech at night, hoping to fulfil an ambition to set up a small business. She gained confidence. And fell madly in love. Roche, infatuated at first, mesmerised by Madeleine's startling good looks and her youth, in time grew tired of her, as the novelty wore off. In February 1986, almost three years to the day that they started the affair, they had a huge row and separated.

"You were aware of the pregnancy?"

The flatmate nods. "Of course. She was sick for the first three months, throwing up every morning."

"Did she discuss it with you?"

The young woman shakes her head. "Madeleine wouldn't talk about the pregnancy. It was like she wanted to wish it away. Any time I brought it up she changed the subject."

"And the birth? How did that happen, do you know? Where did she have the baby?"

The flatmate shakes her head. "All I know is that one day she was heavily pregnant, she disappeared for a couple of days and when she came back she wasn't. That's all."

"Did you ask her about the baby?"

"I did of course, but, as I said, she refused point-blank to talk about it."

"Do you remember roughly when it was that she was no longer pregnant?"

The young woman's eyes open wide. She knows now where this is going. After a long pause she says in a low voice, "About a month or so ago."

She looks at Frankie as she considers the import of what she's just said.

"She continued to live here all the time after the pregnancy was over?" Frankie asks.

"Yes."

"But you never saw a baby?"

"I never saw Madeleine with a baby."

"Where is Madeleine now?"

"I don't know. She usually goes to Derry every Saturday, a daytrip to the market, but before she always came back the same evening. She would usually tell me if she intended staying over longer."

"And she didn't say anything to you?"

The young woman shakes her head.

"Does she have relatives in Derry?"

"She has a cousin ... in the Bogside ... you know, the estate just outside the big gates ... they get on well, but she doesn't like spending too much time there because the place has bad memories for her."

"I take it she was born in the Bogside?"

The flatmate nods. "Yes, that's where she was born and grew up."

"What about her parents?"

"Her father was sent to prison when she was a child, and served a long sentence for firearms charges."

"How did she get on with her mother?"

"Her mother took up with a new partner, after the father was sentenced. That caused a lot of friction. The guy was a bad egg, by the sounds of it, a violent man. He assaulted Madeleine viciously. And sexually. Because of him, Madeleine ran away, crossed the border and came to Father Roche for help."

"And where is her mother now?"

"The family home that Madeleine fled from no longer exists, apparently since burnt out, her mother and brother long gone."

"Gone? Where?"

"To Scotland. It seems they just upped and left after the mother left her violent partner. Derry for Madeleine is just a marketplace. Usually she wouldn't stay long."

"What do you mean ... a marketplace?"

"She goes there to sell her jewellery. She has a stall."

"Jewellery?"

"Yes, she makes her own jewellery, beautiful stuff – she made me this ring for my birthday."

She holds out her hand to display a silver knuckleduster with a garnet inset. Frankie's heart is thumping. The pieces are falling into place. Madeleine Byrne had a relationship with Brendan Roche, was dumped by him, had a child by him, a motive to be very angry with him, a motive to kill. And crucially, she would have had access to a weapon: a jeweller's hammer. Motive, weapon, opportunity.

"Do you have an address for her cousin in Derry?"

The other woman shakes her head.

"Do you know anyone at all who might have an address?"

"You could try O'Donnell's jewellery off Main Street. Madeleine worked there for a year as an apprentice. I know he used take her over to trade fairs in Derry regularly. It's possible they called at the Bogside. Maybe even stayed there, given the state of things in that town. You'd want to be somewhere safe."

O'Donnell jeweller. Frankie jots the name down.

As Frankie walks back to her car she considers the information she has just heard.

Brendan Roche was killed on Monday the 29th of May. Is it a coincidence that Madeleine Byrne went AWOL around the same time the priest was murdered?

"And now, Madeleine is gone," Frankie tells O'Toole.

She locates Joe O'Donnell's jewellery shop, tucked in between a boutique and a butcher's shop, off the main street. The shop is closed. He'll be away on holiday for a week, a notice says.

Due back tomorrow, thinks Frankie. *Well, thank goodness for that!*

She drives back to the barracks.

At Bunbeg Cross she pulls in at the petrol station. As she waits for the attendant to fill up the tank, she drums her fingers on the wheel, anxious to get back to base, preoccupied.

O'Toole fidgets with the car radio, trying to get a reception. "Is there a connection? Between the priest's death, I mean, and Madeleine's disappearance?" He presses buttons, switches the dial, glances at Frankie. "Your radio isn't working."

Frankie pays the attendant. "Car radios aren't supposed to work."

O'Toole gives up on the radio and switches off. "It can't be just a coincidence – I mean Madeleine missing and the priest dead. There must be a connection."

Frankie is already zooming down the road to the harbour. Of course there's a connection!

She has just realised the shocking truth about the murder case. The priest is the clue.

CHAPTER 30

Sarah walks out through the revolving front door of the hospital, flanked on one side by Roseanne, on the other by Mags all spruced up, in her best coat and hat. The sun shines brilliantly in a clear sky. A sea of cameras flash. Sarah blinks. Reporters jostle to get closer for interview, a cacophony of voices, all asking questions at the same time. Someone stands on a wall, pointing a zoom lens at her. Sarah feels faint. The overwhelming joy of release. Of validation.

The *Evening Standard* thrusts a microphone up to her face. "Miss Joyce, how do you feel now you are cleared of all charges?"

"Are you going to sue?" *The Herald*.

"Will you continue to teach in Derrybeg, now you are a celebrity?" *The Mail*.

"How is your health?" *The Independent Daily*.

BBC Ulster wants to know what plans she has now and for the future?

"I'm going home," the young woman says resolutely.

Roseanne pushes herself in front of Sarah. "Please ... excuse me ..." She bats away the microphones. "Have some respect." She takes Sarah's arm firmly in her own and hurries her to the waiting taxi. A group of women holding bunches of white roses and placards that say *"JUSTICE FOR WOMEN!"* form a safe and friendly corridor.

The trio get into the taxi and drive off.

* * *

Frankie drives to the Community Hospital at Kilmacrennan. She parks and walks down the street till she finds a florist. "Can you suggest a bouquet for a friend in the hospital? Something that might cheer him up."

The florist holds up a bunch of orange blooms with bright yellow centres. "Can't go wrong with chrysanths. Our best seller. Very popular."

Frankie nods. *They'll do*. The florist pulls on a roll of cellophane, tears off a rectangular piece, and wraps it around the chrysanthemums. She ties the base with a length of pink ribbon, which she fashions into a bow, scraping the ends with the back of a scissors till they curl into decorative rosettes. "Mums are a great buy. Last for ages."

Belfast accent, Frankie notices. "You're not from these parts?"

"*Naw*, Falls Road." The woman hands the flowers to Frankie. "Belfast."

Lord, she felt she had to tell me where the Falls Road is. Are there people who don't know where the Falls Road is – aliens perhaps?

The florist takes the tenner Frankie offers. "Left the Troubles when I got married to a Prod ten year ago. Lots of us northerners decamped here to Donegal to get away from the war."

Will it ever be over, Frankie thinks, *that war over the 'fourth green field'?* She asks for directions to the community hospital.

"A mile up the road, you can't miss it."

Frankie follows the directions and has no trouble finding her boss.

Moran is in his pyjamas, lying on the bed by a window looking out onto the lawn, his leg – encased in plaster – resting on a pillow.

"Well, aren't you a sight for sore eyes?"

Frankie glances at the chessboard on the bed beside him. *What?*

She puts the flowers on the locker and pulls over a chair. "Jesus. How did you get yourself into such a mess? And what on earth were you doing up in a pub in Lifford cavorting with Shinners?"

Moran, under fire, opens his mouth wide as though to yawn,

but decides against. "Not exactly cavorting. I simply went in for a quiet drink, as one does. And suddenly there is this bunch of rowdies in from Derry. Well on."

"And you weren't?"

Moran wags his finger in mock annoyance at the suggestion. "Don't ask me what happened." He reaches into the plaster with an index finger and scratches. "Before I know it I'm on the floor and one geezer is smashing my leg with a hurley. I don't remember too much of it, to tell the truth. All I remember next is I'm in an ambulance and wake up in hospital."

"Charges?"

Moran breathes in deeply through clenched teeth, shakes his head. He places his hand on the flowers. "Thanks for these."

Without warning, he reaches over, draws her in and kisses her on the mouth.

Frankie pulls away, slides her chair back a little. "*No!*"

A nurse comes into the ward and checks the report card at the end of Moran's bed. "Your consultant will be by in half an hour, Mr Moran."

Frankie glances at the chart. "Did they tell you when they're going to let you out?"

"It seems, my dear," Moran says, making a face, "that when they were doing the scans they found an irregularity with the heart – arrhythmia or some damn fool thing."

"Arrhythmia ... that sounds serious?"

Moran shakes his head in exasperation. "I have to stay in for more tests."

Which means I'm on my own. "Oh, dear!"

Frankie sees an anxiety she's not see before, notices for the first time the greyness of his pallor, how shrunken he seems in the hospital bed, how vulnerable, the strength gone.

"Anyway, enough of this nonsense!" barks Moran, as though aware of the judgement being passed on him, on his diminished status. "Roche dead! Good God almighty! I go away for a few days and the sky falls in. Brannigan called. He says the padre drowned."

"I've examined the body. I saw a mark on his forehead. Like a blow from a small hammer."

Moran frowns. "*What!*"

"Plus the body was found right up near the dunes. The tide doesn't come up that far."

"You saying you think it's murder?"

"Yes, I am. And my money is on Madeleine Byrne."

Moran pulls back. "*Whoa!* Steady on! Analysis, please."

Frankie fills Moran in on her interviews with Sarah and Madeleine's flatmate. She follows Moran's gaze to a seagull and a hooded crow who are battling over crusts of bread beside one of the benches outside, the detritus left over from someone's picnic.

"Go on, I'm listening," he says.

"So here's what I think. A baby is found in the church with a note attached that says: *This belongs to you.* The gardaí assume the reference is to God. My theory is that when Madeleine Byrne hears that there was a message pinned to the child, and finds out what it said, she concludes that the Church baby is Roche's, that yet another woman has been seduced by him, become pregnant and left her new-born in the church with the message to let Roche take responsibility for his actions ..." – the hooded crow is hop-scotching around the bench area, poised to snatch another crust, a sharp beady eye on the look-out – "and murders him for it."

Moran frowns, trying to get his head around the proposition. "He'd have been hard pressed to have fathered *three* babies all around the same time. I mean fathering two – Sarah's and Madeleine's – yes, okay, we'll accept that that could happen."

"It *did* happen," says Frankie.

"But *three*? To paraphrase Wilde: '*To father two babies may be regarded as a misfortune; to father three looks like carelessness.*'."

"I agree it's stretching credibility a little. I'm not saying he *actually* fathered the three babies – we know he fathered two – but you can see how someone emotionally vulnerable could let their imagination run away with them, how Madeleine might jump to that conclusion. And the truth is it's not a completely outlandish assumption. It's entirely *possible* for him to have fathered three children around the same time, even if he didn't."

"Any word on the mother of the Church baby?"

"Yes, a young woman from Fanad has come forward. It's an

emergency case, not a criminal one. She is receiving medical help. She hasn't as yet said who the father was."

Moran turns his attention once again to the renewed crust-fight on the green. "And of course no one wants to have any truck with the likes of little bastards or the women who are a disgrace to Holy Catholic Ireland – even if a priest did get the leg over, well, they have a hard time staying celibate, the poor creatures … " – he smirks – "victims if you like."

Frankie rubs her eyes, too tired after a restless night to take the bait. "Okay, just hear me out. Imagine for a moment this scenario. Outraged at his womanising and rejection, Madeleine calls him and arranges a tyrst." She pauses for a moment. "They meet, she's brought some alcohol, gets him relaxed. Then she kills him."

"But why Port Arthur Strand? Wouldn't that be risky with its connections to the murdered baby?"

"Well, we have to presume she's behaving emotionally rather than rationally. And believes in poetic justice – you know, evil punished in an appropriate and ironic manner."

"But why would *he* agree to meet there of all places?"

"Maybe it's where they usually met? Maybe he likes living dangerously?"

Moran harrumphs, unconvinced. The crow gives up the battle and flies away. Moran turns his gaze away from the window. He pushes two fingers down under the plaster and scratches furiously.

Frankie puckers her brow in annoyance: *Is he paying any attention at all? First he's engrossed with the bloody crows, now it's his plaster of Paris. Have I to do everything?* "Do you have a better theory?"

Moran scowls impatiently and continues scratching his leg. "You're suggesting that this woman – Madeleine Byrne – by all accounts more than a tad unstable, and at any rate a slip of a thing compared to the heft and bulk of Roche – you're suggesting this woman, nonetheless, somehow manages to lure him to the strand and while there is able to overpower this giant of a man, and kill him?" He shakes his head. Draws a deep noisy breath through clenched teeth in frustration at not being able to relieve the itch. "Don't think that is very plausible, somehow."

A trolley lady puts her head around the door. "Tea?"

"Yes, please."

The tea lady wheels a trolley into the ward. She places a tray – complete with teapot, milk jug, a plain mug and a plate with three digestive biscuits – on the table beside Moran. She leaves and closes the door.

"Come on, we know there are hundreds of incidents where small women get the better of strongly built men. Cunning. Planning. I mean she could have poisoned a glass of wine."

"Was there evidence to that effect at the scene? What do forensics say?" Moran lifts the lid of the teapot and stirs vigorously.

"I'm not saying he was poisoned – I gave that merely as an

example. All I mean is, it's not impossible for the balance of forces to be reversed with a bit of cunning. And don't forget that most powerful of weapons – anger that begets revenge."

"And lust that begets babies."

Frankie finds herself blushing. It starts at her neck and travels up slowly. *Christ! Now of all times. As if he knows!* With an effort she brings her mind back to the moment. "At any rate I'm convinced whoever killed the Strand baby also killed the priest."

"Sorry – tea? I should have asked her to bring another cup."

Frankie grimaces and shakes her head. She doesn't want tea. She feels sick. "You've just turned that tea into tar."

"I like a beverage a mouse could trot along," Moran says with satisfaction, as he pours the brew into the mug, adds a splash of milk, and helps himself to a chocolate digestive biscuit. "So Sarah was in hospital when the priest was killed?"

"Yes. It rules her out. She has been released without charge. There is no evidence linking Sarah to the murder of the Strand baby either. Although Brannigan – the fool – still insists she's suspect number one."

"So you're saying this Madeleine Byrne – who Roche had a relationship with and impregnated – killed the Strand baby because Roche had abandoned her, and that she then also killed the priest when she thinks he's fathered another infant by another woman?"

Frankie nods. "There's a pattern to the case."

"There is."

"I'm not talking about the pattern on the murder weapon. First a baby is found beaten to death. And now the priest is killed. Both found on Port Arthur Strand. I believe in patterns."

Moran nods. "Ever the chess player." He bites into the biscuit, dusts crumbs off his jumper. "And all the other leads? Followed up and crossed off, I presume? The Biddies?"

Frankie nods. "The Children of Bríd are basically a peaceable group of matriarchal neopagans rebelling against patriarchy. Their main idea is to commune with Mother Earth by ritually offering her menstrual blood."

Moran grimaces. "It sounded like they were offering it to more than Mother Earth that time you were there?"

"That session probably got a bit out of hand. I'm convinced now there was nothing sinister going on. In any case, the number of babies born there tally. That's the key thing."

Moran pours another cup of tea for himself, adds milk and sugar, sips his tea and digs into another digestive biscuit. "Okay, back to the main event – couldn't this be a copycat murder? Some loon hears about the death in the dunes, murder by hammer, has a grudge against the priest, kills him using the same method, in the hope that the investigation will only look for one person for both crimes?"

"Possible. But I believe we are looking for one person for both crimes. And that person is Madeleine Byrne."

A party of visitors comes into the ward looking for a relative: mother, father and two hyper pre-teens. The children run to the leatherette sofa and jump onto it. The parents quickly realise they are in the wrong place, gather up their offspring and wander off noisily.

Moran shrugs. "Hatred. Plenty of evidence of the anger and jealousy the geezer generated. His serial womanising."

"And that's precisely why I think Byrne killed him. She had motive, had access to a weapon. And I believe she created the opportunity. As far as Brannigan is concerned, there has only been one murder – that of the Strand baby. And I have till Friday to solve that, after which he declares the case closed."

Moran tops up his tea. "So forensics say the evidence offers no clear conclusion as to the cause of the priest's death and yet you saw an indentation on his forehead, that might or might not be from the blow of a hammer?"

"I didn't say I clearly saw it. There were other marks on the forehead as well, as if seagulls had been pecking at the body. It's just that I'm adding in my suspicions. The remains are in a poor condition. On close examination, I saw a strange mark at the hairline, not immediately obvious. O'Toole can verify to seeing it too."

"One way or the other you saw something. Which begs the question – why was the state pathologist so remiss? Didn't he see it? And if he did, why didn't he report the indent on the curate's forehead?"

"That's why I want the body to be examined again. I would

like an explanation for that unusual indentation on the forehead. And crucially, if the verdict is of death by drowning, there must be an explanation as to how the body got up almost as far as the dunes when the tides don't reach that far."

"And Brannigan is blocking all that?"

"He most definitely is."

Moran arches an eyebrow. "Brannigan wants it to be declared a natural death – why? You've had time to think about this – what would your guess be, Mademoiselle Clouseau?"

"My theory is that Brannigan wants to protect the Catholic Church from the scandal of a priest's death by suicide. Suicide is a crime. Neither will he entertain the idea it could be homicide. He must know about Roche's philandering. But he's a staunch Catholic. My guess is he's getting his instructions from either the Church or the Superintendent or both to prevent a scandal. So he insists it was a tragic accident. I believe there's more than a good possibility it is murder."

"Well, that's a theory all right. And it's raising the big issues, that go far beyond a simple murder case in north Donegal. We're looking at the proverbial opening of a can of worms here, Detective Francis, you realise that?"

"I do."

"Well, we both saw how Brannigan – and McGinley too – kow-towed to Roche to the point of obsequiousness. But the pathologist – Johnston? Are you saying there's a conspiracy here?"

Frankie shakes her head. "No. The pathologist says the evidence is inconclusive. It's up to the gardaí to ascertain whether this was an accident, a suicide, or murder."

"But wouldn't he have noticed that mark on the forehead?"

"He says the body's condition allows for no firm conclusion. Johnston did say in the report though that there was alcohol in the system."

Moran pushes the tea trolley to one side and settles back. He screws up his face as if in discomfort.

"Madeleine Byrne has to be suspect number one now," Frankie says. "She had an affair with Roche, has access to ball-peen hammers through her jewellery making, she had a baby and now she has none."

"How do you know that? Couldn't the baby be with a relative, the mother for example?"

"The mother is in Scotland."

"Well, a relative then. What I'm saying is, there's no evidence that Madeleine's baby has disappeared. We have no proof that the Strand baby was Madeleine's."

"Which is why I have to find Madeleine and interview her."

"Okay. Good luck with it. By the way, you never told me how you found out Sarah had a relationship with Roche?"

"When I heard about his philandering, and his affair with Madeleine, I began to add two and two together. In our interviews with Sarah, if you remember, she would never say who the father of her baby was when questioned, but she several times referred to a two-timing bastard. Once I allowed the thought take hold that it might be Roche, everything seemed to point in that direction."

"But you had no proof – what if Sarah had denied it?"

"I was banking on her being angry enough after the third baby was found, to open up."

"Which she did?"

"Yes."

"Well, your instincts proved right. Good work. You have a knack of making young women talk. So good luck with Madeleine."

Moran shifts in his chair and grimaces in response to a flash of nerve pain.

Frankie knows it's time for her to leave.

* * *

Before returning to her hotel, Frankie stops off at a pharmacy. She is one week late. She's pregnant, she's certain of it. And the agonising question – who is the father? She's spent the last number of weeks trying to find out who the father of Sarah Joyce's baby is, now she's pregnant and she's not sure who fathered *her* child. Her menstrual cycle is irregular, so it could be either Rory's or Moran's. How could this have happened? She so wanted a baby but not this way. *That thing with Moran earlier was so weird. Just chance, of course, but it was unnerving. What if it is Moran's?*

As she pushes through the door to the pharmacy, she feels uneasy all of a sudden, vulnerable. The pharmacist, a woman in her fifties, appears warm and friendly, which puts Frankie at her ease. Frankie takes a deep breath and approaches the counter. "Do you have pregnancy testing kits?"

The smile on the pharmacist's face slowly melts, like snow off a ditch in spring. "Oh, I'm sorry, dear," she says firmly, "we don't do pregnancy-test kits here. You'll have to go to your doctor to get that done." It's clear she'll be having no truck with stuff the likes of that.

As she slinks out the door, Frankie feels not unlike a criminal. It's not that the pharmacist was unkind, but there was no doubting her position on irregularities.

Why do women have such a hard time? Stop feeling so bloody sorry for yourself, Frankie.

* * *

Next morning she makes enquiries and finds the local doctor's surgery. The secretary tells her, yes, they can fit her in, but she'll have to wait about fifteen minutes or so, it that's okay – they're quite busy this morning, she'll be called.

Best get this over with, Frankie thinks, the sooner the better.

In the waiting room, she flicks through the only magazine on the coffee table: a Bórd Fáilte brochure on things to do in Gweedore: hill-walking on Mount Errigal, birdwatching in Tory Island, surfing in Gallen strand. After ten minutes, too preoccupied to savour the delights of Gweedore as outlined in the brochure – beaches, mountains and cliffs – she pulls out her notebook. Might as well do some work while she's waiting.

Where are we in the investigation? A priest – father of two babies who have died in the recent past, one murdered – himself dead, murdered too, possibly. Another baby found in the church under suspicious circumstances. Four deaths. One definite murder. One suspected murder.

And the link between them all? The priest. The Church. There is no doubt in her mind about it. But if she opens up a Pandora's box of Roche's philandering, the church's cover-up, and the State's involvement in it, where will it all end? This is, after all, a country where the police force work hand in glove with the Catholic Church. She knows that, everyone knows that, but the question is where will it all end for her? Is she going to be able to topple that century-long relationship single-handedly? The more worrying thought – does her repugnance at the actions of a philandering cleric enabled by both Church and State make her sympathetic to a killer? In murder, as in life, things are rarely black and white. It's the grey areas that need the spotlight thrown on them.

The receptionist breaks into her thoughts and tells her she may go into the surgery now. After a brief discussion, the doctor performs an internal examination. Having once before had to undergo such a procedure, Frankie knows what to expect. She disassociates through visualisation until he's finished. After she dresses, he gives her a receptacle and asks her to go into the bathroom for a urine sample. When she returns, he pulls on a pair of surgical gloves, brings the phial over to the wash-handbasin, and inserts a dipstick into it. Frankie sits by the doctor's desk and waits nervously, palms clammy. She hardly dares breathe. He turns to her and smiles.

CHAPTER 31

Bloody Foreland is shrouded in a damp mist, already forecast. Frankie is following up on a tip-off she received from an anonymous caller. It could very well be a waste of time, but you never know. Nothing is unimportant in a murder investigation, especially one as complicated as this. As she approaches MacAllister's house, she spies Brannigan's car outside the cottage. Brannigan had earlier told her he and McGinley were going to Derry to talk to the RUC. The mystery caller – who turned out to be MacAllister – said the sergeant was up to his neck in it. What exactly he meant by that, he wouldn't say.

She reverses up the road and parks out of view. The light drizzle has morphed into a heavy mist, but nevertheless she's able to make out the two figures who come out of the cottage carrying something between them which they hoist into the boot of a car. Brannigan and McGinley. They get into the car and drive off in the direction of Bunbeg. Frankie follows at a distance, the sheet of fine spray a good cover. They travel south to Dungloe, then east in the direction of Ballybofey. The rain becomes so heavy at one stage, she considers abandoning the whole thing as she wonders what on earth she hopes to achieve; but she feels that compulsion one does at finishing a job once started, even though it might be more prudent to let go on a basis that the effort may not be worth the reward. The rain eases. Frankie is still tailing them fifty-odd miles later when they pass through Ballybofey, and on till they reach the border. Brannigan has been saying from day one that he's been finding bomb caches on information from MacAllister. She's convinced that her suspicions about these so-called "finds" are about to be confirmed.

Frankie watches as both men get out and lift the load – the one they've earlier taken from MacAllister's – out of the car boot. They carry it between them with some difficulty – they almost topple over on the uneven ground at one point – and carefully place it in the ditch.

Frankie can feel her heart thumping so hard she fears she'll have a heart attack. Her mouth feels dry and perspiration beads her forehead. She quickly reverses and, crouched over the steering wheel as though in an effort to make the car go faster, speeds back to Gweedore. Her sweaty palms make holding the wheel difficult and every few minutes she has to rub them – one at a time – on her jacket to dry them. To no avail – almost immediately they become damp again.

She has just been witness to corruption in action: Brannigan, a senior member of An Garda Síochána, and his deputy, planting a bomb. Her thoughts are racing. Did they see her? What if her car breaks down on this godforsaken road? What if they catch up with her? And so what if they do – why should she be worried? Still, her instinct is to get back to base quickly.

She can't get her head around why anyone would risk doing something like this, especially a senior garda with a reputation to maintain? Even as she asks herself the question, Moran's words ring in her ears: *"So that's what Brannigan is up to – looking for the big 'find', so he'll get promoted and retire with a fat pension pot."* So is this another big 'find', a feather in his cap, demonstrating his sterling work in the service of doing down the IRA? Is that another reason Brannigan is in such a hurry to have her gone, so anxious to wrap up the murder case?

What other explanation can there be?

And then the follow-up question – what is she to do with this information?

Focus on the job in hand, Kate Francis, you have enough on your plate without trying to solve the mysteries of a county on the tip of an island divided by a treaty that had a carnival of reaction latent within it from the foundation of the state. Lord! Where did that come from? I've been too much in O'Toole's company lately!

She stops at Duggan's for a sandwich and a coffee, grateful the family-run late-night grocery is open. It's ten thirty when she finally gets to her hotel bedroom. She throws her keys on the dressing table, turns on the bedside lamp, kicks off her shoes and flops onto the bed. She tears off the sandwich wrapper and bites into the brown bread, chicken and salad. The bread is fresh, the meat chunky, and the lettuce crisp. God, she's ravenous! A sandwich never tasted so good. But she mustn't do this, leave long hours without eating. How many times has she sworn to herself she will try and eat at least every four hours? Does she want to end up like Brannigan, self-medicating on antacids?

Her thoughts turn to what's going on in her body. Every time the doctor's fateful words pop into her head *"Pregnant, my dear"*, she tries to squeeze them out of her mind. In vain. But the thoughts persist. Images of what's going on inside her crowd her imagination.

Frankie loved biology at school, loved learning how the body works. The wonder of life beginning. In her mind's eye she sees the millions of spermatozoa, like shoals of miniature tadpoles, surging up through the vaginal channel, each on its own blind evolutionary mission to win, to achieve success, be the one to penetrate the ovum, the successful sperm fertilising the egg and transforming it into a zygote, the cells in the zygote immediately beginning to divide and subdivide, making their way to imbed in the womb. And that moment – that amazing moment when the zygote stem cells differentiate into specific organs that transform the zygote into embryo. How do the cells know which organ to become, she's always wondered – all identical at the beginning of the journey but now somehow knowing which should become liver, which heart, which brain and so on? If she was given a good explanation at school, she's forgotten it now, and so the mystery remains. But more importantly the question – what stage is the life inside her at now? She so wanted a child. But not like this, not knowing which of the two men she had sex with recently fathered it!

This is a nightmare!

Stop! she orders herself.

With an effort she goes into the bathroom and splashes cold water on her face. She brings a towel up to her face and pats it dry, staring at the image in the glass. Her face is drawn and pinched-looking. She goes back into the bedroom. With a mental effort, she turns her attention to the goings-on at the border. Glances at her watch. 11 o'clock. She turns on the TV. More news of an IRA find, no doubt.

CHAPTER 32

Roseanne eases open the half door with her hip and enters, balancing a bottle of champagne in one hand, a cakebox held aloft in the other. Neighbours and friends fill the tiny front room of the Joyce household and spill out into the kitchen and garden. Roseanne navigates her way through the happy crowd, careful not to drop her cargo. "*Excuse me. Excuse me.*" She places the champagne and cake on the kitchen table, already laden with plates of sandwiches, pots of tea, brown bread with smoked salmon, home-made fairy cakes, rock cakes, melt-in-the mouth date fingers, fruit cakes, wine. Friends have not come empty-handed. There's cause to rejoice. They all want to celebrate Sarah's return home.

Mags, decked out in her Sunday frock, worries the work-surface with a cloth, making sure everything will appear spotless under the beady-eyed scrutiny of neighbours. Roseanne spots Hannah by the fireside, silent as always, two small children playing around her feet. Today she appears brighter than usual, dressed in a yellow floral dress with a string of orange beads around her neck. Roseanne cannot remember ever having seen Hannah out of her habitual black – she appears almost young. Roseanne scans the crowd and spies Sarah at the end of the garden talking to the journalist, Pat Mullarkey. She slips out the back door to join them.

"What are your plans now, Sarah?" she hears Pat enquiring of the woman at the centre of all the controversy for the past two months.

In a pink halter-neck dress, ivory-coloured high-heeled sandals, and flame-red hair loose and falling about her shoulders, Sarah appears radiant. An intense vividness shows in every expressive movement.

Sarah smiles and says, "I've applied to Glasgow for a place on the teacher training course," she crosses her fingers, "so here's hoping!"

"But don't you already have a place secured in Limerick?" Mullarkey knows the interest there is in this story: Sarah Joyce is a celebrity now. "Why go to Glasgow?"

Sarah bends down and lifts Goitseo into her arms. The family pet gazes up at her and licks her face. "I want away from here, for the moment. I need to put clear blue water between me and all that's happened." She strokes the dog's curly mop. "A fresh start."

The journalist puts away her notebook, gets ready to leave. "How do you feel you were treated in this case, Sarah?"

Sarah fixes her gaze on the hollyhocks that are in bloom at the back of the garden, fat pink blossoms that sway and nod happily in the light June breeze.

"I don't want to think about any of that anymore."

Roseanne touches her shoulder. Sarah turns, gives her friend a one-armed warm hug and keeps her arm around her shoulder as she faces Mullarkey again. "What's alive for me right now is that I'm back with my friends, my mother, my sister ... they're not suffering any more. I want to put all this behind me."

* * *

Brannigan leans back in his chair. Frankie is pressing for more time. She has a strong inclination to tell Brannigan she's aware of his shady activities at the border, but she represses the urge. Whatever skulduggery Brannigan and his side-kick McGinley were up to, she'll leave to the Super to deal with.

"Just look at the facts," she says. "Roche befriends and seduces a young woman, Madeleine Byrne. Three years later he tires of her and dumps her ..."

Brannigan interrupts. "I'm not listening to any of that nonsense."

Frankie is not going to be fobbed off. "Madeleine tells Sarah he was the father of the child she's expecting, due to give birth at exactly around the time the Strand baby was found murdered."

"The first hole in your theory, Detective Garda Francis," Brannigan barks, "is that you yourself told me you did a thorough investigation of all the births around that time. At no time did the name Madeleine Byrne come up."

"It's possible Madeleine had a home birth with no medical intervention."

"And her flatmate can testify to this?"

"All she knows is that Madeleine was pregnant and then she wasn't. And no baby."

Brannigan takes his pipe out of the drawer and hammers the desk with it, upending the remains of old tobacco.

Frankie involuntarily puts her hand to her nose, in a fruitless effort to ward off the sweet intoxicating stink. She composes herself. "The timeline is important. After Roche dumps Madeleine, he takes up with Sarah. She becomes pregnant. Meanwhile, Madeleine tells Roche she's pregnant. Then Sarah tells him she's pregnant. Roche panics. He threatens both women. He tells Sarah he'll destroy her if she says a word, urges her to go for adoption."

Brannigan fills his pipe, pats down the fresh tobacco.

"Nine months later, Sarah has a botched birth and her baby dies," continues Frankie. "All this we know. What I'm putting to you is that at around the same time, Madeleine gives birth too, kills her baby and buries it near the sand dunes at Port Arthur. She already knows Roche has fathered Sarah's baby, so when she hears about the baby in the church she thinks – it's a likely scenario – this is another of Roche's. And filled with rage, she lures her former lover to the beach where they first rendezvoused. And there kills him with the same murder weapon."

"Outlandish. You've conjured up some mythical woman, embroidered her into a narrative in order to prove your crazy theory. On top of that you expect me to believe the testimony of Sarah Joyce, who, as we all know, has been locked up in a loony bin for the past several weeks." Brannigan snorts. "You are tarnishing the good name of an honourable priest. And with what proof? Where's the proof? This is conjecture, pure and simple. Talk about conspiracy theories!" Having delivered his verdict on the matter, Brannigan sticks the stem of the pipe into the corner of his mouth and puffs rhythmically, emitting small malign plumes of smoke.

Frankie frowns, exasperated. "We must get that mark on Roche's forehead examined and compare it with the hammer mark on the Strand baby. The body was found high up on the strand near the dunes, though the tides don't come up that far. The evidence is there, you just have to look beyond your nose."

Brannigan glares at her. "Detective Francis, I remind you the pathologist has said that no firm conclusion can be drawn about Father Roche's death, no matter how much you would like to consider otherwise, other that he got caught in the rip currents and accidentally drowned. Sarah Joyce's baby's death was due to an accident at birth, the pathologist says. The infant found dead in the church was as a result of a tragic accident also – in fact, as you are aware, some poor divil from Fanad has come forward, and CARE are looking after her." He holds the pipe in the cup of his hand, stem pointing outwards towards the picture of the Sacred Heart. "Which leaves us with one murder – the Strand baby. But – we have found no one responsible for the murder of the Strand baby, despite enormous resources ... and police power devoted to the crime. As you know, Sarah Joyce is no longer a suspect and has been released."

Frankie rolls her eyes.

Brannigan closes the folder on the desk with a slap. "You have till tomorrow, Detective Francis, after which the case is closed," he says, talking out of the side of his mouth. "We are spending no more time or money on this. We have other matters to attend to now. Serious issues." He reaches back to the shelf behind him. "So if you'll excuse me ..."

He's saying no to solving the case. It's not reasonable for him to say no. Clearly he wants her gone even if it means not solving the case. She knows why. Well, she knows one of the reasons why.

But she's not giving up on this case. She'll go it alone, if necessary.

The sergeant lifts down another file and shouts, "*McGinley!*"

McGinley opens the door immediately. "Yes, boss?"

* * *

Frankie's sick of Brannigan and his toady McGinley. As she leaves the barracks, she notices the two old men, one as ever leaning over the half-door smoking a pipe, the other leaning against the wall chatting to him. She ambles over and greets them. They smile broadly at her, delighted with the attention.

"Hello. I'm Kate Francis."

"Aye, we know who you are. You're trying to find out who dunnit."

"I've been studying the sea currents in this area ..."

"*Och*, aye, the poor curate, God be good to him," says the man of the house.

"At the same time, it's not right," says the other. "A priest takes vows."

"He shouldn't break them."

"Sorry, I'm not –" Frankie says.

"We're just saying –"

"And another thing –"

Frankie holds her breath. "Yes?"

"We heard they're saying he was drowned in the currents."

"They must be thinking of Magheraclogher, for there's no channel at Port Arthur," takes up his companion. "No currents."

"Everyone knows that," adds the first.

Everyone knows there are no currents at Port Arthur Strand. So Brannigan is lying. Just as she thought.

Frankie begins to feel more than a little unwell. Cramps have an iron grip on the muscles of her stomach all the way around to her lower back. She says goodbye to the two old men and takes her leave.

As she makes her way to her car, she gropes in her bag for a packet of paracetamol. She extracts the last two from the bubble foil, throws them into her mouth and washes them down with a little water. *Shake out of it*, she tells herself.

The stomach ache subsides a little. *Mind over matter. Don't think about it and it will go away.* She visualises yogi, who have tooth extractions without anaesthetic, who train the mind not to dwell on pain. Well, of course, she *has* taken some anaesthetic.

The sky darkens followed by a cloudburst and downpour. The wipers keep time like a metronome. Her stomach cramps are back with increasing severity. Her back aches. A familiar ache. An old friend of an ache. She can't wait to get home. Bunbeg crossroads looms. She stops at the chemist for stronger painkillers. The chemist is preoccupied with another customer and hopefully won't remember their last encounter. The woman stops in mid-flow to serve Frankie, then back to her intense conversation. Frankie drives straight to the hotel. Once in the room she takes two of the pills with water, climbs into bed, gets under the covers and falls into a deep sleep. She wakes suddenly from a strange dream, which she struggles to remember, but there are only fragments, nothing that makes sense and not enough detail to analyse. Then that familiar smell hits: the whiff of iron. She puts her hand on the sheet and feels the stickiness. The relief! Her panic is over. She is no longer pregnant.

But intermingled with the relief is a sense of loss. A pregnancy now in these circumstances was not what she wanted ... but still ...

CHAPTER 33

As Frankie passes by the Poison Glen, Errigal, enigmatic as ever, discloses nothing of itself. She glances at the lone church, holding the fort still, last man standing, harbouring the secret of the glen. The deed done, a hundred years or more ago. What secrets might Madeleine Byrne be harbouring?

She arrives in Letterkenny at midday, finds a car park near the centre, not a quarter of a mile from where Sarah is incarcerated. Frankie walks the short distance to O'Donnell's. She surveys the recently refurbished shop with its showy front, shuttered over on her last visit. The window display shouts of both flamboyance and taste, traditional jewellery displayed alongside modern pieces: an eclectic mix of unusual silver rings and pendants side by side with more traditional Claddagh ware.

Inside, as she waits for a customer to leave, Frankie observes the proprietor, once Madeleine's boss. Joe O'Donnell is loud both in dress and in manner, but also handsome in an alternative sort of way. He wears an earring in one ear, one of those that display a large hole in the centre. Despite herself, Frankie shudders. She has always felt there is something barbaric about punching a large hole through human flesh.

She flashes her badge. "I'm Detective Garda Francis, from the Dublin murder squad, investigating the death of the baby at Port Arthur Strand."

O'Donnell shudders exaggeratedly, blinking his eyes. "A very bad business, dead babies and all that."

"If you will, I would like to ask you a few questions. I understand Madeleine Byrne was an employee of yours for a period?"

O'Donnell stares at her, smacks his hand on his forehead. "Oh my God, are you suggesting?"

"Routine enquiries, that's all."

O'Donnell comes from behind the counter, activates the TEMPORARILY CLOSED sign, turns the key in the lock and extends his hand. "Let's go in here, it'll be more private."

They move into a workroom. Three of the walls are lined with presses, divided into small box-like drawers, for tools, stones and jewellery cases. Metal shavings crunch underfoot, setting Frankie's teeth on edge. The tang of metal catches her breath.

She pulls out a notebook and pen and leans against a workbench.

"I understand Madeleine Byrne got a position here after she left the government training scheme."

O'Donnell leans back against the workbench by her side, arms folded, appraising her, a little smile playing on his lips. "That's correct."

"How long did she work for you?"

"For about a year. After that, Madeleine decided to branch out, to start her own business."

"How did you find Madeleine? As a worker, I mean?"

"Oh, she was good all right." The jeweller winks knowingly. "Truth is ... Madeleine was a goer, know what I mean? *Nudge. Nudge.*" He nudges the detective a couple of times, eyeing her sideways.

She can smell his deodorant. She steps back from the intimate gesture, draws herself to her full height – she's about an inch taller than the thin slight artisan – and glares at him. Doesn't he know, the idiot, he's one step away from being charged with indecent assault of a police officer in the service of duty?

She takes in a deep breath. "I would remind you, sir, that you are addressing a member of An Garda Síochána." *How did Madeleine cope with this guy?*

O'Donnell moves to one side, palms up defensively. He drums the worktable, looks away from the detective, folds his arms. The front door bell rings. O'Donnell takes a step towards the door, hesitates, opts to remain where he is.

Frankie keeps her eyes fixed on him.

"So she would have had her own jewellery-making instruments?" she asks.

"Yes."

Frankie walks around the workbench. The wall behind, covered with cork tiles from shelf to ceiling, acts as a noticeboard. Frankie goes over to look at the various posts – receipts, clippings, posters for trade fairs in Derry. Some are overlapped. She lifts one or two to read those underneath.

A newspaper cutting tucked under a receipt catches her attention. Her heart skips a beat. It is an obituary of Brendan Roche. Someone has drawn a thick red ring around the photo of the priest with a red marker, and the word YES! underneath. Frankie stares at it. Has she stumbled onto something here? Had O'Donnell a grudge against Roche?

"Did you know Father Roche?" she asks.

O'Donnell harrumphs. "Everyone knew him. He was the local curate here for three years, before he was moved to Gweedore."

Frankie points at the red ring. "Who drew a ring around the image?"

It was on the desk, he says, when he was marking some papers, and he must have accidentally marked the newspaper. *The dog ate my homework, in other words.* This could change things.

O'Donnell and Madeleine worked together. Was Madeleine interested in O'Donnell? If they both had a grudge against Roche, could O'Donnell have been implicated in his murder? Is it plausible O'Donnell would murder a priest?

"And you accidentally happened to write the word *'yes'* too?"

O'Donnell shrugs. "I don't know how that got there."

"What did you think of Father Roche? Did you like him?"

"I don't like priests – not a crime as far as I'm aware."

He's hiding something. Frankie looks at him coldly. Her laser-blue eyes have seen many a criminal pretend and found them lacking in imagination. She walks around the desk, surveying the material on his bench. She selects a small hammer, turns it over in her hand, studying it from all angles, holds it up under the light.

"Is this a ball-peen hammer?"

"Yes."

Frankie taps the hammer on her hand a couple of times, measuring its weight. "What work would you do with a hammer like this?"

O'Donnell sighs. "You hammer out the metal to soften, stretch or smooth it. There are many uses. It's a hammer, that's all," he says, in the tone of one explaining the theory of nuclear physics to a three-year-old.

Frankie puts the hammer down. "I came here to find out Madeleine's whereabouts. I'm looking for an address for her cousin who lives in the Bogside. I understand you went to Derry with her a few times?"

"I took her with me to a trade fair once or twice, that's all."

"How long would these trade fairs have lasted generally?"

"Usually over a weekend."

"And where did you stay when you were in Derry?"

"A hotel."

"Would Madeleine not have stayed with her cousin in the Bogside?"

"I don't know where she stayed. I stayed in a hotel."

"Do you have an address for Madeleine's cousin?"

"I probably have, not sure where I put it."

All the while they're talking, Frankie is riffling through the papers on his desk, receipts, invoices etc.

"Would you mind not doing that, please, searching my papers," says O'Donnell sharply. "Unless you have a warrant."

She has already spotted what she's looking for. Frankie lets the receipts fall over, but is careful not to cover the address.

She puts her notebook in her pocket. "Thank you, that will be all for the moment. I appreciate your help. If you come across that address perhaps you'd give me a call." Even as she's saying this she's memorising the information: *28 Plunkett Drive*.

"I'll get in touch if I find it."

As soon as she leaves the shop, she jots the address onto the back of her hand.

* * *

The trip from the jeweller's to Glenkeen estate takes ten minutes.

Madeleine's flatmate leads Frankie inside.

"I haven't seen Madeleine since you were here last," she says, "To tell you the truth, I'm getting a bit worried something might have happened to her. She really hasn't been herself in the past while since – well, you know yourself."

"So Madeleine has made no contact with you – for what? Over two weeks?"

"Well over two weeks. She didn't take much with her ..." adding quickly – "not that I've been snooping around or anything."

Something inside Frankie soars. She's just been given the cue she was hoping for. "Would you mind if I have a look in her room?"

The flatmate, relieved to have someone else share the worry, nods, opens the living-room door and points Frankie down the hall.

Frankie enters Madeleine's bedroom. The room is not much more than eight foot square. A single bed takes up most of the space by the window wall. A little lamp with a tasselled pink shade rests on the pine locker next to the bed. She pulls on a pair of surgical gloves. Inside the top drawer are some phone receipts. In the next, a folder with magazine cutouts – images of jewellery from top fashion designers, sources of materials for metal work, other fashion ads. In the third Frankie finds a black jewellery box with various handmade items – bracelets, brooches and necklaces. Rings too, mostly silver with crystal stones and other gems embedded. Rings fit for a bishop.

She lifts the red-and-white patchwork quilt and peers under the bed. Nothing there but a thick film of dust and fluff, a pair of low-heel court shoes, runners, an odd slipper. She pulls at the corner of the mattress and raises it. Tucked underneath, she finds a copy of Anais Nin's *Venus of Delta*. On the flyleaf she reads the inscription: *To my darling Maddie*. As Frankie flicks through the worn penguin paperback, several loose pages fall out and flutter to the floor. Something else slips out too and Frankie picks it up. It is a photo of a man in clerical garb whose face has been scrubbed out with a black biro in what appears to be a frenzy of obliteration. Only a rough black blob is left where the image of the face once was. But the body shape is unmistakeable. This was a photograph of Father Brendan Roche.

A plain pine two-door wardrobe is pressed up against the opposite wall. A pair of abalone rosary beads dangles from the handle. Frankie opens the wardrobe. She searches the pockets of jackets and jeans, a long multicoloured raincoat, but finds nothing. She reaches in and pulls out a black duffel bag tucked away at the back. Inside she finds a jewellery toolbox. Within seconds she finds what she is looking for: the ball-peen hammer. She uses a tissue to lift the hammer out of the toolbox, holds it in her hand with a firm grip and brings it down hard on the oak laminate floor – like a gavel. She can feel the force of it resonate back up her arm, the impact. The power. This small hammer could do serious damage. She sniffs. *What is that smell?* She holds the hammer up to her nose. It's been washed with some sort of disinfectant. Parazone? She studies the hammer more closely. Everything else in the toolbox – chisels, wrenches, tweezers, a miniature clamp – is grimy from use. All except the hammer. It's been scrubbed completely clean. Why? Frankie places the hammer in a plastic bag. Her heart is racing. She has evidence, but her training dictates she keep searching. Leave nothing undone.

She sits on the bed and is about to return the rings and bracelets to the jewellery box when she notices that what seems to be the base of the box is in fact a small leather-bound diary, black – same colour as the box – which is why she didn't see it first time around. Frankie lifts the diary out and skips through the entries. It quickly becomes clear this is primarily an appointments record for work: most of the entries are to do with clients and their purchases of jewellery. It does include, however, personal appointments: a dental appointment, visits to the hairdresser, coffee with a friend. Madeleine records the events of her life, in single-line entries. Markers. Frankie can feel the adrenalin coursing through her body as she turns the pages quickly, searching for the 29th of May.

She finds it. Her stomach lurches. There is one entry for that day. *Roche. Port Arthur Strand. 9 p.m.*

CHAPTER 34

Frankie approaches the checkpoint between Donegal and Derry in an unmarked car and in civvies. An armoured personnel carrier blocks her way. She stops. Her palms are sweaty. She rubs her hands along her jeans. To little avail. What seems like a battalion of British soldiers man the border hut. All armed. On the hill more soldiers with semi-automatics. Two approach the Fiat. She rolls down the window. Identification? She produces her driver's licence. Address? Purpose of visit? Etcetera and so on. O'Toole had done the research. She's primed. Nevertheless, she can feel the blood draining from her face with every question. *Will they ask to search the car?*

They wave her through.

She can breathe again.

If she's caught pursuing an investigation across the border without high-level authorisation, it could cause a major diplomatic incident. No chance in hell of getting that authorisation with Brannigan in charge. She will be watched for any suspicious behaviour by the RUC. Not to mention the IRA.

She drives through the city, through the exit gates on the medieval walls and down the steep hill to the Bogside. The contrast between the modest estate of small terraced houses and the formidable stone fortification that overlooks it couldn't be greater. Europe's largest collection of cannons mans the ramparts, all pointed at the working-class estate below. In front of her, and coming into view, a mural on the gable end of one of the terraced houses announces: YOU ARE NOW ENTERING FREE DERRY.

Frankie finds the house on Plunkett Drive without too much trouble. Number 28. *Thank you, O'Toole.* She rings the bell. No response. She waits a moment then knocks. A group of teenage boys kicking ball further along the street stop their play and stare at her. She's beginning to feel conspicuous. Are strangers unwelcome here? Is it a case of *Us* and *Them.* "Who're ya lookin' for?" one of them yells. "If it's herself, she's not in." He kicks the ball hard in Frankie's direction. In the split second it takes for the ball to whoosh through the air in a striker's arc, Frankie is back at school again, team captain, fired up, ready for action. She rises up to her full height, arms out from her sides, positions her head and *WHAM!* with mighty energy head-butts the ball back in the direction it came from.

Stunned silence follows. Then whoops and laughter. Loud cheers. "*Fuckin' hell! A girl!*" The mood changes. "*Your one doesn't be home before tea time!*" one of them shouts before running off. "*Usually goes to Breslin's Bar for a quick one after the market closes!*"

Frankie smiles, gives him a thumbs-up, and drives back to the city centre.

* * *

Madeleine Byrne sits at the back of the Breslin's Bar, a tray of hand-made jewellery in front of her on the table. She looks directly at Frankie with large brown eyes. "What kind of pendant had you in mind?"

A present for her mother, Frankie tells her, something striking, but not too flashy. She looks at the glittering array of precious stones that are displayed in front of her. Emerald, ruby, opal, topaz. Madeleine talks about the merits of the various stones, why people opt for one over the other. Frankie points to an opal. Madeleine hands her the stone to have a better look. The birthstone for October. When is her mother's birthday? It would be bad luck to choose an opal if she wasn't born in October.

Frankie hands it back.

Madeleine picks up a translucent purple. "What about an amethyst – set in silver on a silver chain? Do you think your mother would like that?" She hands Frankie the amethyst.

Frankie holds the stone up to the light, admires the vivid purple. She likes it.

Madeleine goes into great detail about the setting for the stone, the length of chains, gold or silver? Frankie selects her preference. Madeleine makes a note of it, and takes Frankie's name and number. She starts to put her material back into a jewellery case.

"I'll get in touch, when I have it made. By the way, how did you hear about me? You're not from these parts?"

She's from Dungloe, Frankie tells her, saw samples of Madeleine's work in O'Donnell's jewellery shop in Letterkenny, liked them, asked the proprietor, O'Donnell, where she might view some more. He said she often comes here for lunch after market.

There is a flickering at the mention of O'Donnell. But Frankie now knows that O'Donnell is no longer a suspect. O'Toole checked his whereabouts on the 29th of May, and it turns out he has a cast-iron alibi – verifiably away at a trade fair in Leeds for the week. So whatever the reason for the O'Donnell's grudge against Roche – if that is what the cutting hidden on his noticeboard meant – he couldn't have killed the priest.

"And you came all this way to see my stuff? I'm flattered."

"I love your jewellery," Frankie says. "It's quite unique. I've been on the lookout for something different for a while. It's my mother's significant birthday coming up – the big O." A beat. "But I'll be truthful – it was just serendipitous that I saw you sitting there with your jewellery. I had another reason for being here." She smiles, ruefully, bracing herself. "Listen, would you like a drink?"

Madeleine thinks for a moment. "Sure, why not?" She's just made a sale. She deserves it. "I'll have a brandy, thanks."

Frankie orders a brandy and a beer. She looks around, spots a vacant alcove in the corner. "Why don't we move back there so we can hear ourselves talking?"

Even as she's saying this she's aware the bar is by no means crowded.

Madeleine doesn't seem to notice. "Yes, why not?"

Madeleine packs her jewellery in her case, and they both settle into the alcove.

Frankie studies the woman in front of her, the woman who she believes is a double murderer. Madeleine is wearing a cropped black leather jacket and blue jeans. Her dark-brown almost black hair is tied in a knot at the top of her head with a pink toggle. Loose strands fall about her face, framing fine features. She is about five foot six inches in height, Frankie estimates, of slender build. Very well-toned, she notices. This woman works out.

"So what *did* bring you to Derry?"

Frankie makes a face. "I actually came here on a date. Well, that was the plan, but the so-and-so didn't turn up!"

"They're all the same," says Madeleine.

"I wouldn't mind but we'd had a few conversations on the

phone. He seemed very nice. Eager too. And I liked him." Madeleine shakes her head.

The drinks arrive. Madeleine takes a long drink of her brandy. Frankie, sips her beer. "It's so disheartening."

"It's a bummer, alright!"

Frankie needs to get Madeleine relaxed, talking. Off-guard. Which means *she* has to do lots of talking first. She leans back. She intends to keep this party going. "My last long-term relationship ended because I wasn't available enough. He wanted more of my time. He said I was too independent. Problem is – I do like my autonomy."

"What do you work at?"

"I'm a social worker.

"Ah, that probably made it difficult."

Frankie continues reeling. "Then, as bad luck would have it, I had a one-night stand with a married man. A complete disaster! My boyfriend found out and that put the tin hat on it." *Keep things as near the truth as possible.* Who said that? Not Rory anyway! "So the boyfriend left me, the married man went back to his wife – surprise, surprise! And I end up dumped in Derry. Bloody men – they always leave you in the lurch."

Madeleine shakes her head. "You could sing that if you had a tune for it."

Frankie has always marvelled at some people's ability to just keep on talking even when they're not getting much of a response, almost as if they're talking to themselves. She doesn't have this particular talent, but she must keep going. She digs deep. "My view is women are more evolved than men in every respect. Men haven't changed since the dawn of time. They are still chimpanzees – violent, territorial, emotionally infantile, always vying to be the alpha male. It's probably overstating it, but on the other hand maybe not too much off the mark."

Madeleine laughs, finishes her brandy, calls the waiter over and orders a double. She's beginning to relax. She points at Frankie's half-full glass. "You?"

Frankie nods. "But I'm probably talking too much. I tend to do that when I have a drink. What about you? Young, beautiful – I bet you have all the young fellas chasing you?"

Madeleine shakes her head. "No. No boyfriend."

The waiter arrives with the drinks. Madeleine lifts hers and takes a long draught.

Frankie nurses her beer. "Married men are the bane of my life. At my age you keep bumping into them. I always swore I'd have nothing to do with marrieds, and yet there I was after a few drinks and a bit of flattery, hopping into bed with one. He told me of course, that his marriage was over – well, he would, wouldn't he? Charmed the socks off me. Told me I was adorable, special, he wanted me in his life forever *blah blah*, when all he really wanted was – well, you know what they all want! Can you trust what a man says at all?"

"Never trust a man!" Madeleine says and finishes her drink. Frankie orders another double brandy for her.

Frankie rambles on. "You know, my antennae were out to be aware of men who were unavailable, so I could avoid them. I had a little ploy. I would flush them out by asking if they would spend Christmas Day with me" – Madeleine smiles – "that usually got the married ones flummoxed. '*Hamhamahama* ... well, not this year ...' and so on and so ridiculous. But this guy passed with flying colours. Christmas Day would be great, he said, not a bother. I thought I was home and dry."

The third brandy arrives. Madeleine empties half in one gulp.

Frankie finishes her first glass of beer. "If the whole thing didn't make you laugh, it would be enough to make you cry."

People come and go. The waiter passes with a tray full of empty glasses on his way to the kitchen. Frankie lets the silence stretch.

Madeleine has relaxed. She leans back, brandy glass in hand, and sighs. "I was in a relationship with a man for three years. In the end he betrayed me. Just dumped me. Threw me away. One minute he was telling me he loved me, the next I was discarded ... so I sure know what it feels like to be dumped."

Let the hare sit. Frankie says nothing for a moment. "Was he married?" she asks quietly. She puts her hand in her jacket pocket and presses a button.

"No ... he was a ... He wasn't married."

Frankie nods, sips her beer.

Madeleine scowls into her empty glass. Looks around to catch the waiter's attention. "It's horrible to be just cast out like a dog."

"Tell me about it!"

Madeleine orders a another double brandy and a beer for Frankie, which arrive promptly. "On top of everything, I was pregnant when he left me."

"Oh Lord! That's terrible!"

"When I told him I was pregnant, he had no compassion or care. God! I wanted to kill him!"

"Completely understandable." Frankie takes a deep breath. The conversation is flowing in the right direction. She has to guide it to the river. "Killing someone is not so easy, though."

"Not that hard either," says Madeleine, with a little twist of her mouth, half smile, half sneer.

The drinks arrive.

"Mind you, I come from a long line of killers myself," Frankie says, filling in with some wallpaper. "My grandmother used routinely wring a turkey's neck for Christmas."

"It's not so difficult to kill." Madeleine's words are beginning to slur. "All you need is enough anger in you."

"Are we talking here about killing turkeys or humans?"

"I'm talking about killing a bad bastard."

"Wouldn't you need a weapon of some sort?"

Madeleine sits back, brandy in hand. She drains the glass. She hesitates for a moment. But the drink has demolished her inhibitions. "A hammer would do the job."

"A hammer?" says Frankie. "God! I don't know. I can't even bear to squash a spider."

"A little planning is all that's needed. Then before you know it – *poof! It's done!* They're dead."

Madeleine's dark eyes appear enormous. The turmoil inside is manifesting itself on the outside. She has all these secrets, all these experiences she's been through, and Frankie sees she has a sudden overwhelming need to talk about them. For the moment though they are just playing a game.

"But you wouldn't really go through with it?"

Madeleine rises to the dare. "*I would.*"

"What would you do?"

Madeleine smiles tipsily. "Here's what I'd do if a man dumped me. I'd ring him for a rendezvous on a beach in late evening – a secluded beach – I'd bring alcohol. I'd get him drunk and then hit him with a hammer."

"What kind of hammer?"

"A ball-peen would do it."

"But wouldn't a big hulking hammer be hard to hide?"

"I'm talking about a small ball-peen, small enough to keep hidden, but very efficient."

"Oh, I see," says Frankie. "Okay – so you've invited him – the bastard! – to the beach. You've brought alcohol. You kill him with the hammer, what then? Does he die straight away? I mean, not with a blow from a small hammer, surely?"

"He doesn't die. You have to hold him under the water."

"The water? How does he get into the water?"

"He goes for a swim."

"So you come up to him, hit him with the hammer and then hold him under? Till he drowns?"

Madeleine nods.

"This is a fantasy, of course? This could never happen?"

Add enough heat to water and liquid turns to gas – a tipping point is reached when everything changes. Quantity into quality.

Madeleine looks right into her eyes. Shakes her head. "It could. It did," she says drunkenly. The conversation has morphed from fantasy into reality.

Frankie feels a shiver of excitement. "I've often wondered what it would be like to kill someone. To see the life ebb out. One minute they are alive and the next they are dead."

"It's easy. It feels good. Especially if you hate him."

"When you killed him you felt anger?"

"Rage."

"So you did away with him?"

"I smashed his rotten head in."

"With a hammer?"

"Yes."

"And that did the job?"

"No. He wouldn't die."

"So what then?"

"I told you – I had to hold him under."

"The water?"

"Yes."

"Till he drowned?

"Yes, till he drowned."

Madeleine calls the waiter over, orders more drink.

Frankie keeps her eyes fixed firmly on Madeleine, without flinching. In chess, if you take the initiative, you must keep going, you must press home the advantage. To falter, to allow a passivity to enter in, to appear to waver, is to risk giving up that advantage. Make one wrong calculation, followed by a bad move and suddenly everything changes. It's time to move in.

"It must have been easier then to smash the child's skull in?"

The effect on Madeleine is instant. It's as if someone has come up behind and completely blindsided her. She blinks several times. "What?"

"You said you were pregnant? You had a baby?"

Madeleine tries to rise, but falls back drunkenly into her seat.

The colour drains from her face. There's no attempt to challenge Frankie on how she – Madeleine – had been lured into this damning conversation. She stares straight ahead as if in a trance. Her shoulders shake. "I didn't mean to ... I ... I ..." She wraps her arms around herself, shivering as though suddenly very cold. Her eyes redden, and well up. Tears begin to flow down her face in a stream. Finally she looks at the detective through a river of tears.

"Who are you?"

Frankie takes out her badge. "I'm Detective Kate Francis investigating the death of the baby on Port Arthur strand."

Madeleine's shoulders slump, she lowers her head onto her folded arms and sobs.

* * *

An hour later, Frankie leads an unsteady Madeleine out of the pub. An armed soldier outside the pub turns to look at the pair. Frankie puts her arm around Madeleine's shoulders and holds her to stop her from stumbling and drawing attention. Thankfully, the army presence is less than Frankie feared. There are no blocks on the streets. Nevertheless, she breathes in relief when they make it to the car. She drives Madeleine back to her apartment in the Bogside for her things, and on towards the checkpoint and through to Letterkenny.

CHAPTER 35

Frankie calls one last time to the community hospital to visit Anto Moran. The day is sunny and bright, and very warm. A light pleasant breeze from the Atlantic takes the edge off the heat. Cirrus clouds drift lazily across the sky drawing a film of gauze over the intense blue of the sky. A workman in a sit-in lawn mower drives up and down the green in front of the hospital. Sparrows and finches swoop and dive, foraging for easy pickings of grass seed on the shaved green. Frankie finds her former boss outside on a park bench, wearing a baseball cap to protect his eyes from the glare, a chessboard resting on a card table in front of him, his opponent a young man with his arm in plaster.

"You'll definitely get good with all this practice," Frankie says, coming up from behind.

Moran looks up, surprised, not having heard her approach.

"Get good?" exclaims the youth. "This fella is the tops. Won the under-eighteen championship twice in his teens, he tells me. I'm but an amateur in the shadow of greatness."

Frankie stares at Moran. The memory of that night on her birthday comes flooding back. His ploy to get into her bedroom.

Moran, eyes twinkling, puts on a sheepish face, and turns the corners of his mouth down, like a bold boy being ticked off. Delighted with himself.

Frankie throws the magazines she'd bought for him down on the bench beside him. "You *fraud*. You told me –"

The plastered arm, sensing a row, rises. "Listen, I'll be off. We'll catch up later, yeah?"

Moran nods at him and turns to Frankie, a big grin on his face. "Okay, I could play chess already – so kill me. Can you blame a man for using tactics in the service of a little romance?"

Frankie already regrets having commented on his game, or having made any reference to that night. That night was a mistake. She sits beside him and with an effort composes herself.

"How are you anyway? When do you expect to be released? How is your heart?"

"So many questions, detective. My heart is yours, as you know ..."

Frankie, disconcerted, studies the gardener in the sit-in lawn mower, and the green that is beginning to resemble a two-tone organic zebra crossing, warp and weft, the small birds hopping and pecking, heads bobbing up and down.

"Tests. And more tests. They tell me I might have to have a stent implant," Moran says absentmindedly, as if it's got nothing to do with him. He sighs.

The lawn mower chugs to a full stop. The driver works the choke. The engine stalls.

Moran snorts. "Needs to give it a rest or he'll flood the damn thing."

As if to prove him wrong, the engine stutters to life and struggles into action. The gardener moves up to the front section of the lawn near where they are sitting. Moran, fingers up to his ears, gestures to her that they should move. He's already up, lifting his crutches and hobbling inside. They commandeer seats in the lobby by the window, fronting onto the lawn.

Moran positions himself carefully before easing down onto the brown leatherette armchair, He takes off his cap, pulls his hand over his hair to smooth it down. Frankie is about to sit on the chair beside him, also facing the window, but he lifts his crutch and points to another opposite. "Easier on the back if I don't have to twist. Feckin' sacroiliac joint is giving me hell with all this leg-up business."

Frankie sits down on the chair prescribed. He's getting old – talking about sacroiliac joints. He looks older. Or is it that when a person loses mobility they also appear to lose vitality?

Moran drags a small stool over in front of his chair and using both hands lifts his injured leg onto it. He settles into the chair, sighs.

"But enough of all this nonsense," he says. "Madeleine Byrne! *Good God!*"

"Yes, hard to believe. Turned herself in. And then, of course–"

"Chapter and verse, if you please, mademoiselle. I want to hear it all. Every last detail."

Frankie settles into her armchair and takes a big breath. She's still processing all that's happened in such a short space of time. She tells him about her search of Madeleine's room – the hammer, the defaced photo of Roche, the diary with its incriminating entry.

"But I still needed a confession. I had no actual proof she killed the Strand baby. I needed to find her."

Moran stretches his leg out, winces in reaction to a sudden jolt of nerve pain. After a moment he recovers his composure. "And, of course, for that you needed to go to Derry."

Frankie fills him in on her visit to O'Donnell, and the mystery of the newspaper cutting. "But the jeweller had an alibi and O'Toole did the research and came up with a plausible reason for the grudge."

"Good for O'Toole," says Moran. "Not entirely useless, after all."

"Oh, not useless at all, as it turns out. He found out O'Donnell had a grudge because he fancied Madeleine himself. Roche was the competitor, the guy who won the prize, as it were. Though I doubt Madeleine could have had any interest in that jeweller. In any case, O'Toole's done some excellent work. Credit where credit's due."

Moran waves his hand dismissively. "Yes, yes, enough already about the young fella. So you found Madeleine in Derry. Then you somehow magically managed to get her to come back to Donegal to face charges? How?"

"I knew she'd be in Breslin's Bar after her stall in the market. So I approached her about buying some jewellery and got into conversation that way. I made up a story about being jilted on a date, my real reason for being in the pub. That led on to a pleasing rant about, 'Men, they're all the same!' etcetera."

Moran laughs. "Now where have I heard that before!"

"Anyway, we played this fantasy game about what we'd like to do with the men who treat us badly. We ordered drinks. Madeleine was knocking them back. The fantasy turned to narrative, and before long she was telling me how you'd go about murdering a man, telling me how she in fact murdered *her* man. I knew I had to keep up the momentum. I brought up the baby. Asked her how it felt to smash a baby's skull in. That was a rude awakening. The game was over. She became very remorseful. About the baby. Before long, it all came bursting out, the whole story. It seemed like it was a relief to let something out that had been locked inside, like a dam bursting its defences. It was like she just surrendered. She said she didn't know why she did it. She was utterly depressed at the time."

"As she's telling you this, she's drunk of course."

"Pretty well on, yes."

"But you did get a confession out of her?"

"All duly recorded."

"Very good. You do realise getting a statement from someone who's had a lot of drink taken, not to mention clandestinely ... well, let's put it this way, a good defence lawyer will argue that the truth of the confession is immaterial – what is important is how it was obtained – either by oppression or in circumstances likely to render it unreliable ..."

"I planned on taking a formal statement back in Donegal, once she agreed to come back with me to turn herself in."

"But before you got the written statement, she tried to kill herself."

"Yes – she used a sharp-edged gem. She must have secreted it into her clothing before we left Breslin's Bar."

Moran shakes his head. "Was it a cry for help, do you think? Or just a botched job?"

"Who knows. She's in psychiatric care now, anyway."

"She may even be deemed unfit to go to trial. Which could well suit the powers that be ... avoiding the truth about Roche being aired."

"It would be a disgrace if Roche's reputation is protected."

"Whether she goes for trial or not, you have solved the case, Detective Francis. Still many unanswered questions, though." Moran scratches his head. "How did she get Roche to the strand?"

"She rang him and asked him to meet her."

"So she did lure him to the strand. But surely he didn't just hop to it when she asked?"

"That is exactly what happened. She simply rang him, and they met. 'The randy old bastard was always up for it,' is what she said – 'testosterone-fuelled day and night'. You could see the rage in her, by the way her face was contorted when talking about him."

"So – they met at nine. That was very late, surely?"

"I asked her that. She said the strand was always deserted at this time, but it was still light. At that time of year, it takes a long time for it to get dark and there's no full-on darkness. It was their practice to meet late in the evenings, in the summer anyway."

"Illicit liaisons and so on and so forth. So they met at 9pm – what then?"

"Once she started to talk, to open up, once she got going – about killing Roche – there was no stopping the momentum. She'd brought some stuff – biscuits, peanuts, crisps, junk. Wine. After they'd had a few glasses, he suggested a swim. Madeleine told him she needed to go first, that she'd follow him in."

"She needed to go?" Moran frowns. "Meaning?"

"For a pee."

"Oh! I see."

"So she went into the dunes and he ran down to the water. The tide was in, she told me. Roche was floating near the shore when she came down to join him. I asked her how deep the water was. Not very deep, she said, she couldn't remember exactly."

"Enough to drown in anyway," says Moran.

Frankie nods. "She approached the sea with the hammer behind her back, waded in and just as he was turning to look up, hit him on the temple. Hard. It caught him by complete surprise. He was stunned. It was easy to hold him down after the blow to the head. He sank without a struggle."

"And drowned?"

"Yes."

"She must have hit him a mighty thump. Probably where she hit him did the trick."

"Exactly. There's a spot on the temple ... well, we both know that."

Moran flicks his hand for her to get on with the story.

"I asked her how she managed to get the body up the strand, to where he was found, Roche being a big man. She said she dragged the body up as far as the marram grass. Her intention had been to bury it in the dunes, but she couldn't manage to drag it any further. She had to stop often to get her strength back. I told her I found it hard to believe that someone as slender as she is was able to drag someone of Roche's bulk that far. It wasn't easy, she told me, but she practises Tai Chi. And indeed, though slight in build, I'd already noticed how very well-toned she is."

"In any case, her rage would have given her strength," Moran said.

"True."

"'He ruined my whole life,' she said, 'as well as ruining Sarah Joyce's. Then I heard about the third baby found in the cathedral with a message pinned to it – I was convinced that it was yet another baby he had fathered. I just snapped. I didn't want this to happen to anyone else.'"

"An avenging angel," says Moran. He shifted to a more comfortable position in the chair.

"She was."

"What about drag marks?"

"The tide next morning took care of any marks up to the water line. She'd used her jacket to brush away the marks on the softer dry sand up near the dunes – where the body was buried."

"All that took a lot of planning."

"She said she didn't plan it at all. She did intend to kill him but didn't know exactly how she'd do it. Her original idea was to get him very drunk, or that maybe he'd fall asleep. Killing him in the water made things a lot harder for her, having to drag him back up to the dunes."

"So, what about the baby?"

"'Why didn't you go for an abortion which is legal just across the water in England?' I asked her. She just kept shaking her head, as if that was something she'd never considered. When she was describing how she killed Roche, you could see the anger that was driving her. She was beside herself with rage. But her whole attitude changed when I confronted her with killing her baby. The belligerence evaporated. She crumbled. In the end there was no resistance. She volunteered to hand herself in. But I still needed her to actually admit it – to get her to say 'I killed the Strand baby'. I asked her if she'd planned to kill the child all along as soon as it was born? 'No,' she said, 'I had no plans.'"

"But she finally admitted to killing it?"

"Yes, she confessed she killed the child because she couldn't bear to keep it. But she said she was all over the place, didn't rightly know what she was doing." Frankie pauses. "Almost certainly post-partum blues, but that will be for the doctors to ascertain."

Moran looks her in the eye. "So now she is in psychiatric care."

"Yes."

"Well, that was some investigative work, Detective Francis."

"It's sad though. She was a victim."

"Maybe. Nevertheless, the mystery of the murder on the dunes is finally solved."

A doctor comes into the day room. "Mr Moran, good morning. How are we today?"

"Is that the plural 'we', the royal 'we', or do you mean the nurses 'we'?" bats back Moran.

Frankie stands. "Listen, I'll leave you to it for a few minutes. I'll be back."

She wanders outside and over to the seat she and Moran vacated a short while previously. The gardener has finished mowing, and the place has the appearance of a bowling green. She can smell the pungent aroma of cut grass, a pleasant smell that reminds her of childhood days, the exhilaration of rolling down the slope of a meadow near the family home when summer days were invariably sunny and stretched out to eternity.

When Frankie nailed the Border Weasel, she felt the exhilaration of a job well done. There was a sense in which she'd done something worthwhile, solved a mystery, and left the world a better place with the Weasel behind bars. This time is different. She feels conflicted. Madeleine was a victim all her life. She left a troubled childhood in Derry, sought succour as housekeeper in what appeared to be a safe place – what *should* have been a safe place – only to have been taken advantage of by a self-serving philanderer, a man of the cloth, who she had every right to expect she could trust, but who instead betrayed that trust. She was a murderer, true, but with Madeleine locked away in a psychiatric ward had anything really changed? Was there a better way to make a difference?

She takes a few deep breaths and rejoins Moran. The doctor has left.

"Everything okay?" she asks.

Moran waves his hand in the air, as if to dismiss any reference to his fragility. "You solved the case, Detective Francis. Again, well done!"

"You know, I feel sorry for Madeleine. When you think of the life she's had, her father interned, her home beleaguered, the war, the violence, the abuse ..."

Moran raises an eyebrow.

"No, don't worry – because I have sympathy for Madeleine doesn't mean I condone her murderous actions."

"Well, I should certainly hope not." Moran harrumphs. "She was capable of murdering the man, villain though he was. Murderers who have psychiatric problems can't be allowed to go on because they suffered abuse in the past. Most of them probably have."

"I know. Madeleine's mind is disturbed. I had a responsibility to arrest her either for trial or psychiatric help."

"Your job was to hand Madeleine over, which is what you did. And if I might remind you – you're a police detective not a social worker. And even if you *were* a social worker, you would have been doing Madeleine an injustice by not getting her treatment."

Frankie nods. "But the bigger picture remains unchanged. There are forces at work in Irish society that I cannot really touch. The Church will go on moving its problems around, will still work hand in glove with the State ..."

"Ah, for the love of God!" says Moran. "Detective Francis, you're beginning to sound like a pinko, if you don't mind me saying so. If your aim is to change the world, you should immediately hand in your badge and join one of those protest outfits that keep popping up here there and everywhere." He chuckles, amused at his witticism. "Obviously, I'd strongly advise against."

Frankie smiles and shakes her head.

"But enough of this nonsense. Loose ends, we can't be left with loose ends," he growls, "not good for a sick man. I hear from the grapevine that Brannigan could be in trouble?"

Frankie nods. "MacAllister rang me again. Anonymously. Supposedly. It seems that when Brannigan and McGinley found cannabis in his house, they used this to put pressure on him to do their bidding."

"He would be the fall guy, if their plan went wrong?"

Frankie nods. "McAllister did as he was told and bought tons of fertiliser. Brannigan then coached him on to how to use the stuff to make a bomb."

"And that's what you saw Brannigan and McGinley taking to the border town?"

"Actually, the day I followed the pair of them to Ballybofey, what I saw them planting looked just like a big bag of fertiliser."

"So much for McAllister's bomb-making skills," says Moran.

"It's laughable when you think about it, that the IRA with all their expertise – who have Charlie Haughey quaking in his boots that they might one day march down O'Connell Street to take over the Dáil – would be relying on the likes of Mike McAllister to make bombs in a coffee-maker, capable of bringing down the British Empire. Did Brannigan really expect the top brass to swallow this preposterous story, when the big 'finds' were investigated?"

"Or imagine if McAllister – instead of contacting head office – had gone to Martin McGuinness, Commander-in-Chief of the IRA in Derry?"

Frankie shakes her head, bemused. "Lord! What a thought!"

"In any case he took his courage in his hands and contacted you," says Moran.

"I told him I knew who he was and that I also knew he was being blackmailed."

"*Mnn*. How did our trusty volunteer react to that?"

"He did what he should have done from the word go."

"Contacted Dublin."

Frankie nods. "I told him he should speak out and it looks like that's what he's done."

"And you? Have you decided what you're going to do about that whole bad sorry business?"

"I'm mulling it over. But don't worry, I will act on it."

"I have no doubt, Detective Francis. Brannigan, be afraid! Be very very afraid! There could be a tribunal in it yet!"

Frankie tries not to seem pleased by the thought. "There could, indeedy."

"All those dead babies came at just the wrong time for the sergeant, when he wanted to bring his own scam to fruition. In any case, bang go dreams of a big pension pot for Liam Patsy Brannigan! You couldn't make it up! Sergeant in small town picks a vulnerable youth, threatens him with incarceration for smoking weed if he doesn't do his bidding. Youth does as he's told and makes bombs which the sergeant then places at the border. Sergeant subsequently makes a big 'find', which is trumpeted far and wide and earns the said sergeant no end of laurels – promise of promotion, etcetera and so on ..." Moran smirks, having no trouble at all with schadenfreude. "How the mighty have fallen!"

A young nurse comes into the day room, pops a few pills into a phial, smiles, and hands them to Moran with a glass of water. Moran raises an eyebrow resignedly, receives the medication and thanks the nurse who leaves. He's definitely changed, thinks Frankie. In the past, he wouldn't have been able to resist flirting with that young woman.

Moran tips the pills onto his hand, tosses them into his mouth and slurps some water to wash them down "And what's to become of the Boy Wonder now the case is closed?"

"It seems O'Toole has taken up with young Lara from Burtonport. Totally smitten."

"He smits very easily, that fella. At one stage, I thought he was fixed on you. But then ..." – he sighs – "weren't we all?"

Frankie restrains a smile. "What about you?" she asks. "Any plans?"

Moran leans back in the chair and sighs. "When I get out of here, I'm planning to take early retirement. I could put a word in for you for my job, if you'd like?"

Frankie smiles, says thanks. Would she like? She'll reflect on it.

"I think it's time for me to leave. I'm ready for it," Moran says.

Frankie is not surprised. The life seems to have gone out of him. When they arrived in Gweedore, he was animated, energetic, a powerhouse. Now he seems diminished, defeated. The attraction is gone.

And what about her? How has she changed? Her experiences since she came here have forced her to zero in on what she wants out of life. And where she was conflicted before, about her aims, about her emotions, suddenly everything becomes clear. For the first time in her life, she feels grounded. She has a firm idea what she wants to do. She also has a clear sense that being with Rory feels like being home.

As if reading her thoughts, Moran says, "And you? What are your plans?"

Frankie smiles. "I have plans."

"Involving the bould Rory, no doubt?"

They do indeed involve Rory, but Frankie has no intention of letting Moran in on her plans.

* * *

Sarah takes the boat from Belfast to Glasgow. She arrives in Cairnryan ferry port and after some enquiries finds the bus station. She has her homework done, has an address to go to.

She feels excited. And free.

Before long she will settle into college life in this strangely familiar city, will make friends, begin a new life. She will embrace this new life with energy, enthusiasm and curiosity and savour all that university has to offer. But she has another mission too. Unfinished family business. For the first time in her life, she is passionately curious about her heritage, her identity, who she is, where she came from. The trauma of the past year, having survived it and come out the other side, has given her a new energy, a new insight into the world and what it's all about. For the first time ever possibly, she feels agency, like there are things she wants to do with her life and she will do them. And one of those things is to trace her father.

It was her aunt – Hannah's sister – who, in the end, filled Sarah in on the circumstances of her birth. Sarah found out that her father was no stranger, as rumour would have it, but none other than her uncle, Mags' brother. Mags was the oldest in a large family of ten. This much Sarah already knew. What she hasn't heard before was that Niall, the youngest, and twenty years

Mags' junior, was only two months old when Hannah was born. Hannah and Niall were practically reared together. The youth followed in his father's footsteps and became a fisherman, pulling hauls of herring into Bunbeg harbour at night. During the day, he often took Hannah out on the boat with him to the islands. They fell in love. Hannah became pregnant.

The disgrace of it, in a tightly knit, deeply religious community, was too much for the family and Niall was pressured to take the boat to Glasgow. Hannah, broken-hearted, never recovered from the break-up. Mags reared the young Sarah. The story put out in the parish was that Hannah was raped by a stranger, some blackguard who absconded to Scotland, which was why she was so depressed. All Sarah had ever been told about her Uncle Niall was that he emigrated and lost touch with the family.

Will she be able to find him? Will he want to see her after all this time? And what difference will it make? Sarah doesn't know the answers to any of these questions. But she feels a compulsion to at least make some effort to find this man who gave her the gift of life. Her happiness doesn't depend on it. It's simply something she feels compelled to do among many other things. Like steel tempered in fire, she feels strengthened by the ordeal she's been through in the past few months and firmly resolved to move on: to grasp life, explore, expand, reach for the stars.

* * *

It's time to leave Donegal. As she packs up her things. Frankie reflects on the two women whose lives got entangled with Father Brendan Roche, a man the church protected until they couldn't any more. On the one hand, Madeleine: a victim who in the end turned the abuse outward, and then inward, who could well end up incarcerated in a mental institution for the rest of her life, as a sacrificial lamb to protect the Church. Sarah Joyce, in contrast, managed to transcend what had happened to her, and in the process grew through the experience, her horizons now expanding.

Gweedore has been Frankie's home for the duration of the case and it's time now to move on. Shortly she will meet up with Rory in Dublin. There will be changes.

* * *

One last time, Frankie drives down the long narrow road to Port Arthur Strand. She parks near the pier and makes her way over to the grassy path through the dunes to get to the beach, smiling wryly at the memory of her dangerous trek over the slippery wrack-covered boulders the first time she arrived here.

Brilliant yellow birds-foot trefoil – that holy trinity of plants – pokes its way up through the sandy path as she winds her way down to the strand. To either side of her are masses of orchids resplendent in their episcopal purple – she chuckles as she reflects on the irony of it – and the ubiquitous harebells nod their heads agreeably in the gentle breeze.

The air is balmy. Small white clouds scud over an azure sky. Frankie feels at peace.

She stands for a moment looking out to sea. She can see Gola and Umfin and the other islands floating in the Atlantic. The tide is coming in with a gentle *whish-whish* up and over the golden sand creeping ever closer to the high-water mark of shingle and seaweed and small broken shells. A solitary seagull squeals and dives for herring, the sound reverberating over the vast expanse of strand that is so bright it's almost white. She turns and looks up towards the dunes where the marram grass sways lightly in the sea breeze. Frankie sighs.

THE END